CHILDREN OF GOD

CHILDREN OF GOD

Philip Loren

Published by Black Moss Press, 2450 Byng Road, Windsor, Ontario N8W 3E8. Black Moss gratefully acknowledges the assistance of the Canada Council and the Ontario Arts Council.

Black Moss books are distributed in Canada and the United States by Firefly Books, 250 Sparks Avenue, Willowdale, Ontario.

All orders should be directed there.

Canadian Cataloguing in Publication data:

Loren, Philip, 1923-

  Children of God

ISBN 0-88753-006-0

I. Title.

PS8573.0715C55 1995   C813' .54   C95-900371-1

PR9199.3L648C55 1995

Black Moss Press

To Candy and Margot and my beloved Roselyn

PROLOGUE

It was in the land of the south where it all began. A barren stretch on the fringe of the desert, far below Gaza's Brook which flowed in its sandy bed to the Mediterranean sea. Further inland and to the west, roving shepherds wandered with their flocks for the land was parched, fit only for pasture, with scrub and rubble, desert flowers, and barley growing wild.

It was in the days after the death of the patriarch Abraham, who had been laid to rest in his tomb beside his wife Sarah in the cave of Machpelah. Still some three hundred years in the future lay the exodus of the Israelites from Egypt to the promised land of Canaan.

Down from a hill Zadok, Gaza's prince, had followed the spoor of a lion. As midday drew near, the high peak of the sun had heated his brow, and below in a valley he had found a place to rest in the shade of a ledge of rock.

He had beckoned to his party of hunters, his nobles and cousins who had joined in the hunt, and he bade them sit and refresh themselves. As he passed among them they bowed their heads before their lord which pleased him. He smiled and pressed his bearded lips together. He watched while his servants distributed the oatmeal-cakes, the olives and fruit and roast onions, the fresh cheeses and goat-skins full of thin sour milk.

Though he was only thirty years of age, the young ruler had the bearing of a king, stately and full in the flesh. He was well-favored among men, taller than most, his body slender. He had the arms of a warrior, his chest full and strong. A leather jerkin studded with bronze discs hung from his broad shoulders, a dagger in its scabbard strapped in his girdle, gold armbands gleaming in the sun. His beard, curled and brown, thinner at his cheekbones and heavier below, swept round the corners of his lips to his chin. His youthful eyes took the measure of men and it was clear that he felt worthy of his high place among them.

Gaza, the strong citadel, powerful and prosperous, was foremost among the white-walled hill cities in the southland of Canaan, and often in a fanciful dream, the young prince ruled not only Gaza but all the land to Babel's river.

He waited to one side until the hunters had feasted on the wealth of provisions, then bade them rise up to continue the hunt. He knew that the lion whose spoor they followed would seek shelter from the midday sun and he led the troupe on a rocky path into the depth of a ravine which stretched round and behind the cliff. The hunters were watchful with spears and bows at the ready lest the lion suddenly spring out from ambush. From the ravine they pressed southward toward the desert. They searched for the prey in the high ground and the low, but the trail had disappeared.

Thinking back, Zadok believed that destiny had led his every step. Had he known what pain lay in store he would have searched no more. He would have turned his face away from the south. He would have turned back to Gaza's hill, to the world he knew and ruled, back to his walls and gate and Dagon's temple newly built on the slope above the shore.

A demon lured him on, a demon in the shape of a jackal with its pungent smell and narrowed snout, a messenger of dark from the underworld which pointed out the path toward the desert. Zadok saw the beast with its dog's head and bushy tail at a distance, running sideways parallel to the shadow of his camel; then it disappeared among the rubble where it joined a concert of jackals howling, screaming, barking, as if a legion of demons were fighting over some lost soul.

This was the first of three signs of evil which he saw that day.

The second was borne on the breath of a soughing wind from the south. Deep in the canebrake where he sensed the lion lay hidden, he heard the wind like a moan or a wail. It was as though someone called his name and he turned his head toward the sound.

The third sign flew from an arrow he loosed from his bow. An eagle had circled high overhead, soaring, floating black-winged on the wind. He had sped the arrow high into the arc of the wind but the arrow turned on itself. It curled in the air, and from the rise of a slope where it pierced the crust of the earth, he saw sheep in a distant field. He shouted to alert the others and pointed the way with his lance for it meant water to slake their thirst. Clucking his tongue he urged his riding beast forward; and it stretched its neck and lengthened its stride.

Two herdsman, who had rolled away a stone from the mouth of a well and were watering the sheep, turned courteously to greet Zadok and his party as they drew near.

"Peace." Zadok returned their greeting. "Shalom." With his hand to his forehead he bent forward.

Together the herders bowed as if they were one and offered water for the camels. "In the name of the master," they said. They led Zadok to a grassy mound where a house of goat-skin stood tethered to the earth by wood and rope. One herder lifted the carpet at the entrance to the tent and cried out loudly, "Lo, a stranger, master."

And from within came the answer, "Bid him welcome."

The house of hair was cool and dim. Three earthen lamps on little stands with ivory footings served as light, the flames flickering in the gust of wind from the entrance.

In the myrrh and musk-scented tent, Kadesh, the shepherd-chief, sat in the comfort of carpet and cushion. A ridge-filled face, graybearded. Small keen eyes squinting in the dimness. Two deep furrows ran from his brow to the bridge of his nose. He suffered in his foot which was bandaged to cover the reddened skin. The old man stiffened. The demon in his foot was restless and pained the toe-bones and the ankle but the shepherd-chief courteously extended a wrinkled, thin-fingered hand from the folds of his garment.

"Welcome, stranger, welcome to my household."

Zadok bent forward, palms extended to the elder. "Peace, old father. My thanks for your welcome. May the goddess Astarte shower you with favor so that your sheep drop twins and the wives of all your sons bear more sons, and may your life be lengthened into years and years without end."

"God does all," replied Kadesh indulgently. "Peace to thee, stranger. And may Jehovah, God the Highest, the Shepherd of the flock, look upon you with favor." And he bade Zadok sit and take rest from the breathless heat.

To welcome the stranger was God's way, in Jehovah's heart, Kadesh said. When he learned that it was Gaza's prince who had come to this watered place he drew himself more erect. Despite the pain in his bandaged foot he would stand, he said, to honor his guest.

Limping with difficulty, the shepherd-chief made his way to the carpeted entrance and pointed out the place where the hunters were to pitch camp. A distant field hidden by a glade, away from the sacred stones and the altar-table where the tribe sacrificed and served the God Jehovah. Kadesh extended his hospitality without prejudice, provided, of course, that no craven gods be brought within the shepherds' sight. Not the image of Astarte holding her tiny breasts in both hands, nor the god Dagon dressed in his shiny cloak of fish scales.

The shepherd-chief called out to Eliezer, his eldest servant, who came without delay and bent himself first to his master, then to Zadok, the guest.

"My trusted servant, the overseer in my house," said Kadesh. "He will guide you and your retinue to the fallow field. It will be in his hands to provide beasts of burden laden with those things needed to pitch camp. Tents of hide or woven goat-hair, food and water for your comfort."

Even as Zadok gathered his hunters and followed Eliezer, Kadesh called out to his household servants, "Prepare meats and fruits and the sweet date wine. Bring the sons to a feasting. We will break bread with Gaza."

In the fallow field, Zadok watched as servants raised the tents. He had barely time to sit and rest when cymbals rang out in the shepherds' camp. Within the hour, a young boy with spindly legs appeared astride an ass and piping on his shepherd's flute, he led Zadok and his men to the place of feasting.

To honor Gaza's prince, the people of Kadesh, both kin and herdsmen, had washed their hands and limbs, anointed themselves and put on their festal garments. In a shaded spot under a tree they had prepared a banquet table where Kadesh sat and clapped his hands to the musicians' din.

And the sons, eight together, came to bid Zadok welcome, led by Asa. the eldest, a bull of a man with a bushy beard, already grayed at the temples. Then came Hira and the others, until the eight were named and numbered, and all the wives came and the mothers with babes and sons and daughters. In an ever-widening, bustling group they bent their heads before Kadesh and the prince of Gaza.

The last to come forward was Yaffia, the daughter of Kadesh. Her smile was like the summer sun in a cooling wind, her eyes a deep blue like the great sea at Gaza's shore. "Blessed," said Kadesh. "She has been blessed with the beauty of angels." He motioned with one hand for the musicians to heighten the shrill and tempo of their strain. "Dance, my maid," he said and her feet stirred in welcome to the flute and drum.

On a measure of earth within sight of the banquet table she bent and swayed, her fringed skirts swirling to reveal the skin of her thighs as her dancing feet spun high and round and back and forth to the rhythm of the drums.

Kadesh watched with pride that his old loins had conceived such a beauty as this. He rose up before his guests and lifted his hands high above his head and clapped in tribute to his daughter's skill and grace. Though it was not the custom to show such esteem for a maid he could not restrain himself. "Unmatched," he boasted to his guests and clan. "Unmatched in all the land of Canaan, to the east or north or even beyond."

Yaffia raised her arms sensuously. Twisting this way and that, she favored the lord Zadok with a glance, and Gaza's prince rose up from his place and applauded.

Eliezer led the maid to Zadok's side at the banquet table while Kadesh smiled and nodded and tapped his fingers in rhythm to the drums.

"A great honor to break bread with Gaza. Eat, eat," urged Kadesh and he bade Yaffia fill Zadok's cup again and again.

Zadok raised the cup of polished horn inlaid with gold as Yaffia called for a second wineskin to serve the guests. "My lord Zadok, refresh your weariness with food," she said, and she set a dish of meats and oat cakes before him.

Zadok smiled and turned toward her as if drawn by a spell. He could not take his eyes from her. He had first seen her near the well where the shepherds had rolled back the stone and watered the sheep, and the dogs had barked and leaped around the flock. She had stood in the field amid the bleating sheep, desert flowers in her hand, the wind flowing in her hair and in the folds of her garment, a yellow smock gathered by a cord at the waist. She had brushed her black hair from the wind and her face as he approached. Zadok had made no sign to her nor she to him; it would not have been fitting, but their eyes had met for one brief moment and the man-need in Zadok had stirred in his loins.

As Yaffia sat by his side, his manhood was stirred again at the thought of her form beneath the cloth, at the thought of her thighs and the red buds peaked on the mounds of her breasts.

Smiling, Yaffia refilled his cup. She brushed his arm. Their fingers lingered one upon the other and there was a flame between them and a fire in their flesh.

It was not long before Kadesh had second thoughts that his daughter sat so close to Gaza's side. When he saw that their hands touched on the wine cup, he flinched as if some evil clung forever to a heathen's skin. He made little signs to Yaffia with his eyes. Hospitality to Dagon's kind was one thing, but for his daughter Yaffia to walk hand in hand with Gaza, to spread the seed of God into Dagon's world, that would be a blasphemy, a mockery of God. Kadesh was revolted at the thought of giving his seed outside the clan, to be lost forever in Satan's world. A waste of the blessing bestowed by God.

To Kadesh, Dagon was little more than the worms which swelled his toes and joint inflamed with gout, a curse of Satan sent to plague him. As for Gaza's people who knelt before Dagon's image, these were heathen men and women and unless they broke their gods of stone, they were best kept apart from the followers of Jehovah.

The banquet table was still laden with food and drink, the sabbath guests and Gaza's prince still ringed round with a festive air, when Kadesh beckoned to Eliezer who bent his ear low to listen to his master.

"Yaffia," Kadesh said simply, "and the heathen-king."

Eliezer understood at once. The elder servant, too, had seen the sparkle in Yaffia's eyes and how she sat close to Zadok's side. Deep reluctance crossed Yaffia's face when Eliezer called out to a maidservant to lead her from the banquet table. "Make ready her tent and see that she rests," the steward commanded before he turned to Zadok and bowed stiffly from the waist.

"It is the time and the hour." he said. "My master has spoken. The feast is done." Eliezer saw Zadok's disappointment and he bent his head still lower above his hands. "It is my duty to guide you and your nobles to the encampment."

"So be it," said Zadok. He called out to his hunters who rose up as one man and followed the prince and the elder servant to the fallow field, but Zadok's heart was with Yaffia where she walked with the handmaid. Her sweet scent had vanished and he could think only of when he might see her face again and feel her touch.

Had Kadesh been willing, Zadok would have offered gold for the shepherd maid. Gold and more gold. A vast amount. He might have bartered cattle and jewels, even wide estates, vineyards and fields, but he said nothing. He knew that Kadesh would not agree.

In the end, it was Yaffia who took matters in hand and led the way under the black of night. In the dark hours she came to Zadok's tent. She sat by Zadok's side, eagerness in her shining eyes, a flush of warmth in her cheeks. It was meant to be, she said. Jehovah's own plan. God's beast had led Zadok to her. The lion whose spoor he had trailed to the field and the watered place of her father's tents. She had prayed for love, and God had brought love to her side.

She took Zadok's hand in hers and she pressed his fingers close to the soft of her bosom. There was no shame in her eyes at his touch. No shame for the desire she felt. It was God who had molded her form and her flesh to receive Zadok's love. It was a sign that she was to him as Eve was to Adam, his flesh and his rib.

As they lay side by side, he put a flower in her hand as a pledge of his love. The lamplight sputtered and began to fade, for no oil remained to light the flame in the lamp. She untied her sash and loosed her robe and he pressed his manhood against her thighs. She received him again and again with so deep a tenderness and strength of desire that tears rushed to his eyes with joy.

"My beloved," he said. "Heart of my heart, you are more to me than life itself."

She caressed his chest and felt the swift beat of his heart, the flesh of his arms, his strength. "Walk with me," she said, and she led Zadok from the tent into the solitude under the dome of dark. "Love," she said, "is a wonder of wonders sent down by God who knows all our dreams. He must watch us from above."

Zadok felt the warmth of her touch, the love, but it was as though her heart had suddenly paused. Between them there was a sadness then, a sadness for her father who would be torn at the thought of Jehovah's seed and a heathen breast to breast. Her hand was already promised, she said in whispers. Betrothed since childhood to a man of God, old but pious, who lived farther up between the mountains in a valley. A righteous man who walked on the right of God. There was no hope that her father would have a change of heart. He would not reverse himself for a heathen. Not even for the Prince of Gaza. She had no choice but to leave her house, her tribe, under the cover of dark.

With hushed voices, Zadok's hunters led the caravan from the camp in the field. Servants driving pack animals and young boys leading camels on a long rein brought up the train in a silent march. On her riding beast Yaffia followed Zadok's lead. Far behind them, the shepherd's campfires disappeared from sight. The darkness hid them; and by dawn they had reached the safety of Gaza's walls.

One day of bliss, then came thunder.

Kadesh, gout and all, appeared before the walls of Gaza with some fifty of his kin and herders, all geared for war. Soon after the first glow of dawn, the maid had been missed. With angered cries the sons had burst into the old man's tent and pulled the father from the semi-darkness to the open light, then led him to the daughter's tent where he put his head through the flap and peered inside.

Gone!

"Stolen!" the eldest had cried with his bull-necked roar; and the youngest, still beardless and slender, and the wives and all the maids who pressed behind had added their shrill cries of anger.

They believed that Zadok had torn Yaffia from her couch. He and his henchmen had tied her wrists while God's eye was still shut. She had been bound and gagged, flung onto the saddle in the night blackness, dealt with as a common slave, not as a child of Jehovah. Zadok, the high and mighty, already had the choice of many beauties lolling in his garden-house, dusky bosoms from the farthest south and fair-skinned maidens from the mountains of the north. Must he also have this sister and daughter?

Now, as Kadesh looked to Zadok high above him on the walls, his anger mounted like a sudden flame in tinder. "Robber!" he shouted. He churned the earth, the bandages unravelling from his sickly toes. "Wolf who devours the lamb and leaves nothing but carrion! You sat in honor at my table. Is this the reward?"

Yaffia took her place beside Zadok on the high tower above the walls. Bewildered, she looked down on her father. Certainly she had expected that he would be incensed, that his nose would be reddened at her impure choice, but she had thought he would come down to Gaza's gate only after his first anger had cooled. "Child!" he might have sighed. "Is this your place? In this ungodly house, this lust-den of dancing maidens and slaves? Not as a true wife but only as another in his queenly house to serve his lust? Turn your face from the wooded mount where men and maid howl to the moon as if possessed. With nails pointed like claws, they gash their breasts to curry favor of their gods who relish the sight of blood. Hear me, my maid. Turn back."

This she had expected after a month or a week, but not this madness, this howling, before Gaza's walls! It was as though the sight of her empty tent had suddenly twisted the old man's mind and he had lost his reason.

"Vandal!" thundered Kadesh and struck at the bronzed ribs of the gate with his shepherd's crook. "Release the maid. Yaffia," he called up to the foursquare tower. "Jump down to me. God will grant you wings. Better to be crushed than to lie ravished in the arms of a heathen."

"Hear me," Zadok shouted down to the old man. "Hear me, and be content. Her God shall stand high. He shall stand where she stands, and sit where she sits, as high as this tower and equal to all." All this and more, he promised. He asked only that Kadesh bless their bed and be reconciled; even to the condition that Zadok's foreskin be shortened after the custom of the tribe. He would moan and bleed if it would please the father's heart.

"Blasphemy!" raged Kadesh at the concessions to Jehovah. "Fool!" he screamed. "Fool! To sacrifice the fragment of your manhood will not make of thee a child of God." His bowel boiled up with disgust at the thought of Yaffia's naked thighs exposed to Dagon's lust. He retched with loathing, the green slime rolling from his mouth. "Water," he gasped and the sons fetched water in an earthen jug to cool his anger.

"Dear father, be at peace," Zadok called down. "Jehovah shall dwell in the highest tower, equal even to Dagon's sacred house. Only bless us, father. Bless our bed."

"No blessing!" Kadesh screamed. "A curse! Cursed be your bed forever! Cursed be your house, your walls, your city! Lord Highest, throw down Thy flames! Send down a bolt upon the vandal!"

His final curse, and there it ended.

A bolt came down, but not from heaven. From the walls it came — the bolt, an arrow.

Kadesh toppled. The shaft struck his heart. He died where he fell.

And the land was stilled.

Zadok closed his eyes to the horror. The name of his friend and captain filled his throat. It was Eliphas who had loosed the shaft in a sudden fright.

Yaffia paled and covered her face with her hands. She wavered as though she were faint, but she shook her head when Zadok reached out to support her.

"Dear God", she said, turning to the high land and the wind, "I have sinned against my father. Dear God, forgive me. May he now sleep in peace."

She went down among them, her brothers, and she touched them and wept with them, saying, "It was in my heart, of my making." They were to cast no blame on Gaza. "I will remain," Yaffia said. "It is my wish."

And the shepherd clan went their way with Gaza's gifts of gold and grain and cattle and they bore Kadesh to the land where Jehovah lived.

BOOK ONE

THE CURSE

Chapter One

Fires burned in the streets of Gaza before every threshold, on every hearth and altar. Fires against the dark of night that swarmed with demons and spirits risen from the grave; their greatest enemy was fire which put them to flight and dispelled their power. Night by night, Gaza's people built their flames. They sent up prayers and set their little gods before their doors, then crouched in the darkened corners of their walls where they bent in fear.

Three years had passed since Yaffia's father, the shepherd Kadesh, had stood below Gaza's walls and cried up to God for vengeance. He had cursed the city, the bricks, the mortar, and who could know what evil would come, where it would lead, into which house, which bed. They saw death in every black-edged cloud. They feared a hail of fire and brimstone raining from the sky.

Then, under the black wing of night, the evil came. Word of it spread from mouth to mouth throughout the city. The queen lies stricken! The evil has crept to her couch!

In the temple, Zadok stood alone before the red-stoned eyes of Dagon, lord of the sacred house, with no priest to serve him, no ministrant to make fire and kindle the pellets of incense. With his own hands he put incense in the dish and struck the flint. As the yellow mist of smoke rose up from the pan to Dagon's navel, Zadok raised his hands and made service to the sacred stone, his god of the sea and air, half-man and fishtail below, whose power was born of the waters of the deep and the storm-winds which swept over the world.

While the sweet odor curled round in whorls to Dagon's nostrils,

Zadok confessed his fear of the evil which had rooted deep in the hollow of Yaffia's side. He knocked on the breast of god as if it were a door of stone. "Hear me!" Zadok pleaded.

He had brought gifts to Dagon's altar. This coffer of gold was to revive her limbs; this silver to restore her withered flesh. These jewels for her bosom to be made full again. This blue jewel for her eyes; this red one for her cheeks. All this and more, if it please the god.

"Shield her, lord. Wrap her in heaven-strength. Purge the evil from her flesh. Destroy it. Crumble it into dust that she be freed from the power of the curse."

Zadok bent his neck and kissed the sculpted stone of Dagon's fish-tailed feet. He was as nothing in the sight of his god, no more than the dust on the floor of the sacred house, and he spread his arms, like a gull its wings, that Dagon might see his tattered cloak.

"Go as a beggar," the high priest had said. The god would have more compassion for a beggar than a king. And Zadok lay himself down at Dagon's feet. "Let me die in her place," he pleaded. "Let her live. Let the curse be on my head alone."

"Kadesh, hear me," Zadok cried to Yaffia's dead father. "Have mercy." Twice he called to the dark of the wind where dead spirits roam. "Hear what lives in my heart. I repent!"

Like the sudden sweep of a morning light, memories opened the door of the past, and it was as though he spoke to Yaffia's father again, when the old man had stood below Gaza's gate, his bitter anger rising from his throat.

"Forgive us," Zadok begged. "Forgive that we went against the tenets of your God in the dark of night. Roll back the curse. For Yaffia is young and barely three years have passed since the seed of our love stirred in her womb."

Three years . . .

Had he known then where it would lead — the hate, the curse, the evil which lay twisted in Yaffia's bones and flesh — had he known...

"Go back," he would have begged. "Go back to your father's house. Back to the fields and the shepherds' flutes. You will be safe though we must weep apart and my heart will break each night when another will know your flesh and touch. Go back, my love, to the betrothed of your father's choice. Though he is old and with bony feet, he is a man of God, a priest, and it will be a blessing on your womb and seed.

With his head against the stone of his god, Zadok humbled himself. He took the hem of his cloak and tore it to shreds until pieces of the cloak fell in rags to the stone. His heart ached with the pain he had seen in Yaffia's flesh, the trembling of her arms and hands which she pressed to her bosom, her bewildered eyes which clung to his heart.

In his despair, he raised his voice to the heavens. "Gods, let her live. Show me a sign," he begged. He called to Astarte, the goddess of the moon, to stand with Dagon, lord of the sea, the moon and the sea against the evil in Yaffia's bones.

Then he turned his face to the eastern mountains, to Jehovah, God of the desert. "Father of shepherds and of Yaffia, my queen, let her rise up this day. Heal her, Lord, and a great tower I will raise in Thy name."

* * * * * * *

With his head between his knees, Zadok prayed until the sunrise. He clung to the hope that the powers of heaven had heard his plea and would send a sign without delay, but the wind was still in the early morn, the clouds a thin white fleece without form or movement. At the palace gate, the guard lowered his spear and shield before his lord, and within the courtyard two slaves drew water from the well. Otherwise Zadok met no one and saw no sign in the great hall or on the stairs to his chamber. He lay himself down and fell into an exhausted sleep. He would have slept until the sun circled red to the west had not a sudden shout from the door awakened him.

"A dreamer is coming!"

Zadok raised his head with a start. In the doorway he saw his steward Enan, mouth bawling as he slapped the fatness of his paunch with his excitement.

There was no need to explain that it was a dreamer with a vision who approached the Great-House. Two or three such prophets lived close by. One, a leper in a hut by the sea; another in a hovel hidden within the walls of the city. Like moles, they came out in times of evil with their god-warnings and prophecies.

"How near is the dream?" Zadok asked.

"The flight of an arrow from a good strong bow," came the answer.

"Bring him cakes and wine," Zadok ordered. He leapt from his couch and covered his nakedness with his robe. His heart was pounding. The world seemed to tilt as he ran down to the pillared hall and into the open court, where he waited for the dreamer to approach.

It was high noon, the arc of the hours lost since dawn. The sun in the sky was a high, white flame, a blinding glare. Zadok squinted at the leper-prophet's rags and filth, at his hobbling feet bound with shreds of cloth and string. The old man gripped a gnarled staff in veined hands, his fingers like twigs. His humped back was so bent with age that his chin and beard lay on his breastbone. Now and then he looked up to the sun, his lids blinking in the burning heat.

A noisy throng had followed the leper like bleating sheep who sense danger in the wind. The crowd drew back when the steward came running out with cakes and wine.

The old man stopped. Wagging his head as old ones do when they approve, he took the wine from the steward's hand and raised the jar, his lips ready and cupped to the rim. Then with the hem of his tattered cloak he wiped away the last driblet of wine which had bled into his beard. Leaning heavily on his staff he moved slowly toward the gate.

Suddenly he teetered. The people cried out in alarm as he stumbled.

Zadok ran out from the court, but before he had counted five steps, the dreamer fell. The staff tumbled from his open hand. His fingers clawed at the wind. The yellowed whites of his eyes rolled up. The old one shuddered and fell dead at Zadok's feet.

Zadok heard the shrieks of the crowd, then his own voice shouting. "Speak, old man! Speak!" He bent close to the leper. "Quickly! What dream?"

His captain's voice called out softly above him. "He will speak no more, my lord. The man is dead."

Zadok rose up and stood in silence. Stunned, he looked down to the leper-prophet who lay sprawled, his mouth open, the tongue of the dream smothered in the sand. Then, from the earth a black fly darted. From the leper's lip to his tongue. It flew off, then lit again. Round the rim of lip. Clinging, squatting on the juices.

Zadok shrank from the mark of evil. He stepped back, then turned and fled toward the garden. "Gods! Protect us!" he cried.

At the gate he looked back to see if blackness followed, but he saw nothing, no whorl of dust, no wind. But as he hurried through the garden, a black-tailed fly lit upon his hand and clutched his skin with its hairy feet. Frantically he brushed it off. It buzzed away, then lit again.

His heart sank. His feet were leaden as he walked into the shadows of Yaffia's chamber.

She was lying on her couch, half-raised, her limbs outstretched. Her face is pale, he thought. Waxen and pale. "The pain?" he asked. He listened as she answered that her pain had eased somewhat. But her breath is weak, he thought, and her eyes heavy, weary.

"My night was somewhat sleepless," she said. "Come, my lord, sit by me. Your hand upon me will bring me comfort."

He sat down. He touched her brow, but the warmth was in his own fingers. Her skin is cold, he thought. Shadows beneath her eyelids. Too little sleep, she said.

"God stands by me," she murmured, "in light and dark. He is my guide in all things."

Zadok listened as she spoke of God, of His house, the mountains. Always God's will and God's doing in all things, as it was in the beginning world.

"God is my judge," she whispered. She pressed his arm to reassure him, but he saw how her flesh had thinned and her arms hung limp, weakened, fingers lying almost lifeless on the woolen covering around her thighs.

He held her head and gently rocked her back and forth. He caressed her face while she spoke of flowers, of the desert, of the shepherds' flutes and moonlight, of love and of Tamuru, their child.

His tears welled up and he struggled to restrain them. The anguish within him was like a lion clawing at his heart. "You must rest," he said. He kissed her cheek. Then he left her and fled to the Great-House beyond the garden.

He closed the door to his chamber. He shut out the light. And in the darkness, he held his head and wept.

* * * * * * *

Gaza's people had gathered in the market square before the great copper-shielded gates. They stood in small anxious groups between the stalls and the donkey carts. Merchants and the poor huddled side by side, every heart frozen with fear. Each man sucked in his breath and looked cautiously around to his right and left.

Whatever it was that the leper dreamed, the sign was clear. All Gaza had seen the mark of black in the leper's mouth. His left hand had dug into the earth and a cloud of dust had risen to the wind, a footless spirit which veered south toward the desert.

"We are doomed," they whispered.

"The power of the curse," an elder said.

The poor gave themselves up for dead, their lives being all that they had to lose, but the rich ran off toward the temple and bowed down before the high priest Kohath. "Our fields!" they wailed. "Our fields!" In every omen they saw their land endangered; always their land, which in their greed they considered first above all. "Protect us, most holy one!" they cried. "Here is gold for the gods. Lay it at the feet of the fish-tailed Dagon and his sweet one, the Moonhead. And there is more gold if needed. Save our lands from drought and famine!"

"Speak to the gods on my behalf," each begged of Kohath, though all the world knew that in a time of drought one field could not be spared while the others suffered. Later, in the farthest corner of their gardens, each secretly buried a sackful of gold and silver, knowing that in famine one piece of silver was like one measure of wheat.

Kohath smiled to himself as he counted the gains to Dagon's house. In the late hours of the afternoon he paced in the shadows near the temple gate and pulled absently on his straggly beard. Now and then he glanced toward the street, hopeful that Zadok would soon come riding forth with precious gifts. He studied the tablets which the underpriests had brought to his hand. As high priest it was his place to interpret signs and omens, whether it be birds that flocked overhead or the speechless dark of the leper's mouth. He knew the concern that would bubble from Zadok's mouth, but the omens revealed no harm to Yaffia, the shepherd maid.

On previous occasions, Zadok's gifts on Dagon's altar had pleased the god. As for the leper's dream, the signs were clear. The leper's hand had pointed to the south, and in these latter weeks, the wind blasts had been warmer from the desert and the rains scant. Kohath considered his answer with the greatest care and rehearsed the words while he waited for Zadok to appear. "The meaning is clear," he would say. "There will be drought."

He sent a fledgling priest to mount the walls to keep watch and call out at the first rise of dust and clatter of Zadok's chariot wheels, but the sun slipped west to the golden swell of the sea and still no herald or envoy came from Zadok's gate.

It was the fault of Yaffia, Zadok's queen, mumbled Kohath. Her doing. She had turned Zadok from Dagon's house into the ways of the desert god. Kohath had known the truth from the first hour that Zadok brought the shepherd maid to Gaza's walls. There would always be contention between her god who had no face and Kohath's god, for Jehovah's gain was Dagon's loss and Kohath's greed was such that he was not content unless the storerooms were filled with grains and fruit and the temple coffers overflowed with silver and gold.

He snorted his disappointment as he walked in the night shadows beyond the temple. Let Zadok cling to his shepherd maid if he so pleased, but in the end Dagon's priests and Astarte's maids would regain their full share of Gaza's wealth.

*   *   *   *   *   *   *

In the blue hours of dusk, the physicians passed in and out of the house of women. They had come in haste soon after they were told of the leper's death. They said only that Yaffia was not healing as expected and for the time being they would say no more. They stood before Zadok in the courtyard; a haggard group with perplexed faces. They had poured pure water upon her from a pool which no hand had touched. They had brewed their potions, ground the root of saffron with salt and fat as ointment, but there was no sign of healing.

"No such illness have I seen before," said one to his lord. "An evil of great fury rages against her soul. Only the gods can aid her."

"It is embedded deep in her flesh," said another, "beyond the reach of my humble hands."

Zadok's face paled. Though he heard them and what they said, he stood bewildered. "Why can you not heal her?" he demanded with sudden anger. He glared at the helpless physicians. "Are my gifts less than the gifts of others?"

The physicians stood pallid and dumb before him. He saw that they were afraid lest he strike them, and his anger left him as suddenly as it appeared. "I must pray," he said, and left the courtyard.

He walked back through the garden, back into the shadows of Yaffia's chamber. There he held her once again. Her breath was quiet.

"Lo," she whispered, "a dark angel seeks me. Hold thus my hand, my love. Hold tight my hand. I must leave thee soon."

Yaffia's tears rolled swiftly on his breast and he wept with her. A silent weeping in the shadows of her chamber, and he rocked her in his arms until her tears were dried and she slept.

He stepped back from her couch toward her door, then back to her side again, where he lingered. His fingers brushed her cheek. Then he left. He followed in the same path where he had walked before. Backward into the shadows of the courtyard to the altar he had built to Jehovah. Like the leper, he fell upon his face and he ground his beard into the sand, his tongue and mouth filled with dust.

Later, in the darkened hours, torch in hand, blade drawn, he stood guard near the wall of Yaffia's chamber. The lintel was smeared with the blood of a suckling pig, and the door with plaster and bitumen. He had hidden the child, Tamuru, from the face of the curse. He had whispered to the slave Shatah, the second mother, who had covered the little maid with a shawl and smeared the babe's face with earth as though she were the child of a slave, not Gaza's princess. A little wall of pap had been spread round the couch, and a kid-offering near the door to lure the demons away from her body. Under a coverlet in the maidservant's lowly bed the child lay still, eyes closed.

"Kadesh!" Zadok called to the dark beyond the garden house. "Mercy! Spare the child at least," he begged. "Hear me, and hear the words in Yaffia's heart. How she speaks to the child of her love for you. How she tells Tamuru over and over that no man was more worthy and devoted to God. Three times have the shepherds gathered with musical pipes and wine to mark the festival of the wool shearing and the hour of your death. Year after year we have stood beside your grave with gifts and prayer, hand in hand with Tamuru, your grandchild."

Zadok's thoughts drifted back to the day when last they had stood by the hollowed rock. "Your sweet grandfather," Yaffia had said to the child. "It is there that he sleeps in peace." Yaffia had pointed to the darkened house of death near the base of Jehovah's mountain. She had pressed her forehead on the round stone which served as the door to the sepulcher, as if her warmth could touch her father's brow as he lay at rest.

Tamuru had run beside a gamboling lamb to the stone entrance. She had mimicked Yaffia and kissed the stone as though it were her grandfather's face.

Yaffia had clasped the child to her breast. "His walls are dark where he rests," she had said. "Even as your house was dark when you slept in the womb walls of my flesh until an angel brought you out into the light. Gather a swimming sunbeam in your frock and bring a pocketful of sunlight to light his house that he may see your eyes and know your heart."

The memory of the mother and child beside the grave twisted the sinews of Zadok's heart. Though the wind was cold, his brow was studded with beads of sweat. Fatigued, he rested on one knee. He leaned on the hilt of his sword, the point of the blade piercing the earth. The dark hours faded, and before the twilight of the dawn, he had closed his eyes.

Chapter Two

Yaffia recovered. Her heart was wearied but her tears were dried when she called out to Zadok in the first hour after the dawn. It was a demon which had burrowed into her flesh, Yaffia said, and not the curse as all Gaza had believed. The Lord Jehovah had heard her prayers and driven the evil from her side.

The slaves and women who had been paid to wail and grieve cast off their mourning shrouds. They shook themselves free from the ash of grief. Hand in hand, they danced and sang round and round the garden and in the Great-House.

The sun had slipped to its lowest slope under a cloud of gold and red when Zadok returned to Yaffia's side. She was standing by her bed, pale and weakened, but smiling. Zadok kissed her cheek. He fondled her hair and caressed her arms, but she sensed his fear. She saw that his face had tensed. She knew what lay deep in his mind — the threat of the curse which still hovered like a sword over their heads.

Yaffia pressed his hand. "The pain is no more," she said to reassure him.

"But the leper is dead. His dream is lost," Zadok said helplessly. "How shall we escape? And our child? What magic can keep her safe?" The water of his fear stood out on his brow.

"The Lord God will show us the way," Yaffia replied. "Such things lie in His hands. Noah was forewarned by God and built the ship."

"But Noah lived in the days when gods spoke to kings," Zadok said.

"And the leper," Yaffia replied, "was his not a vision from God? Who can know how or when God will speak?"

Hand in hand she went with Zadok to the leper's mound which had been dug by a wall near the shore. Zadok bade her stand a distance from the grave lest poisoned vapors seep out from the depth. He made a sign to ward off evil spirits which might be lurking near the dead and bending low to the mound where the leper slept, he cupped his ear to hear the wind.

"Leper," he called, and he tapped with a stick. "It is I, the king. What dream?"

A stone clattered to his feet. He listened, then tapped again. But the wind was still.

"Do not fear," Yaffia said. "Have faith. Jehovah will provide the answer. A man has but to listen and he will hear.

*　*　*　*　*　*　*

Under a cloak of dark, Zadok lay in his bed and listened to the myriad of sounds that filled the night. "I am the king," he whispered to the dark. "Leper," he called. "Speak!"

The lamplight flickered, and where the shadows leaped, it seemed to Zadok that the leper danced and hopped, an idiot's jig, knee to knee and toe to heel. "Speak," Zadok begged.

But the vision wavered and disappeared.

Far-away shadows fell into the well of sleep. And Zadok dreamed that the leper wakened in his grave and escaped into the light.

Far down in the desert, Zadok saw the leper running toward Gaza from the south. The sun was fierce, beyond all flame. A small stone image of the goddess Astarte was cradled in the leper's hand.

And Zadok shouted: "Stop! What dream! What evil from this desert land! Why the goddess under the blaze of sun?"

But the leper would not speak. On he ran. The sand slipped in streams from his flying heels. Then a sudden wind, and the leper's breath choked with sand. His tongue stuck out between his lips. The tip turned black, and the black grew wings, with beetle feet clinging to the leper's lips. First one. Then ten. Then hundreds filled his beard, his mouth.

Suddenly he disappeared. Only a whirling cloud of dust was left.

The cloud filled Zadok's beard. His throat was parched, without breath.

In a fit of coughing Zadok wakened from his sleep. He coughed and coughed until his body shook. Deep in his throat, he hawked and spat. A thin rivulet of blood and phlegm spilled out. He stared with fingers clenched and wiped the last spittle from his mouth. A thin streak of red clung on his flesh. A shred. But it was his blood, his life!

"Leper," he gasped. "Come back! Speak! It is I, the king!"

He listened. But there was no answer from the night. The wind was still. No voice. . .

With the dawn, the alarm went out. A courier stood ready at the open gate. "Run!" Zadok ordered. "Blow the ram's horn at the temple gates. Let the high priest Kohath hear the call to the Great-House. Run!"

Without delay the high priest summoned the four elders of the council who sat huddled round their warming pots in the chilling morn. Though their bones were cold, they rose up and followed Kohath to the Great-House and into the inner hall where Zadok raised his hand in greeting and bade them sit.

They praised his foresight in calling out to them for counsel. They would serve him with their knowledge of the stars and their wide experience in the realm of omens.

"The leper," began Zadok in a lowered tone, and he told them of the strange happenings in his dream. But there was more to tell, he said. He had wakened in a fit of coughing and spat out blood. "Blood," he repeated and held out his hand.

"A dream of great importance," offered Kohath.

The counselors nodded.

"A portentous dreaming," mumbled one ancient prophet.

They requested time to think on it. There were certain scrolls here and there which must be studied.

They delayed an hour. The sun had already risen above the mountains when Kohath led them back to council. "My lord," he said, "we are gathered here, the five as one, and five times five are the number of tablets which explain the dream." The swarm was locusts, he went on. Locusts would be the scourge of Gaza. That was the meaning.

The sages nodded. They were all agreed. Perhaps their lord was not aware of the intricacies involved, the delicate weighing of every thought. It had required such insight that only the five together had been equal to the task.

"And the blood?" asked Zadok.

"Unimportant," they answered. "A man in a fit of coughing might spit out blood."

"True, my lord," rasped one wrinkled scholar. Whereupon he coughed, then spat on his hand, and there was blood. Did that mean death? No, of course not.

Locusts, they insisted.

A unanimous decision — except for Zadok.

There must be more, he thought. They had failed him. They had blundered and failed. How could they speak of locusts when he had choked and spat out his life. They were blind, these old ones, and that ancient bone who coughed had pestilence in his lungs; with each cough there was blood.

The elders sat patiently at Zadok's feet with the expectation of thanks but Zadok remained silent.

His silence did not sit well with the wisdom-circle. Disappointed, the high priest stroked his beard. "There is more to be fathomed," he declared, stepping forward. "Did the lord Zadok not remember that in his dreaming he had seen Astarte's face? The goddess was pointing to the sacred house, to her priests and her maids. The sign was clear." It was only in her temple, he said, with the aid of oil gazing or the reading of livers that the full meaning could be revealed.

"Let one hour pass and the east light fill the sky before my lord follows to the sacred house where the pots and oils and all things needed shall be prepared."

* * * * * * *

"Enan," cried Zadok to the steward of his house. "Bring the gifts for Astarte's table and place them in a donkey cart. Choose the harness studded with silver discs."

Enan watched while slaves set the gifts within the cart. Then, thumping his staff on the ground with importance, he marched in front to guide the creaking cart beyond the Great-House and open court to the temple walls.

Deep within the heart of Astarte's temple, the high priest waited. Dressed in his high-coned hat and white linen, he strutted about with anticipation. He rubbed his hands and prepared for feasting. He was smiling as he kindled incense on Astarte's altar. He knew that Zadok was not one to deny an Astarte vision. His lord had always taken the greatest care to please the Mistress. Many times before he had laid gifts upon her altar; the best of meats, and scent of sweet incense.

Kohath nodded knowingly. Often in the past, hidden in the long shadows of the torchlight, he had watched while Zadok pressed the flesh of his manhood close to the stone of Astarte's navel and looked into her eyes. She stood on the back of a sculptured lion, rings in her ears, breasts bared, a thin skirt covering her stony thighs. The silvery disc of the moon crowned her hair. In one hand she carried flowers, in the other, a spear and serpent — the sweet and sour which was the way of the goddess, favor or disaster.

Kohath beckoned to an underpriest who stood behind him. "Leave the chamber," he instructed, "and stand by the temple gate to greet the Lord Zadok."

Soon after sunrise, Zadok dismounted from his chariot at the temple gate where the underpriest walked before him and led the way through the heavy portal and into the inner court, then to the stone steps leading down to Astarte's chamber.

Zadok paused on the threshold. He drew a deep breath. He was thinking of Astarte's spear and serpent. No, he thought. He had always served her well. Her anger would be undeserving. He shook his head but with the shaking, his neckpiece rattled like the bones rattling in an augur's cauldron.

"Whatever you command shall be done," Kohath said, bending low before Gaza's lord when he entered.

"Cut for me a sheep," said Zadok. "The purest and the best to lay before Astarte's eyes. Prepare the cauldrons and the oil gazing and whatever else to aid the oracle."

Fledgling priests scurried here and there according to Kohath's instructions. Three up, four down, each carrying a jar of oil or water. Four jars of wine and ten loaves of bread were brought for the sacrifice. The priests stood and swayed in a pensive circle, Kohath in their midst. The sheep they burnt as offering; the liver they read for pox and boils or whether the gall flowed from the left or right.

Then came the answer: "Rejoice! It is not from the goddess that tears will come."

Zadok was smiling as he left the temple. That was satisfactory, clear-spoken and straightforward. No mention of... He paused. Not through her that tears will come? Tears? If not from the Mistress, then from whom!

"What means this!" he whispered.

Chapter Three

A man ran along the narrow road to Gaza. Northward from the south he ran. Barefooted, heels flying up and down, panting as he sucked his breath, his beard matted with blood from a cut high on his cheek. He stumbled into the dry bed of a stream. Up a bank. Past a shepherd and grazing sheep.

From afar, they saw him. A farmer and his oxen stared. A man, bending with hoe and rake, looked up. A shepherd's fluted whistle ceased. From a hillock, shielding eyes from sun, they beckoned, waved their arms.

"Who runs?" they shouted. "Why and where?"

But the runner would not stop to answer.

Down came the watchers from the hill. A fisher left unmended nets. Another joined him, then another. A woman with earth-stained hands, a ragged urchin, children, a barking dog. A goatherd left his herd untended.

Alarm spread through the gathering throng. They pressed close behind, then closer still as the strength ebbed from the runner's limbs. They groaned at his staggering steps. The runner tottered. His knees buckled. They raised him up and urged him on; they bore his weight to Zadok's walls, where he fell senseless to the ground.

Swiftly the captain Eliphas was summoned, and the steward Enan and slaves and soldiers. And Zadok came down running from his tower. He had heard the clamor of the crowd, the cries of shepherds. He followed a wedge of soldiers who drove the people to one side.

The throng grew still.

Zadok stared at the runner who lay sprawled and limp. It was as though he saw the leper once again. "Speak!" he demanded.

"He still lives, Lord," said Eliphas. "He breathes, but he cannot speak."

They carried the wounded runner to a shaded place where they raised his head and washed away the blood. "His lungs have burst with all his running," they whispered, and they poured heated wine between his lips to restore his breath.

The runner coughed. He turned his head. He choked and coughed until his body shook and wine-stained strings of gall spilled from his mouth.

"Speak!" Zadok ordered.

"Egypt is coming!" the runner gasped. He raised himself weakly and pointed south. "Chariots as far as the eye can see. Soldiers, a swarm. Like locusts in a field." Of three brothers, he alone still lived, he said. They had built a blaze against the cold where they had grazed their flock near a running stream. From the darkness came flashing knives. Only he escaped. With flaming torches, Egypt had searched for him among the stones and brush, but burrowed like a mole in sand he had hidden under Egypt's feet.

"Kill all!" he heard them growl. "Leave no survivors to spread the warning!"

They were coming. And under Egypt's feet they would all be buried.

* * * * * * *

"Egypt is coming!"

Alarm swept through the city streets. People ran. A mother held her wailing child. A master and his slave hurried side by side. Crowds gathered near the city gates and in the shadow of the temple.

Before the midday hour they saw a cloud in the distance, a round rim of dust which hung on the southern horizon. Slowly the cloud rose higher. Then the rumbling sound of a beginning thunder; louder and louder. They knew that it was the thump of marching feet, and the neighing of horses, the pounding of hooves, the grinding wheels of chariots and carts.

The people looked south from Gaza's hill to the cloud of dust. Soon it was so near they could see the movement of the approaching horde. They could see the platoons of spearmen and archers following in the wake of the endless columns of chariots.

The people wept. They raised their hands to heaven. They prayed for a miracle to stave off evil, for a plague to descend upon the Egyptian soldiers to sicken them with crawling demons in their lungs and bowels. They prayed that the earth would open up its jaws to swallow the invaders.

Then cries of "Zadok! Zadok!" broke from the pressing mob. They turned to the walls where they had always turned at every threat, whether a roving desert band bent on plunder or brigands who infested the roads and valleys. Zadok had always been their rock, their lion-shield. He would come out and stand above them on the tower's height. They would cheer him as he raised his fist, cheer the anger flashing in his eyes, the defiance from his bearded lips, and they would raise their hands to their lord, their prince, to lead and they would follow.

But now Zadok looked down on the people from the height of the walls, Yaffia by his side, and he shook his head. "Where can I lead them? What can I say in answer to their calls?"

Still the cries of "Zadok! Zadok!" rose through the wind.

"Too late," he said.

He knew, now, what his dreaming had meant, why the south, why the sand. Egypt! These were the beetles he had dreamed and the blood which he had choked and coughed.

"Cursed is my house!" he called aloud. "My kingdom and Gaza's city."

* * * * * * *

In his pride as prince and leader of the people, Zadok accepted his duty to stand against the approaching threat but he was overwhelmed with a feeling of helplessness at the vast force gathering below Gaza's slope. With no hope to match Egypt's might, he instructed the captain Eliphas to muster all available soldiers and deploy them on the walls and at the city gates.

Through the next hours Zadok paced nervously in the hushed silence of the Great-House. At the evening meal, he left his food untouched but drank cup after cup of wine. Later he met with Eliphas in the courtyard. "Egypt will not choose to attack in the dark," Zadok said in lowered tones. "Most likely they will march with the morning light."

From the courtyard, Zadok returned to the Great-House, then went to the chamber where Tamuru slept. The child wakened at his caress and stretched out her hands to him. He gave her drink from a golden cup, then kissed her eyes and face. "Close your eyes and sleep, my love," he said. He lingered there a moment longer as if to cling to the memory of her face. Then a last kiss on the child's cheek.

All the while Yaffia had watched Zadok's every step. She knew what lived in his thoughts, his dread of the hour when he would be forced to meet with defeat face to face, and her heart ached to reach out and give him comfort.

When the bronze flame of the sun turned down below the rim of the world, she danced for Zadok. In their bedchamber where the earth was still. Silently, her shadow swept into the flickering light of the oil lamp standing near the wall.

Softly the cloth flowed and swayed as she turned with her steps. She let her shift fall from her shoulders and breasts. The thin wisp of cloth slipped to her thighs and her feet.

Zadok watched from where he lay on his couch as she bent and curved and raised her arms. She danced for him without a sound, her flesh opened to his eyes, her love exposed; until she kneeled by the couch and swept into his arms.

His robe was opened to the softness of her body. And he took her as if it were the first night again and their first hour, and there were no men of Egypt swarming below.

As he rose to leave the bed, Yaffia reached up to touch him. She hid her fear from his eyes. She pressed his fingers and kissed his hand as he left.

"Lord God," she prayed. "Creator of the universe. Soon the dark horse of war will thunder below the hill. Shield him from the invading horde. Great Jehovah, take my life for his. Only let me hold him in my arms once more."

BOOK TWO

EGYPT

Chapter Four

E gypt's soldiers by the thousands and thousands had come to stand before the walls of Gaza. It was nightfall of the first day by the time the tents were raised and the dust had settled and the camp was lit with the flames of campfires and rows of torches like a vast sea of twinkling lights.

In the centre of the camp the god Amun-Ra had been sheltered in Pharaoh's tent, away from the cold of the desert night. But Pharaoh Thutmosis, having rested and taken food, commanded that the image of stone and gold be brought out into the dark, and the priests clothed the bearded god in a blue striped woolen cloak and carried him to an altar covered with an embroidered cloth.

The idol was small in stature for he was only a replica of the god in Thebes, but he wore the same high plumed headdress of red and blue with the golden sun disc set between. Small as he might be, the god's eyes were here and through these eyes the god in Thebes could see, though it was a thousand leagues to the heart of Egypt, the land of Keme.

By day, the god's vision was clear for he was the Sun, the glorious Amun-Ra. He was the father of all Pharaohs and the reward he bestowed on his children-kings was life after death, to sail forever across the sky in the sun-boat with the father-god at the helm.

"We have arrived," said Thutmosis as he stood beside the image of Amun-Ra. "There lies Gaza," and he pointed into the darkness to Gaza's hill.

Of Gaza, he had spoken many times before. Here was the place where it would all begin. Gaza would be the first to bend its knee. Gold would fill the sacred house at Thebes. The severed hands and heads of the defeated would be piled at the god's altar. This would be the first tribute to the power of Amun-Ra, soon to be known in all the world. Thutmosis bent his head and vowed it.

When he whispered into the god's ear, no one could hear the words Pharaoh spoke. For he had sent off all the royal ones of his inner court. From the dark they watched. Only the Keeper of the Royal Axe stood as sentinel nearby. But he, too, was some twenty paces back.

Under Gaza's night, Pharaoh sat cross-legged by the high peak of flames, his blue war crown reflecting the fiery light. There he would doze at the feet of Amun-Ra until dawn flowed from the god's eye rising in the east, when Pharaoh would once again point above to Gaza's hill and the walls where the battle would be fought.

*　*　*　*　*　*　*

A dark broad cloud drifted across the silvery face of the moon. On the parapet above Gaza's walls, the shadows of Zadok and his captain Eliphas mingled and melted into one.

Death, thought Zadok as he looked to the Egyptian fires below the slope. He saw death in the row upon row of flames. His destiny was unchangeable, his life bound to the curse on his house and bed. "I go alone to meet with Egypt," he said.

When Eliphas begged to lead the way, Zadok took the captain's arm in his. In this, he must stand alone, he said, but for his friend, there was one last task. "Eliphas," he said, turning away from the eyes of his captain. "If I do not return, see to it that Yaffia and the child are dead rather than slaves to Egypt's king."

Then the two comrades in arms were silent. There seemed little more to be said.

At dawn Eliphas watched as the great copper-shielded gate was opened. Alone in his chariot, Zadok rode out and the city gates closed behind him. Without arms, without a shield-bearer, Gaza rode out to meet with Egypt, who had come from across the desert with an eye to conquer and a will to sit highest in the world.

The fires in the Egyptian camp were dead. Dawn was breaking on the slope. Shield to shield, Egypt's soldiers were waiting. From a sentry post the word had come down: "The gate has opened." The lords, bejeweled and silent, had already formed a glittering arc of gilded chariots about Egypt's king.

Zadok threw down the reins of his chariot and went out toward Egypt's host. He bent his neck. He swallowed pride though the weakness within the man was pride. To no man would he bend or yield, his mother had said. In the world he would stand high.

Before Pharaoh Zadok bent low. He stretched out his hands and bowed down in the manner of Egyptians and said, "I recognize in your Majesty the highest of the high. None higher has been, nor ever will be."

Above him stood mighty Pharaoh, silent, tapping his golden whip on the chariot rail. The strength of the man was visible in his well-muscled arms and shoulders. A coat of brazen armor was strapped round his chest. Pharaoh's high cheekboned, clean shaven face had remained rigid like sculptured stone.

A nobleman at Pharaoh's right, eager to see Gaza's head rolling in the dust, took up his axe, his fingers clasped round the golden figure of a hawk inlaid upon the ivory handle.

Thutmosis turned, then thrust out his hand to restrain the zealous lord. A decisive gesture, as if to say: "The decision is mine, not Egypt's nobles." Besides, the royal axe was readied should it come to that — and it might or might not, as it pleased him.

"Let Gaza speak!" declared Thutmosis. He would hear more from Gaza's mouth. The highest of the high, Gaza had said. Admirable and most fitting. A clear recognition of what the world soon would know as truth.

Zadok steeled himself to keep his voice from trembling. "Wherever the sun shines, great Pharaoh and his god shall be known," he said. "To the ends of the earth, and for all eternity."

For the moment Pharaoh was blinded by the flattery. Not that the words were new. He had heard the same high praise many times within the walls of his royal house, but it seemed to him that Egyptian tongues had lacked the sincerity that flowed from the tongue of foreign Gaza.

"Let Gaza speak on!" Thutmosis ordered. "He has come to bend his head, and I would ask him why."

"For Gaza's sake," murmured Zadok.

"Then you choose to die to spare your people?"

"It is Pharaoh's choice," said Zadok. He bit his tongue lest he spit out a curse that could end only in disaster. "It is Pharaoh's choice, for the world and all its kings and cities will lie at Pharaoh's feet and be blinded by his splendor."

Pharaoh's inner eye applauded. It was his secret inner vision. He thought of it as an eye looking inward deep into his brain. Useful in detecting false pretenses. "A most reasonable man, this noble Gaza," Pharaoh said. He turned to his royal circle and raised his hands as if to say, "Do you not agree?"

Then, turning, he said, "Gaza, you have recognized quickly what the world soon will not fail to see. For this, you deserve reward. What shall it be?"

Zadok bent his head and was silent.

"Gaza," Pharaoh said again, "I have spoken. I have said it. What reward? Is it so difficult a choice?"

"I would choose an easy death," Zadok answered, "but if that displease the great king, then I would choose to live, to bear witness to his power when he goes forth to battle. I would live to tell of it to my children and their children, that his might and glory be recorded and remembered for all eternity."

Pharaoh's inner eye blinked with delight.

"Then bear first witness now!" Thutmosis cried out. "Gaza, bear witness now to my might and let all Keme's nobles hear it and remember. Gaza shall live as his just reward. Here no blood shall be shed. His city shall suffer neither fire nor sword, and his house is free. He shall pay a tribute of gold and jewels into the temple of my celestial father who now shines upon us and who has led me to this foreign land. Gaza shall provide foods and wine for my charioteers, archers and spearmen, fodder for my horses. Lastly, my noble prince, your god shall step down from his pedestal, and his house from this day forward shall be the house of Amun-Ra, lord of the universe, whose divine son I am for all eternity. Open your gate and lay the city at my feet. Live, Gaza. This is your reward from Egypt."

At Pharaoh's signal, a procession of drummers and trumpeters and soldiers with banners flying led Egypt's king along the road to Gaza's gate. Behind the royal chariot, Zadok walked in the cloud of dust raised by the wheels. His feet were dust. His robe. His beard and mouth were filled with the dust lifted by Pharaoh's steeds.

On the stony ground below Gaza's gate, Zadok kneeled.

While the world watched, the priests of Amun-Ra raised their chant to heaven and gave a basket of Gaza's earth into the hands of Pharaoh, who held it high and poured the dust of defeat on Zadok's head. The earth and sand swept into Zadok's beard and on his face until the basket was emptied.

Zadok had shut his eyes so that he saw no one in the bitterness of his defeat. Now he rose from his knees and shook himself free from the flow of earth and sand. Stepping forward to Gaza's gate, he raised his fist against the copper, striking at it with the violence of his trembling hate.

"Open, Eliphas! Open!" he shouted, and struck his fist until the skin was broken and blood marked his rapping. "Peace is made!" He raised his hand with the blood running from his knuckles. "Proclaim a feast. The great king has been generous in his terms."

"Open, Gaza!" cried Thutmosis to the soldiers on the walls. "Have no fear. Your women and children have been spared."

* * * * * * *

Pharaoh Thutmosis had risen up to sit upon the throne of Egypt where his father Amenhotep and his father's father had sat before him, but unlike his father who had been a docile man, Thutmosis had a will for power which drove him north from Egypt to conquer distant lands. It was not for plunder; the wealth of Egypt's coffers and stores of grain were already his. The driving force, the key to his ambition, was a hidden thorn, deep and ever present.

Thutmosis suffered a secret inner pain, for a blemish on his birth had left a blemish on his honor. Though he was born a son to Pharaoh, she who gave him birth was merely a concubine in his father's elegant pavilion; a minor harem-maid whose enticing hips had caught his royal father's eye. Out of this union, Thutmosis had been born, a Pharaoh with a blood heritage of half-royalty. A blemish in the eyes of Egypt. However slight, still a blemish.

Though he had risen to the highest, the son of the great Amun-Ra, Thutmosis was not satisfied. He would frown, purse his lips, and his inner eye would see the truth: he was still the son of Sonisonbu, a concubine, though she had been proclaimed royal mother.

Thutmosis was determined to prove himself doubly worthy of the throne of gold and his place in the Sun. Not only to himself, not only to

Egypt, but to all the world. In the temples, the priests of Amun-Ra would chant his praise to the Sun: "Greatest among all kings is Pharaoh Thutmosis!" This was the dream of glory which led him on his path of conquest.

*   *   *   *   *   *   *

Leading Egypt's horde, Pharaoh in his chariot rode through the marketplace and streets of Gaza. Drums and trumpets blared. Heralds called out what Pharaoh had shouted to the walls above the gate.

"Gaza, have no fear. Your women and children have been spared."

A benevolent Pharaoh. Lenient terms, but the lenient terms of a conqueror who, for the moment, was inclined to be indulgent toward his newly subjugated vassal prince, but a benevolence subject to change at a whim or a careless word.

He liked a man of reason, Pharaoh said later to Zadok who had been summoned to the royal presence in the temple. He insisted that he and Zadok had this one thing in common: they were both reasonable and farsighted.

And there were other things besides.

"I have been given to understand that your house has been blessed with sweet fruit in the form of a child princess who is loved, even as my own royal house has been blessed with a princess of royal blood, Hatshepsut, who one day will sit as queen."

"May your royal life be blessed with yet more fruit," Zadok replied.

"And may your own efforts be fruitful with your shepherd maid or another of your choice. May we both be blessed with sons," said Pharaoh, who seemed to know everything about Zadok's household, even to the privacy of his bedchamber.

For all his benevolence, Thutmosis was perverse to the core. Many were the things he wished to know and from Zadok alone would he accept the answers.

Not that he was unaware of the political structure and natural topography of the land. He was well informed. A host of scribes of Thebes and other cities had recorded all that was known of the various regions of Asia. The borders of the tribal kingdoms were noted, as well as their names both in Egyptian script and foreign. The Zahi, people of the sea, dwelled in the coastal region and Gaza. The Kharu inhabited the mountains and the valleys, while further north, a great host of tribes and kingdoms were gathered into the collective term Rotanu, with the further subdivision of Upper and Lower. All this had been written in red inks and black in neatly ordered lists. The caravan routes and roads, passable and impassable, were mapped, and for the military, the positions of the many local fortresses were noted.

These things Thutmosis knew, and many others, but in his pretense of ignorance, many were the things he insisted he would like to know.

"The rain?" he asked. The waters of the heavens, he called it. To him, it appeared adequate for the soil but unreliable. Certainly not so fruitful as the yearly inundating wave of Egypt's great river.

"Are you not of the same opinion?" he asked, raising his eyebrows and expecting the proper answer. "Your god," he went on, "your Dagon, half-fish and half-man." Here Thutmosis smiled. A god of the sea and sky and air, all in one. "Quite strange," he remarked. "But the fish god, too, must learn to bow down," he added sternly.

There were seemingly endless questions, each unmistakably phrased in such a way as to leave little doubt which land was the more civilized. Thutmosis did not specifically refer to the Zahi as barbaric, but there was always the innuendo that this seacoast land, this Canaan-Zahi, had much to learn from Egypt's far-advanced culture.

The kingly questions, with their mood of half-interest, were clearly intended to let it be known that Egypt was well enough informed not to be duped. Pharaoh would not look lightly on any attempt at deceit, especially where it concerned the subjection of the Zahi god and his homage to Amun-Ra. There was to be no secretive uplifting of the vanquished Dagon. In the temple he would remain, but only as servant to the divine golden disc, celestial father of Pharaoh.

However, when it came to questions of the goddess Astarte, Pharaoh's attitude of half-interest pointedly grew into full interest. Here he lingered, refusing to pass over her briefly. Her form and figure, clothed and unclothed, her rites, the priestess and maidens of the mother-cult, their pleasure giving — all this he wished to know, and his eyes sparkled as he listened.

The son of Amun-Ra forgot himself for the moment and took on the characteristics of a son of man, parting his moist lips with anticipation. All of it ended with a come-and-see type of conversation, once Zadok realized that this had been Pharaoh's intent from the beginning.

It was clear that Thutmosis was not adverse to sharing his manliness, kingly and divine though it was, with others less divine than his royal spouse. At home in Medinet, the palace at Thebes, this man-side of him had not been evident, though his pavilion of women was far from empty and contained many who lolled and painted themselves while they waited his pleasure. He had always proclaimed quite loudly, and always within earshot of his spouse, that he did not care to waste himself on others, but he had shed no tears when he stepped aboard his ship and left behind a half empty couch at Thebes.

At Memphis, he had forgotten all about his former declarations when the virgin daughter of the high priest of the temple was brought before him. Her parents, overjoyed at the honor which had come into their lowly house, clapped their hands for joy.

She was a young, dark-eyed, timid maid, who was frightened and confused, though she understood full well the honor and duty which lay before her. Perhaps she was too young, or perhaps it was the suddenness with which she was whisked away from her garden to the royal barge, but she shuddered when she knelt before her king. She shuddered when she stood up. She shuddered when she lay upon his couch, and even whimpered a little, which was scarcely pleasing behavior for a maiden who had been chosen to please Pharaoh. In his disgust, he picked her up bodily and dropped her overboard into the water. Had it not been for the alertness of the captain of the watch who lowered a rope, she would have drowned.

Thutmosis had fared better when he went ashore at Zalu, the Egyptian border fortress on the military road to Gaza. It was here that he first came into contact with a moon-maiden of the foreign Astarte goddess of whom he had heard so much; a maiden who more than once had followed priest and priestess to the sacred hilltop grove where the tribe performed their frenzied ritual to the moon and fertile earth.

She was a brown-skinned maid, fierce-eyed, not ugly at all as he had expected these barbarians to be, but as shapely as he had ever seen. An under-officer of a marauding chariot squadron had taken her captive, bound her hand and foot, and rolled her squirming body toward Pharaoh's feet as he might a bundle of faggots. In principle, all booty taken, whether slaves or goods or gold, was the property of Pharaoh, but it was usual that a slave be given to the soldier who had made her captive as reward for duty and valor. Thutmosis had already raised his hand to bestow this gift when he suddenly changed his mind and gave her to himself, throwing the soldier a gold chain in her stead.

Her robe was torn and ragged. She was not clean like the timid maid who had been brought to him at Memphis but he soon had her made clean, oiled and painted, and clothed in fine white linen. A small gift of a bronze bracelet brought her first joyous smile and a burst of foreign gibberish, which was proof enough that she was pleased. A feast of fine roast meats, wheat bread and wine made her openly affectionate. A fierce and lively affection which gave Thutmosis intense pleasure; so much so that he had her brought out of Zalu on the march to Gaza. Now, in Gaza, he wished to learn more of these desert moon-sprites with Zadok and the high priestess as his guide.

"It will be arranged without delay," replied Zadok.

"Tonight?"

"For Pharaoh, this very night."

"And the wine-feasting as you have called it?"

"All that will be arranged, my lord, and more."

And Thutmosis crowed aloud his pleasure.

Chapter Five

Though the sands of defeat had been strewn freely on Zadok's head, still, there was much grumbling among Egypt's nobles who had come up from the land below to this city of great wealth. The lordly circle were vexed that Zadok still ruled in Gaza, and they looked askance at this unexpected turn of events. A man of Egypt should rule in Zadok's stead. Pharaoh should have chosen one of them. They came before Thutmosis with their grievance, though they kept it subtly hidden.

"Of noble Gaza," they said cautiously. "That Gaza lived was the decision of king and god." There was no question of Zadok's head being lopped off and placed in the golden lap of Amun-Ra who now was seated highest in Dagon's city. They were all agreed that Gaza should live, for his gates had been opened and no Egyptian blood had been shed. Save five spearmen or perhaps ten who in their drunkenness had fallen and struck their heads against stones but through no fault of Zadok's. He was truly a worthy man of reason.

"This Zahi prince," they cried, "this Adoni as his servants address him. He is a man defeated, and no doubt bitter in his defeat, and a bitter man is not forever reasonable," they said to Pharaoh, who listened but remained silent.

"Bitterness is the end to reason," offered a lean, wry-necked noble whose eyes were poised on the city's wealth.

"True," nodded Pharaoh. He sensed what lay behind their tongues. He knew they meant to swallow Gaza and his inner eye winked and twinkled at the eagerness of his lords. He grunted as if to give approval, then cupped his hand over his nose and mouth with an air of doubt.

"Still," he frowned, glancing from lord to lord, "Gaza bowed his head with proper humbleness during the ceremonies which celebrated his defeat."

"Merely for the moment, Oh great Pharaoh. Merely forceful self-restraint." They crowded round, eager to defend their position.

"But self-restraint is a mark of reason," declared Thutmosis. "Surely none of my nobles doubts my insight concerning Gaza's most reasonable qualities. In any case, we shall see." He raised his hands and dismissed them with the inference that it was too soon to judge. "Meanwhile let Gaza's folly condemn the man, or let his reason prevail. We shall see," said Pharaoh again. "There will be ample opportunity."

Opportunities for Zadok to lose his self-control were arranged without delay by Egypt's nobles. Elaborate preparations with flute and horn. A glittering host, captains and under captains. Priests clad in lion skins draped closely round their left shoulders clashed their cymbals as they marched around Amun-Ra, the golden god of Egypt seated highest in the temple. Zadok, prince and vassal, was brought forward to bow down and pay homage.

Pharaoh and his courtiers watched closely as Zadok stretched himself out before the god. They watched as he rose up, sidled backward and bent to Pharaoh. But Egypt's nobles were disappointed that Zadok remained humbled and silent.

"There he lies, your fish-tailed god!" jeered one lord of Egypt. He prodded the broken stump of Dagon's tail. "What worth a fish out of water! He must be rubbed with salt, or soon he will stink."

Zadok bit his tongue. He refused to fall into their trap. His memory turned back to the prophecy of the goddess Astarte. "Not through her that tears will come," he whispered to himself, "but through weakness in the face of Egypt."

And Zadok sang out praise to Pharaoh, calling him 'chosen one' and 'god above all gods'. He sang loud and long to the pleasure of Pharaoh's sensitive inner eye, which in turn led to bilious dispositions among the royal lords of Egypt. Some fumed, others were astounded that Zadok retained his composure. Not one fault, not one flare of contempt. Having failed to set him down and have one of them set up in his place, they were doubly angered and refused to let the matter end.

The malevolence of Egypt's inner circle now became more vicious and daring.

* * * * * * *

Black was the hour when it became clear to Zadok that the door of his garden-house had been opened wide to the eyes of Egypt. It happened on a day when he was absent.

A lion hunt had been arranged for Pharaoh. Runners shouting "Make way for Pharaoh!" led the procession of soldiers and hunters to the west gate. A perfect opportunity. The lords of Egypt could not resist. No sooner had the sound of drums faded in the distance when three men of Egypt burst into the garden of Zadok's house of women. They obviously knew which door was closed, which was open, and where to find Yaffia near Jehovah's altar.

In a moment they had swept her up, her eyes wide with fright. A muffled scream, and they fled with her in a waiting chariot as swiftly as they had appeared.

When Zadok and Eliphas returned, they found the household in an uproar. The slave Shatah came running with tears and cries. "Three men of Egypt have carried Yaffia off!" She had seen them as they fled. Three noblemen. Three highborn. The sun had glittered on the gold of their armbands and their jewelled neckpieces.

His heart pounding, Zadok leaped to his chariot and raced to the temple which now served as Pharaoh's royal house. On the stone steps, he saw Yaffia's red cloak in a crumpled heap, but a detachment of black-skinned soldiers from the forests of Nubia stood shoulder to shoulder, barring the temple gate.

With a sword in each hand, Zadok sprang to the attack but pharaoh's guards raised their shields to form a wall. Egypt's lords watched and waited expectantly from a nearby alcove.

"Open!" Zadok bellowed.

The clatter of arms brought Pharaoh from his quarters. "Hold!" he shouted.

Zadok's voice rose to a shriek. "Where is she?"

"Why the turmoil? Your sister is safe," Thutmosis replied. "She sits in comfort."

"She is not my sister. She is my wife," Zadok gasped. He fell to his knees before Egypt's king.

"So?" Thutmosis appeared surprised. "My nobles said only that she was sister to Gaza's king. Be at peace. No harm has come to her. Why, then, make so much of it between us? She is only a maid. Of what importance is a maid between men?"

"She is my queen," said Zadok.

"A beauty indeed," replied Thutmosis. "You have kept her well hidden. I will buy her," he declared.

Zadok humbly bent his neck. "Even a man defeated cannot sell his heart." He could say no more. Fear stilled his tongue.

Thutmosis studied the man. He sucked in his lips. His inner eye had suddenly wakened to the plot. He frowned. It was clear that he was annoyed with the scheming mischief of his lords.

"Bring her then," he ordered the soldiers on guard and when Yaffia appeared in the doorway, Pharaoh turned to Zadok. "Take her back to your garden," he said. "Go."

He beckoned to the lords of his court who gathered attentively. "Pharaoh thanks his noble servants. The beauty of Gaza's queen deserves to sit at Pharaoh's side. My Majesty found her presence most pleasurable." He smiled. Yaffia's sweet scent lingered in the antechamber. He had caught a glimpse of her thigh where the cloth of her robe had been torn away. He thought of his hand on the high haunch of her limb and the strength of his groin wakened.

"Such beauty is truly deserving," he said to his lords, "but the abduction was an error. The fright could close a maiden's heart to Pharaoh. What need for violence? There are other ways to win the maid."

* * * * * * *

Egypt's herald appeared in Zadok's court at sunset of the following day. "A great feast has been proclaimed. Hear Pharaoh's voice!" the herald cried. "Call out to Gaza's queen in her house. A litter awaits to carry her to the great king's side, while Gaza's prince will follow in his chariot."

Suspicion crept into Zadok's mind but he said nothing to Yaffia as they made ready to depart.

Servants with flaming torches led the way to the temple where the highborn of Gaza and their ladies had already gathered with the lords of Egypt in the brightly lit banquet chamber. The richly bejeweled guests were seated according to their importance in rows of single and double chairs around small tables. Scantily clad slaves distributed dishes and napkins and offered jars of wine and silver bowls laden with fruit. Pharaoh sat enthroned on a low divan in the centre of the room.

A fawning chamberlain ushered Yaffia to the place of honor at Pharaoh's side. Zadok was directed farther back.

Reluctantly, Yaffia sat by the side of Pharaoh. She chose an orange from a bowl of fruit and slowly peeled it with a small bronze knife, the handle inlaid with blue and yellow gems. Thutmosis edged closer moment by moment. She leaned backward but Pharaoh took her hand in his and deftly pressed his knee against her. He lightly touched her arm, then her shoulder. He brushed against her breast as if by accident.

Yaffia drew back. Her body tensed.

Her reluctance only spurred Pharaoh to caress her further. Stealthily he moved his hand to stroke her thigh, and he smiled with his pleasure.

The color drained from Yaffia's face. She would have pulled herself free from his grasp, but she feared lest Egypt's king take it as an insult and injure Zadok. To her relief, Pharaoh's attention was diverted for the moment by the lords of the inner circle who had approached. With honeyed smiles, they gathered round Pharaoh. They had brought a work of the greatest art. Rare gems of lapis and jade encrusted on a bed of gold plucked from the wealth of Gaza's god.

Thutmosis pressed the priceless gift to the hollow of his neck where all the world would see its wealth, but he was soon distracted by the ringing clash of cymbals followed by the swirl of temple dancing girls. They were joined by a high-born maid of Gaza, dark haired and voluptuous. Her body swayed. She kicked her limbs high. Her breasts swung freely with every twist. As she brushed near Egypt's king, he reached out to clutch her arm and he pinched her breast. She cried out in pain and turned away. Pharaoh laughed aloud. Refilling his wine cup, he drank again and again. He grew more boisterous with each hour that passed.

Yaffia could not escape his hot drunken breath and his red face bedewed with sweat. As she tried to draw back from his touch, she caught a glimpse of one noble snoring lightly, his head slumped on the table, his wine cup still clutched in his hand. In desperation, hoping that Pharaoh might fall into a drunken stupor, she began to ply him with more and more drink.

Before long, Pharaoh felt unsteady. The room spun round and round when he turned his head. He clutched his brow and clung to the edge of the table. Summoning his strength, he forced a smile and pressed

Yaffia's hand in his. "Another festive time will come," he said. "A private hour when we will sit side by side, touch to touch, with no watching eyes to mar the bliss." Then he raised his hand to his herald who thumped loudly on his drum as a signal that the feasting time had come to an end.

* * * * * * *

A deep resentment had filled Zadok's soul throughout the festive night. Egypt's nobles, in their animosity, had spoken no word to him. He had tried again and again to see the place where Yaffia sat, but his vision had been blocked and he had seen nothing of Pharaoh's brazen lewdness toward her.

Now, as Yaffia stood silent beside him in his chariot and the temple walls faded from sight, the light of the crescent moon shone on Yaffia's face and he saw that her lips trembled. "The great king touched me," she said. She remembered the heat of Pharaoh's hands pressed on her flesh. "Here, and here," she said, looking downward to her thighs.

Zadok's eyes darkened. He could feel his anger coursing through his blood. He felt helpless. In a sudden wave of fury, he seized his spear and broke the shaft, then flung the broken pieces below the wheels of the chariot. Like an animal caged, he viciously struck at the guardrail of his chariot with his whip.

"Take care, my lord," Yaffia said, and caressed Zadok's shoulder. They had passed through the gate into the courtyard. "Restrain your anger for the sake of the child. Pharaoh is now the power in this land. He holds the royal axe in his right hand."

Late that night, Yaffia lay by Zadok's side in the upper chambers of the Great-House. Her body trembled in her sleep. Her arms twisted restlessly. In her dream, she saw herself alone with Pharaoh in his private chamber. He had flung her down on the bed. He reached out to her breast. She tried desperately to resist.

Zadok gathered her in his arms and she wakened from her nightmare. "Have no fear," he said. "You are safe here with me. I will find a way to shield you from Egypt's might. Even if I must beg the aid of demons of the underworld. I will pay whatever price they might ask."

"I have little trust in the aid of demons," Yaffia replied. "I choose to place my trust in God. We must go together to the altar and pray."

By the light of a torch they went to Jehovah's sacred table which Zadok had built near her house in the garden soon after Tamuru's birth. He had sent word to a priest among the shepherds of the south to bring the altar-stone from God's mountain. No heathen hands had touched the cart or the donkey which had carried the sacred stone from the south. With the help of sons born of priests, the holy man had laid stone upon stone in Zadok's garden, then anointed the altar with fine wine and oil. Thus, the altar, kept pure and untouched, had been consecrated to the god Jehovah.

Zadok and Yaffia removed their sandals. In the dark of night they kneeled together before the sacred stone. With her hands folded before her face, Yaffia prayed. A rising wind rushed through the trees and Yaffia stood erect. She listened.

Then Zadok felt her touch on his arm. He looked up and saw pain in her eyes. Tears dropped in quiet streams on her cheeks. Her head drooped. "God's voice has spoken to my heart," she said. "I must return to the shepherds' fields and the brothers' tents. I must leave both you and the child. I must turn back to Jehovah's house."

From the altar, Yaffia went to Tamuru's chamber. The child wakened with the sudden light of the torch and Yaffia sat beside her on the bed.

"I must leave you," she said in a low voice. "It is God's will, but the day shall come when Jehovah will bring us back together." Yaffia gathered Tamuru to her breast. "Remember always that you are a child of God."

"I love you," she wept, "but I must leave you now. Close your eyes and sleep. I will pray that God watch over us until we meet again."

*　*　*　*　*　*　*

The stillness of the early morning lay upon the high walls of the Great-House. The doors were locked and silent, the slaves asleep in their beds.

Near the outer gate of the courtyard, the captain Eliphas and the

lord Zadok whispered side by side. Eliphas held two riding asses and a pack animal by the reins. He wore the rough mantle of a farmer, only a dagger at his side.

"You are my most trusted and loyal friend," said Zadok. "Yaffia's life is in your hands. Guide her to the lands of her kin and the tents of her brothers, then return to me with word that she is safe. Speak to no one on the way or beyond the city gate. To the Egyptians who guard the south gate, you will be a farmer and his wife newly married, returning to their village after the celebration at a nearby inn. Take care. No one must know who she is. Protect her and guard her, my friend."

They turned at the sound of footsteps. From the garden, Yaffia approached dressed in a coarse peasant's robe and a woolen shawl which covered the black sweep of her hair. She walked with head bent to hide the tears she had wept while she held the child Tamuru to her breast.

"My lord," she said. Her voice trembled. "I have said my farewells to the babe. Keep her gently. I will pray daily that Jehovah protect you both." She caressed his brow, as though the tenderness of her fingers touched his soul. The weight of a stone filled her throat at the sadness in his eyes. "My love, have faith," she said. "Jehovah will bring us together again at the time of His choice. Great is the god of Pharaoh in the eyes of men for he is of gold, but an even greater power is the Lord Jehovah, the Creator of the Universe."

* * * * * * *

Some hours after dawn had lit the morning sky, Zadok called out to the steward Enan to make ready his chariot. Then, in a burst of speed, he raced off to the temple amid the clatter of hooves. At the temple gate, a groom seized the bridle and Zadok leapt down. "I must speak with Pharaoh!" he demanded of the captain of the guard who came forward to meet him. "Guide me to the great king."

The captain knocked loudly on the door to the inner chamber, then beckoned Zadok to follow. Zadok pressed his forehead to the ground before Pharaoh. He turned his eyes upward to Pharaoh's face. "My queen, is she here?" Zadok brow was furrowed in a pretense of concern.

"Not in this house," answered Pharaoh. "Not within these walls. Nor among my lords. Why do you seek her here? Is she not in her garden?"

"Great king of kings, I have searched everywhere. My last hope was to find her here." Zadok glanced furtively at Pharaoh's face. "Great lord, I fear Yaffia has fled. I should have suspected something was amiss when she met with shepherds in my courtyard, her kinfolk among them. I believe she has run off with a lover. My house has been dishonored by a shepherd maid, and I am left to look the fool and remain the butt of laughter before great Pharaoh and the world."

"You should have sold her to me when I offered to buy her," said Pharaoh. "Now you have neither her nor the riches you would have gained. But console yourself, Gaza. Willing breasts abound in the world. There is no lack in pleasures of the flesh. My Majesty gives you permission to leave. We will not speak of your shame again."

Zadok sidled out backward, head down. In his chariot, he breathed a sigh of relief.

Later, when Eliphas returned with word that Yaffia was safe, a thankful Zadok poured a libation of the purest wine on Jehovah's altar.

* * * * * * *

Zadok suffered Yaffia's departure in silence. To Egypt, he put on a smiling face, but he suffered deeply in his soul, and the man's heart hardened without his love by his side. For Yaffia's sake, Zadok laid the best of meats before the Lord God and made fire daily in the twilight hours.

In his wisdom, he kept his distance from the temple on Gaza's hill which now served Amun-Ra. Clearly, the great Dagon was dead. The god lay on his side in the temple probably never to rise again, even though his broken fishtail could be repaired. The high priest Kohath had been driven off. Not one underpriest remained to serve the stone. Only the goddess Astarte and her priestess had survived and awaited Pharaoh's beck and call.

Not one day passed when Zadok did not bow down to the glory of Amun-Ra. In the light of the sun, Zadok raised his hand to the searing flame and cried out to the height of the sky, "Hail to the mighty Amun-Ra who rises in the horizon of heaven and shines with joy over the world!"

He said it aloud both within his own courtyard and without. It was for Egyptian ears to hear, and the spies in the pay of Egypt's lords that he was certain infested his house.

He had a shrine built to Amun-Ra in a small room adjacent to his bedchamber. A statue of the god stood on an altar, a tripod for incense burning beside it. The flames of two torches played their shadows on the walls. A shrine to please Pharaoh.

Zadok would have been ashamed before Yaffia, but her eyes were in another land. She saw only God's mountain and she was safe from Pharaoh and Egypt's lust.

Chapter Six

The captain Eliphas tapped on the entrance to Zadok's chamber. "Adoni," he called. "A merchant is here. The man Caleb. He brings an amulet for the lady Copperakh of the garden house."

Zadok looked down on the man who was brought before him. A thin wisp of a man with crooked nose and small peering eyes. He was dressed in a black and gray striped mantle slung over one shoulder and drawn in at the waist with a cord. A long white scar ran from the lobe of his right ear to his throat. He combed his beard as though to hide it.

The captain bent down and spoke in a low voice to Zadok. "This merchant is well known in the city. He deals in Egyptian wares for the most part."

Zadok's eyes narrowed at the word 'Egyptian'. It was clear he was not pleased. "Merchant, this amulet you bring for the lady Copperakh, from which land does it come?"

"Not from the land of Egypt, lord," the merchant answered. "Not from that impure earth. The God of shepherds led me to it. Guiding my small caravan through the barren hill country, I was attacked by brigands. As I defended myself, I called out to Jehovah for aid and the robbers fled. It was then God led me to a bush aflame yet not consumed by fire, where the amulet lay on the earth under the red glow of twigs and leaves. Without burn or pain, my hand plucked the stone of power which I now bring to the lady Copperakh."

Zadok's brow furrowed. "And this God of the eastern mountains and desert," he asked, "did you see His face?"

"Nay, lord, He is unseen. He lives in the clouds."

"And His voice? Did He whisper your name?"

"Nay, lord, not in my ear. His voice is thunder, without words, so they say."

Zadok knew the God was Yaffia's. She had spoken of a burning bush on Jehovah's mountain. "You may come into this courtyard with your wares," he said to the merchant. "My captain will guide you. Your goods are welcome in this house."

"My lord is kind," said Caleb. "Lead me, dear captain," and he followed Eliphas to the garden gate.

In an arbor beyond, the lady Copperakh waited half hidden in the shadow of the trees. She beckoned to Caleb, who took the amulet from the folds of his robe. She clutched it tightly in her fingers and gave the merchant a purse in return.

"The love potion which I promised," he whispered, "soon I will give it into your hands."

* * * * * * *

Copperakh had come into Zadok's house at the age of twelve, the daughter of a chieftain who lived in the northern forests. A precocious beauty, whose copper-coloured hair was her greatest pride. None other had hair with such sheen, like the flame of sunset on a cloud. At one time, before Yaffia, she had been Zadok's favored. She had already born him a child; but a stillborn princeling with face as puffed and red as was her hair, and over the years she had hoped for a second son whose blood was strong.

That night, with the amulet pressed to her breast, she followed the steward Enan's torch through the darkness of the Great-House to Zadok's bedchamber.

Zadok heard her footsteps in the corridor. "Who walks in the night?" he called.

"It is I, your handmaiden," she answered, and stepped into the dim lamplight of his inner chamber. She loosed her mantle and her copper-colored hair, unplaited, fell sweeping to her shoulders.

"I sent no word to the garden," Zadok said. "You should have waited with the others. Have you no wisdom within your copperhead? Demons fly about in the dark night air."

"I have no fear of demons," she insisted. "See my lord. I have this magic amulet."

Copperakh revealed the charm. A black stone, thin and flat. It dangled from a beaded rope knotted about its narrow middle. Wind the rope round and round your thighs, the merchant had instructed, and lay the stone flat on your flesh, on the belly-mound below your navel when your shift is open to your lord.

She took Zadok's hand in hers to touch the sacred stone. He felt the softness of her skin, the warmth of her limbs. The flesh of her thighs quivered.

Zadok succumbed; he led her to the couch.

* * * * * * *

Freshly robed, the merchant Caleb stepped from his threshold into the morning sunlight. He lived in a small house not far from the market. A poor hovel, shabby, but well suited to his meagre habits. He made his way through the market to the south gate of the city where two merchantmen of Egypt waited, one tall, one fat. The tall Egyptian took out a small vial which had lain hidden in his inner garment.

"We have procured it at great expense" he said. "The love potion which the lady Copperakh requested for the lord Zadok's cup. The magic moon-dust to ensure his love. Very precious. You should gain considerable profit, even more than gold. Perhaps a red gem and a blue."

"A thousand thanks," said Caleb and humbly bent his head, but his eyes were sparkling with his success.

"In five days we will meet again for payment," said the elder Egyptian. Then the two men of Egypt turned abruptly and walked away.

"A thousand thanks!" cried Caleb again, and pressed the vial to the innermost folds of his garment, close to his breast.

The vial felt warm in his fingers. He could feel the heat against his flesh. Love, he said to himself. Love is warm.

As a child, Caleb had never known love. Neither a mother's love, nor a father's. He was beaten almost daily with a stick by an elder brother who died of hate. His mother and father, hardened with a life of poverty, knew nothing of love.

His slave met him at the doorway to his hovel. He had allowed himself the luxury of this one slave since her cost was small. She was of common desert breed, neither old nor young, neither short nor tall, but somewhat fat. She was without the ability of speech, her tongue having been firmly fastened in her mouth since birth. Otherwise she was whole and willing and served well to prepare his food and wash his feet. She walked backward, smiling, nodding, pleased at his return.

Dreaming of the magic in the vial, Caleb wondered if she knew the warmth of love. Not likely, he thought to himself. Born a slave as she was. But with the warmth of the potion against his breast, Caleb saw his slave in another light. The vial was small. Two drops would go unnoticed. There would still be enough.

Carefully he took the vial from the folds of cloth and poured two drops into a cup of water. Ah! Three drops! No matter. A murky cloud spread through the water. "Drink this," he said, and offered the cup to his slave. "Yes, drink it." He nodded as she took the cup. He watched as she drank. "Good," he said.

Eagerly Caleb waited for the cloud in the water to work its magic, but his slave suddenly cried out in pain and grasped her side. Her face drained white. She fell to her knees and retched, her hair falling round her face and neck.

Caleb clapped his hands to his beard and shrieked in fright. "Ahi! What is this!"

With a cloth and a jar of water, he wet her brow over and over, until the water ran from her chin and hair. He brought goat's milk to ease the pain in her bowel. Not knowing what else to do, he bade her drink more and more, which eased her pain and her retching stopped.

Caleb helped her to a bed of straw where she lay down and closed her eyes. "Sleep," he said, and covered her with a woolen shawl. "Rest," he said. "Whatever the evil, it has been driven out."

With the vial clutched firmly in his hand, Caleb closed the door and left his house. He hurried through the market, half-walking, half-running toward the south gate of the city, then down Gaza's hill to the sand dunes where the sea washed the shore.

In a secluded spot he stepped into the surf. His feet sank in the sand below the waves until his robe and knees were wet. He emptied the vial into the water. A black cloud spread round and down to his feet. Two fish floated to the surface, belly to the clouds above, and they were dead.

"Poison!" Caleb compressed his lips.

The two Egyptians! They had conspired to poison the lord Zadok. They had deceived him with their tale of a love potion for the lady Copperakh. He had very nearly killed his own slave for the sake of love. Viciously Caleb flung the empty vial far from the shore.

When he returned to his house, his slave had wakened. Smiling, she took his hand, as if to say she was grateful he had fought for her against the monster who had battled in her flesh. She pressed his hand gently to her breast. He felt her warmth, her love. Tears, the first in many years, sprang to his eyes. A strange world, he thought. Even for love, there was a price to be paid.

* * * * * * *

In five days Caleb met again with the two men of Egypt as they had requested. Spies! he said to himself. Jackals! He took care to hide his anger. He lightly bent his head toward the ground like a man concerned with other thoughts.

The Egyptians leaned forward.

"Freedman," said the fat Egyptian, "what profit?"

"The lady Copperakh has not yet put payment in my hand," replied Caleb. "She gave the potion to a soldier of the guard. It was he whom she loved, not Prince Zadok. Tragically her lover died soon after with a demon-pain in his side."

Caleb watched the two Egyptians. Their faces had drained white.

"The potion was most precious," said the elder merchant. "Precious," he said again. "Difficult to replace." They would have to go back to Egypt. "We may not return to Gaza for some time." With that, they turned and left and Caleb knew he would not see them again.

No sooner had the Egyptians turned their backs than Caleb ran off to Zadok in the Great-House. "Lord", began Caleb, "you must hear what I have come to say. Evil days are come among us. My ears have been open in the market square. Egyptian spies are everywhere. They walk freely in the market. I have heard whispers. Be wary. My lord must not drink a potion from any hand. From any hand," he repeated. "Even wine may be filled with death."

Startled, Zadok listened. He saw the sincerity in the merchant's eyes. "Caleb," he said. It was the first time he had called the freedman by name. "You have proved your loyalty to my house. I grant you the status of trusted courier, to travel on my behalf to the shepherds in the southlands. Your reward will be measured in weighty gold."

"Greater than gold is the honor to serve my lord," replied Caleb.

And Zadok grasped the shoulders of his new-found friend.

Chapter Seven

In the days after Caleb's warning, Zadok lived with watchful eyes. Now, a scribe who spoke Egyptian sat crosslegged on a mat in the shadow of the outer gate and recorded the birthplace and names of all who would pass into the court. The captain Eliphas doubled the guard. An elderly slave who served as taster of wines sat always by Zadok's side.

Zadok wore a mask of calm, but the well of resentment grew deep in his heart. Egypt's presence was everywhere. Egypt's soldiers strutted near the city gates. Foreign faces crowded the streets and market square. Egyptian caravans thronged the coast road both north and south. The people no longer shouted "Zadok! Zadok!" in the streets as he rode by in his chariot. Now runners with sticks drove the people to one side and shouted "Make way! Make way for the lords of Egypt!"

Egypt ruled this land.

Egypt was master.

Zadok changed, even in his face. Glancing at his reflection in a burnished shield, Zadok saw the change. His brow was furrowed, his face tensed. He thought to escape Egypt's power over his life, but where could he hide? Where could he escape the sun? The islands of the sea were far away over treacherous waves. Who could know what he would meet on a distant shore? Perhaps giants wielding massive blades. Nor could he abandon the child Tamuru, so little and delicate, so vulnerable without his protection.

His only choice was to submit to his master, Egypt.

Day by day, he listened carefully to Caleb who came unsummoned to the Great-House. Caleb's tongue bubbled with the rumors rampant in the market. "War!" he said. "Egypt will soon march against the cities to the north." Also from Caleb's mouth, the name Sakhiri, a captain of Egypt newly appointed head of the garrison in Gaza. The son of a noble who stood close to Pharaoh. A youthful officer who was born with a mark of purple on his neck which some said was a streak of royalty hidden in his blood.

Then one day, at the hour of noon, the newly appointed captain drove his gilded chariot into Zadok's courtyard. He came, he said, with Pharaoh's command that Zadok join a council of war in Astarte's temple.

Pharaoh had called, and Zadok, the servant, head bent, came promptly as directed. He was surprised that he had been included. At the temple, he followed Sakhiri into the great hall where Egypt's nobles were gathered around Thutmosis, some by his right hand, some by his left. It was clear that they were perturbed at Gaza's presence.

"We broach a note of concern to Pharaoh," said an elder lord. He turned with a backward glance of contempt at Zadok, as if Gaza's prince had no more worth than a camel dealer in the market. "Surely your Majesty will not allow this Adoni to remain perched on his walls. He is a hazard at our backs while we march forth to conquest."

Dismay grew in Zadok's throat as he listened.

"Surely," another protested, "this danger must not be permitted."

"My thanks to all my nobles," Pharaoh answered. "My Majesty is grateful for your foresight. Let Gaza provide the answer to your concerns. Adoni," he called out. "My Majesty extends an invitation to Gaza. Nations wait to be conquered."

"Willingly, lord of heaven," said Zadok. "Permit me to be in your vanguard against the world."

Pharaoh searched Zadok's face. These were brave words from a brave man, and Pharaoh had always valued courage. Pleased at Zadok's reply, he raised his hand in salute. "We march at dawn," he declared. "Gaza's prince will join the battle in the forefront. Even in the second chariot behind Pharaoh. As reward, he will receive a share of the spoils."

To mask their disappointment, the long-faced circle of nobles applauded the royal decision. "Amun-Ra leads us all to victory!" Thutmosis shouted, and the nobles joined in with their cries of "Victory! Glory to Pharaoh and Amun-Ra!"

Four hundred thousand men of Egypt marched from Gaza into Canaan. Four hundred thousand men with spears and arrows, chariots, banners flying, oxcarts, provisions, slaves, women, and straggling beggars who gleaned droppings from the marching columns. For two days a cloud of dust hung low on the northern horizon, covering the vineyards and the valleys.

It was the hour of a changing world. Egypt's god sought glory on the field of battle. He thirsted for blood, and his priests for gold. So came this plague upon the land of Canaan.

One by one the cities crumbled. From south to north, walls were cracked and gates left open. First mighty Megiddo fell, the hands of her princes heaped high at the feet of Pharaoh. Then Carmel, then Acre. Then Quodshu of the Amorites with its barrier of wide ditches filled with water. The fortress walls were shattered, the princes left to vermin and vultures. Into the land of rivers, where Babylon the lion trembled and sent precious gifts to Pharaoh and offerings to the god Amun-Ra, and peace was made by Babel's river, which to Egypt was the farthest edge of the world.

* * * * * * *

Trumpets blared Pharaoh's return in triumph. Gaza's gates were thrust wide open. Three days of feasting were declared. Wine without end flowed freely in the temple. Egypt's nobles toasted victory and valor and Pharaoh who was the highest in the world.

As an afterthought, they toasted Zadok, but the same old bone stuck firmly in their gullets. Though Zadok was defeated, he still ruled on Gaza's throne. To belittle him in the eyes of Pharaoh, they raised their cups in a toast to Zadok's liver instead of Zadok's honor. "Adoni," they mocked. "It is a fine upright liver that you must have. It soaks up the wine of your valleys like a bale of cloth. Perhaps it is a vineyard keeper that you should have been. Think on it, Adoni. It is lighter to be a servant than a prince."

The air was warm with the breath of men. Having drunk wine to excess, Egypt's lords reeled as they followed Pharaoh to the outer court where the air was cool, but their mockery continued. "Adoni," they called, where it should rightfully have been "My prince" or "Noble Gaza".

Before long, a charioteer dared to follow their example. "Adoni," he cried as he swung himself down from his chariot.

Pharaoh turned. Mockery from Keme's highest was tolerable to a point, but from the mouth of a charioteer it had overstepped the mark. His whip cut across the disrespectful soldier's face.

At the sudden movement, the charioteer's horse reared up and neighed. Its flailing hooves sent one groom sprawling. A second rolled on the ground out of harm's way. The horse tossed its head wildly and stumbled backward, knocking Pharaoh to the cobbles. Thutmosis cried out in fear.

Zadok leaped forward. Seizing the horse's bridle, he turned the horse and chariot to one side.

Pharaoh rose up, unhurt. He glared at the state officials of the court, at the keeper of the royal breads and wines, the chief scribe who recorded Egypt's might, the bearer of the royal axe, and others both lesser and greater who were permitted to stand near his majesty. Not one of Egypt's lords had thrust himself forward to shield him from the unruly beast. Zadok alone had braved the rearing stallion.

The sun-circle stood mute as Pharaoh raised his arm toward Zadok. "Gaza!" he declared. "Bravery deserves rewarding. Come, Gaza, stand by me." From his own hand he took a gold ring set with a red gem. "A gift from Pharaoh," he said to Zadok, "and there will be more."

"My thanks to thee, great one," sang out Zadok on his belly, his feet stretched out, his nose and forehead scraping before the toes of Egypt's king. The veins in his neck filled out as he bent his head but his blood rejoiced at the envious looks of the inner circle. For the first time since Egypt marched on Gaza's hill, defeat was less a burden to bear.

*   *   *   *   *   *   *

The next morning, Thutmosis sent the captain Sakhiri to the court-yard of the Great-House. "Make ready, my lord Zadok," Sakhiri said. "Pharaoh has decreed that Gaza's prince be rewarded further and be honored with a gilding. All has been arranged."

Zadok listened in disbelief. A gilding! "To become a man showered with gifts of gold" was the phrase used by the people of Egypt. The highest honor accorded to grand viziers, first ministers of the royal court and other individuals of high authority.

He sent Caleb to procure Egyptian garments. Dressed in a fine folded linen kilt, a modish apron and elegant sleeved coat, in the manner of a nobleman of high rank, he rode off in his chariot to the temple.

In a grassy spot in the garden court, the lords of Egypt stood as witnesses to the ceremony. Women struck tambourines and ranking retainers of the court dressed in finery of white linen bowed and cheered. Pharaoh stepped forward, reached into a chest and tossed out a shower of valuables into the grass at Zadok's feet. Gold in the shape of lions, flasks, cups, collars, miniature hatchets and daggers. Zadok could not gather them all. He had two slaves leap out in front of him to collect the golden hoard glittering in the sunshine.

"A gilding by command of Pharaoh is an honor to be remembered for all time," said one lord. "A great thing!" he cried.

"A small thing," declared Thutmosis peevishly, having recently suffered from a watery irritation of the rectum. "A small thing," he insisted. He pointed to Zadok. "Small or great? What says Gaza?"

"Great, lord of heaven," replied Zadok. "A great thing, if it please you, yet it must be small in the eyes of Pharaoh. For my greatness is small to him who rules the world."

Pharaoh applauded. "Truly spoken. Both great and small and truth demands recognition. Stand down," he said to a lord of Keme. "Stand up," he said to Zadok.

He scanned the sun-circle, whose faces had gone pale at the setting-up and setting-down. His ever watchful inner eye glistened. Pharaoh had not forgotten that not one of his lords, only Zadok, had rushed forward to shield him from the hooves of the unruly stallion.

"It is Gaza's destiny to stand higher," declared Thutmosis."My Majesty has said it, and so it will be."

Egypt's lords stepped backward and to one side, and Zadok was swept into the inner circle. His face flushed with his sudden triumph. He drank wine when wine was offered. He coughed when there was no need for coughing, and he laughed when he heard laughter.

A door had been opened. The unexpected. Pharaoh's words rang in his ears. It is Gaza's destiny to stand higher: so sayeth the pig-eyed son of god who is Pharaoh. But how high is high? High is a tower, but higher is a mountain. High is the prince of one city, but higher is the king of many cities.

"There are affairs to be settled before my Majesty returns to Egypt," Pharaoh said casually to Zadok. "The question of a Regent to rule all the newly-won kingdoms."

Zadok listened, his heart pounding with the hope of rising higher in the world. To rule all the land from the cedar forests to the desert, from the blue sea westward to the Sea of Salt and the mountains.

Later, alone in the garden of the columned temple court, Zadok stood with the gold of favor gathered in a box at his feet and he thumped his thigh with his mounting expectations.

* * * * * * *

Since the day of the gilding, the word Regent kept ringing in Zadok's ears. Hour by hour, he was taken with a dilemma which kept coursing round and round in his brain: How to please Thutmosis even more, how to curry greater favor of the mighty Pharaoh, lord of the world. The answer came as Zadok lay in his bed, his eyes open to the dark. He had a vision of Pharaoh in days gone by and his lustful craving after Astarte's maidens.

At sundown of the next night, Zadok came to the inner chamber of the temple with a gift to Pharaoh. He brought a precocious moon-maid with wide eyes and gleaming teeth. She fell on her knees before the son of Amun-Ra and seized his thighs as she had been instructed, which so excited Pharaoh that he stamped his feet and tugged her hair. At a signal, a female servant led the moon-maid from the room.

"She pleases me," said Pharaoh to Zadok, "and you have chosen an opportune time."

Pharaoh had taken his evening meal in his inner chamber. A jar of wine and two silver goblets sat on a low wooden table carved with snakes winding round its rim. "Come drink with me," Pharaoh said, and filled the wine cups.

He had already chosen a gift in return. He led Zadok to the back of the room where the small statuette of the god Amun-Ra watched from his altar. There, Pharaoh presented Zadok with a precious collar fashioned with sacred symbols of a whip and mace and a golden uraeus, such as Vice-Regents and Grand Viziers wore on days of festive celebration.

"Were I the greatest king, I could not be more highly honored," said Zadok, and he kissed the hem of Pharaoh's mantle, as if he had already been proclaimed Regent of all the land to Babel's river.

"The time of my departure draws near," Pharaoh said. "The great river Nile soon will rise, and the royal court will leave for Egypt to greet the sacred wave. My Majesty will set aside a day of celebration to bestow a farewell gift, my reward to Gaza."

While Thutmosis prepared for his return to Egypt, Zadok, joyful, waited for his day of days. "Come," Pharaoh would say. "Honor Zadok." Trumpets would blare from the highest tower. Come. It is Gaza's day, Zadok's hour.

He yearned to tell Yaffia of his expectations. He thought to send Caleb with a message. At the last minute he reconsidered, fearing that spies in the pay of Egypt's lords would follow Caleb and discover where she dwelled. So Zadok held his tongue and waited.

Then it came — the day and the hour when he would receive the parting gift expected from Pharaoh. A great array of guests assembled in the temple. A fine procession with wives and sons and daughters, their slaves bearing feathered fans. The reception hall rang with song and laughter.

Zadok stood with Egypt's lords at Pharaoh's right, the place of honor. At Pharaoh's left stood Ezamar, the daughter of Ashcalah, a nobleman of Gaza.

So! thought Zadok. The jade! Not surprising, this worming her way up to Egypt. At one time he himself had been the centre of her schemes. Perhaps she had set her mind to sit in Pharaoh's house of women. Or as chief priestess in Astarte's house which Thutmosis proposed to build in Thebes. Let her suckle then, on Pharaoh's pride, if it please her. The harlot, he thought, but he greeted her with courtesy, as if she were already a queen of Egypt.

"This moon-sprite has given me great joy," said Pharaoh and pressed her arm. "She has great talent and great art. She is the pleasure of the moon alive on earth. The mystery of the goddess burns in her veins."

His praise went on and on while Zadok waited impatiently for his time of honor. Nervously, Zadok shifted his weight from one foot to the other until at last Thutmosis took his place at the forefront on the dais above the host.

"Gaza!" called Pharaoh. "Stand before me!"

Thutmosis raised his hands before the gathered throng to command silence. "My Zahi friends and lords of Egypt, Pharaoh has a farewell gift to Zadok, one which will bring him the greatest joy."

Round went all eyes and turned to Zadok — the lords of Keme with their drooping noses, and Gaza's highest, envy behind their smiling faces, having heard the rumors of a Regent to be proclaimed over all Canaan.

Zadok had steeled himself for this moment. He had prepared himself. He would hold his head high with honor. But now that the time had come, he clenched his fists. His knees felt weak. Great Lord of the Sea, let me not quiver and quake before Egyptians! He was about to be proclaimed Regent, and he was trembling like a frightened novice. He had rehearsed his speech, measured each word. The great honor... Great Pharaoh, great son of heaven, father of splendor and gold. I am undeserving. King over all Canaan. This greatest reward...

"You," called Thutmosis and pointed to Ezamar, who stepped forward.

"You," cried out Pharaoh. "You are my gift to Zadok. You will reign as queen at his side."

And Zadok stared, his mouth dropped open.

BOOK THREE

THE SERPENT AND THE FLOWER

Chapter Eight

There was a time before Zadok had brought Yaffia, the desert flower, as queen to the Great-House that Ezamar, Pharaoh's gift, had set her eyes on Zadok's tower. To sit as Gaza's queen had been her aim, and step by step she had formed her plan.

She had sent her father, Ashcalah, to the courtyard of the Great-House. It had been Ezamar's words that Ashcalah spoke to Zadok. "I have a gift in mind for my lord Zadok," he said. "For my lord's pleasure. What greater gift than my daughter whose breasts have just blossomed out with life? Her hair a raven black, limbs white and lithe. If the fire in her eyes is lurking in her flesh, she will bring a man such delight he will never forget. My lord has but to come with open eyes and see."

The invitation to visit Ashcalah's house and garden was not refused.

In her scheme, Ezamar had planned that Zadok would spy on her while she bathed. Ashcalah had led him round by a hidden path to an arbor where Zadok had peered through a leafy break in the shrubs. Pretending she was unaware that he was watching, Ezamar had slowly shed her garments one by one. As Zadok looked on, a vision of her flesh next to his had made him shiver with his lust.

Until her father had unwittingly revealed her scheme. All the while that Zadok had watched, Ashcalah had hovered near, his thin blade of a nose and white-tufted beard eager with the prospect of success. He forgot that Zadok stood close by. He clapped his hands and whistled through his nose. "My clever maid," he whispered to himself, but more loudly than he thought.

It had not been meant for Zadok's ears but Zadok had heard and understood at once. It was a plot. He should have guessed. It pricked his pride. The deceitful wench! In silence, he followed Ashcalah from the hidden arbor to the house.

Later, Zadok turned toward Ezamar as they broke bread together in the dining chamber. There was a pressing matter he had neglected, he said. It was regrettable but he must leave at once.

Anger flared in Ezamar's blood. She restrained herself, but her eyes grew steely cold. Rising up from the banquet table, she made excuses to her father, then motioned to her servant Akab to accompany her from the chamber. If Zadok could have looked deep into her heart, he would have seen the fury of a leopard that lay wounded in its lair, but her mouth was sweet again with smiles as he made ready to depart in his chariot. "Farewell," she called from the threshold. "May the Mistress shine down on my lord with her light."

Minutes later, Zadok tumbled from his chariot and struck his head. Somehow a wheel had broken from its axle. Four slaves carried him back to Ashcalah's courtyard. Ezamar herself gently daubed the bruise while Zadok groaned and cursed and held his head.

"An accident," Ezamar said, and glanced at her black slave, Akab.

"An accident," echoed Ashcalah, who knew no better.

Perhaps, thought Zadok. He had caught the glance between Ezamar and her black slave, and he left by litter with guards both front and back. So it had ended. Zadok had escaped her net. He was grateful and sent a gift to Dagon in his temple. Years had passed, and Ezamar's shadow had not crossed his path until he saw her standing at Pharaoh's side.

* * * * * * *

His gift bestowed, Pharaoh bid farewell to Gaza. No Regent had been appointed to govern Egypt's conquered lands. It was Pharaoh's decision that the newly won kingdoms would be ruled from the royal house at Thebes. With an Egyptian in command, each conquered city would be secured by a garrison of Egyptian soldiers who would also keep the roads safe from brigands and defend the people against marauding bands. In Gaza, the young captain, Sakhiri, would have control of all matters of the military. To Zadok remained only the lesser duties of a judge and ruler, his power now subject to Sakhiri whose soldiers watched from the city walls and stood on duty at Gaza's gate.

Late that night, alone in the darkness of his bedchamber in the Great-

House, Zadok drank cup after cup of wine to drown his rage. His skin grew hot with the fire of the wine and his eyes heavy. In anger, he struck his fist sharply against the wall. Shame! The word rang like a clarion call in his brain. A failure. A would-be Regent. Humiliated. His honor drained.

A vision of Ezamar sprang to his mind. Harlot! How she must have stood shameless, stripped of her shift that Pharaoh might see her beauty and agree to proclaim her Gaza's queen in return for the favors of her flesh. To Zadok, she was no better than a temple prostitute who waited for a lusty son of the land to share the mysteries of Astarte for the price of a he-goat or a walking staff with a silver knob.

Now this whore was his queen! He would have no choice but to take Ezamar into his bed and wallow in her flesh, lest the Great King learn that Gaza's prince was displeased with Egypt's parting gift.

In a half-drunken stupor, Zadok staggered into the room where the statuette of the god Amun-Ra stood in its shrine. Zadok's hand trembled with a sweep of anger. He would have torn the god from the altar and flung it to the ground, but at the last moment he restrained himself. Fear stayed his hand.

Suddenly, in the darkness of the chamber, a sadness filled his heart. He thought of the days when Yaffia sat by his side. "Eyes!" Zadok spoke aloud to himself. "Eyes!" he said again like a man feverish in a delirium. "Let me see my world as it once was. Here in this Great-House, within these walls where love once ruled my life. Let me see Yaffia again, though the wind and the walls are dark."

From the Great-House he went into the garden, to the altar which he had raised to Jehovah. Alone, he knelt before the sacred stone. "Great Lord," he prayed. "Without Yaffia at my side, I am as nothing. From the time that she left the garden house to this very hour, I have not seen her face for fear that Egypt's spies would follow my steps to her tent. Lord, grant me that my arms enfold her once again."

* * * * * * *

From their threshold, Ezamar and her father Ashcalah had watched as an endless stream of pack animals, camels, and oxcarts followed Pharaoh's chariot down from Gaza's hill on the long journey back to Egypt.

Now, Ashcalah grinned with pride as he sat by Ezamar in her chamber while she waited to be taken to the Great-House. She reclined in comfort, leaning on soft cushions, her zither by her side. Her black servant Akab, ever present, stood behind her. She smiled, smug with her success."I have won," she said to her father. "I have achieved my purpose. I am queen."

Toward the hour of sunset, she left in a grand procession led by shining banners and Egypt's soldiers who marched to the thump of drums and blaring of trumpets. The towering Akab walked beside her litter. At the garden gate of the Great-House she dismounted, then followed Akab to her chambers in the house of women.

She waited expectantly for Zadok at the time of twilight. She heard his steps, hesitant, uncertain. She laughed. Her cunning had finally closed the net.

Uneasy, Zadok stood upon her threshold.

Ezamar spoke quietly as was fitting. She was pleased to be his bride, she said — and queen of Gaza.

Zadok edged towards her. He sat down, then lay beside her. The thought of Yaffia swept through his mind. He was filled with self-loathing that he was about to betray his love and with a flaring hate toward Pharaoh who was to blame. If he had the courage, he would have fled from Ezamar's side, but in a sham of passion, he took her.

*   *   *   *   *   *   *

At first light after Zadok rose up and left the chamber, Ezamar spat upon the bed where she had opened up her thighs to receive him. "Fool! He is a fool!" she muttered to herself. He would soon learn that she was not one to be treated with contempt. She had not forgotten how he had scorned her after he had watched her bathe. She would repay that slight. Like the goddess Ishtar in the legends of Babylon whose love was scorned by Gilgamesh, the king.

The mighty Ishtar, the Morning Star, had raised her eyes to the beauty of Gilgamesh who had adorned himself and put on white garments. "Come, Gilgamesh, be my husband," she called. "I will place you in a chariot of lapis and gold, with golden wheels and mountings of onyx, and you shall be drawn in it by great lions. Kings shall bow down before you. They will bring the gifts of the mountains and the plain to you as tribute."

But Gilgamesh heard her with contempt and apprehension, for he knew of her vindictive ways. He rebuked her, saying: "You loved the shepherd Tabulu, then turned him into a leopard; his servants went in pursuit of him and his dogs followed his trail. You transformed Ishullanu into a dwarf, then set him up on the middle of a high couch. He could not rise up, he could not get down from where he was. You love me now; afterward you will strike me as you did these others."

The mighty Ishtar fell into a fury at his scorn and he felt her vengeance. She marred his beauty of which he was so proud. She covered him with leprosy from head to foot and made him an object of horror.

And Ezamar was an Ishtar come to life. Her anger against Zadok's scorn still festered. She, too, sought vengeance. If Zadok thought she would sit quietly as queen over shrubs and trees and fishes in the lily pond, he was sorely mistaken. She was not done with Zadok. He would feel her claws. She would not be avenged until he was completely stripped of his power and she would begin by taking control of the Great-House.

The first thing to be done was the induction, as she called it, of the ever-fattening Enan, the chief steward. He was the only slave with access to every wall and nook. She would have need of his ears and eyes. It was he who would carry her commands through all the house.

Ezamar remembered him, bloated and oiled, dressed in clean linen, his copper-tipped staff at his side, his gleaming bald pate bent toward her as she was carried through the gate. She had already devised a plan which would ensure his unfailing loyalty.

*   *   *   *   *   *   *

Ezamar chose the first day of Zadok's absence from the Great-House to initiate her plan. No sooner had Zadok left than she sent her black slave, Akab, to command the steward to her inner chambers in the second hour after high noon.

"It will be an honor to serve my queen," said Enan to her eunuch. He held his staff at arm's length. He was both pleased and flattered. Like a boastful cock, he strutted through the courtyard. The great one had called. Perhaps he would glean a reward, a gift to add to his growing store of treasure which he had buried in a small box in the farthest corner of the garden. These riches were a great joy to him. The weight of gold in his hand made him feel less a slave. He hoped that the new queen would be generous.

But gifts or no, he had always come running to the garden if the opportunity presented. Whenever he kneeled before the ladies of Zadok's harem, he would savor the fragrance drifting from their bodies as their robes fluttered in the sunlight. The nearness of their flesh would rouse his manhood. He yearned for these scented beauties of the garden no less than he yearned for jewels and gold. A slave for a slave's bed was all that he had ever savored, and then usually a whimpering slave.

If only he were king! he thought. In all his dreams, he saw himself as ruler over many subjects; the rich land was his, and the vast blue sea and all the ships that sailed. This great stone house was his, and the great hall with its banquet tables and hundreds of gold and silver trays and goblets. In his dreams, it was he that the desert flower Yaffia loved. It was he that Copperakh desired, and he had lewd visions of her unclothed, her copper-colored hair sweeping to her shoulders. There was yet another who stirred his blood, the blue-eyed Delia, youngest of the fragrant circle, with ripe full bosom, nipples pouting through the cloth. He would dream of pressing the softness of her bosom, pinching her breasts and nipples until she screamed, then covering her with his weight whether she was willing or not.

Enan grunted as his thighs were roused. He slapped his paunch as he walked among the slaves in the courtyard, and he went off to a secluded corner to make his water. Gathering up the skirt of his steward's apron, he examined it carefully to be certain that he had not stained the cloth. Then, thinking about Ezamar, the queen, he thumped his staff down sharply to restore his air of importance.

She must not be kept waiting. A steward could expect no praise or reward if he were not prompt. He hurried to the door of his chamber which reeked with odors of medicinal ointments, for he went often to seek the advice of healers and nurtured himself with powders and potions. Having oiled himself and changed his linen, he strutted until the appointed hour, then went back through the garden to the house of women.

In an inner chamber, Ezamar sat in the comfort of her chair. Her black servant, Akab, waved an ostrich-feathered fan above her head. She smiled and in her hand Enan saw a chain of gold.

"This is the first gift from your queen," she said and she gave it into Enan's hand. "As steward, you have great worth. You have appeared promptly." The responsibilities of a steward, she went on, are wide in scope.

Enan nodded. He could feel the weight of the chain of gold. This gift, he decided, he would not bury with his other treasures. He would wear it round his neck where all could see. A great honor given from the queen's own hand to his, and a first gift implied a second.

Respectfully he kissed her robe before he left.

The next summons came at the time of dusk. Come, she ordered, when the sun has set.

Shadows gathered in the garden. The path was dark, the trees giant in the cast of night. And Ezamar waited in her nest. She was lying restfully on her couch. No Akab, no maids in sight. A single lamp flickered on the wall. She was dressed in a gown of thin white linen, one bosom and shoulder covered and the other bared.

Enan hesitated on the threshold, but Ezamar raised herself and beckoned. "It is my wish to extend my friendship to the steward of the house," she declared. Was he aware, she asked, that with the proper opportunity a devoted steward could rise up in power?

Enan listened. His ears pricked up with interest.

"I see by your face that you have considered such a possibility," she said, and praised his foresight.

Enan reddened. He rattled the chain about his throat. "I am a humble servant and a slave," he said.

But Ezamar refused to allow him to belittle himself. She bade him sit. "Here by my side," she said. And the intimacy of her smile disarmed him.

In some men, greatness is hidden, she said. Did he think that she, Gaza's queen, would permit a common slave to speak with her in her private chambers in the twilight hours without eunuch or maid? That was the prerogative of the king.

"I am your servant," Enan mumbled, but his face had paled at the nearness of her flesh. In a panic, he looked to the door.

Gently then, Ezamar said to herself. This fat one must be enticed, not frightened like a rabbit. She put her hand in his. Like a temple dancing girl with a virgin youth, she touched his flesh. "Come, rabbit, be a king!," she whispered under her breath. "I will lead the way." And from the softness of her couch, she dubbed him king.

Great was Enan's hunger, having lusted in his dreams these many years. He foundered into her net. To the cunning Ezamar, it had been an easy task. And the rabbit-king could not escape.

* * * * * * *

The morning dawned, dim and lucent from the east, and with the rising sun came Ezamar's crowning of the king.

"Rabbit!" Ezamar shouted the epithet into Enan's ears. She trampled him even while he snored. She abused him, she kicked him, she spat on his face which had yellowed and become blank. "Rabbit!" she shrieked. "You should have fled!"

And Enan would have fled had he known where to run.

Ezamar seized his linen apron which had been clean but now was crumpled. She pulled him backward and he thumped down heavily to the floor where he sat stunned, his eyes sticky and puffed with sleep.

"From this day onward," she said, her teeth clenched, "should you even think to disobey me, you will feel my lion claws. In the corridors of the house, the people would hear my outcry: 'The chief steward has attacked me! The fiend came to my bed in the dark of night while my servant slept!' The guards would seize you and place you in fetters. Your offending part would be cut from you and thrown into the sand and your body left to vultures." She struck his face, then pointed to a basin. "Slave! Wash my feet!"

Enan's fat quivered as he wet her toes.

"Now drink!" she shrieked. She kicked the basin, and water overflowed the brim and spilled on the floor where Enan sat. His steward's apron, crumpled and wet, clung to his thighs. "Drink!" she shouted; and Enan splashed his mouth and robe.

"Akab!" she called out.

Enan bent his neck, awaiting death. The golden chain slipped from his neck and clattered to the floor. He felt himself being lifted up and carried out. He fell roughly to the ground, his knee sharp against a stone. Behind him, he heard Akab laugh.

A moment later, the chain of gold struck Enan's foot. He groaned, retrieved it, then crawled away into the shadows of the dawn.

Two days Enan lay upon his bed, his feet frozen cold with fright lest Ezamar breathe one word and he was dead. Two days he lay without food or drink, his dry breath puffing in and out, the chain of gold wound on his wrist and pressing into his side.

To Zadok, he said: "An affliction of the heat." He groaned when his lord appeared. He pressed his hand to his pate. It was the golden sun, he explained. The flame and the heat. There was a demon in his head.

Two days Enan scarce moved lip or limb. The dreams of the man were dead. He lay in a pit, a gull betrayed, in ruin, a sickened greed-fat, would-be king. The pain jabbed in his ear and nape. He lay wry-necked until the pain was drained.

Hate remained. An inner rage against Ezamar and her cunning, and a fury against Akab and his black face and wide flaring nose.

Enan cursed himself for a fool, a dupe. He had been seduced by Ezamar's bewitching flesh. He was trapped, bound to her with his very life, a slave to her every breath.

She bade him recover without delay.

"I obey," he said. "I am your slave."

"Come," she said, and he obeyed.

"Go," she said, and he went his way.

* * * * * * *

Zadok woke one morning and saw that he was a stranger in his own house. The steward Enan seemed distant and morose. He clung close to Ezamar's side. Day after day, his sharp voice was heard berating the slaves in the court and house. The servants in the main hall and the adjoining loggia and banquet chamber walked with careful quiet steps. Overseers with whips stood grim and unrelenting in the storerooms, kitchens and workshops. To thwart Ezamar's slightest wish brought the pain of the lash, and the walls rang with the cries of slaves. A tyrant queen ruled the garden, the court and the Great-House.

If Zadok was concerned that Ezamar had usurped his authority, he

said nothing. He looked the other way. What else could he do but live with the gift which was Pharaoh's. Amun-Ra ruled here, and a vassal prince must take care what he might say or do. Only one thing he dared.

He ordered Yaffia's chambers sealed, that none, even she who was queen at the behest of Pharaoh, should walk where Yaffia had walked, nor live where she had lived.

In silence, Ezamar watched the stone masons squat with chisels and listened to the click and clack of brick and trowel. Click. Clack. Seal the shadow of the desert flower. Stupid! Of what use was a shadow? What comfort? Had it breasts or thighs? Be sealed and be damned!

"It was my own wish," she said later to the ladies of the garden. "To my lord, I said: 'Let no one walk on her memory. Let her house be sealed. Let it be so, according to my will.'" But anger sat with Ezamar through the day. Zadok had denied her the queenly chambers that were justly hers. From the garden house she surveyed her queendom and was not content. She was consumed with one thought: Vengeance! Somehow she must find a way to weaken Zadok's power, to sour his world. Hour by hour, she searched every facet of his life, she probed for any vulnerable point but Zadok's throne stood secure; he had found favor in the eyes of Egypt.

Then suddenly a potential weakness came to light.

She had ordered the steward Enan to spy out Zadok's every step. Then one night in the darkness of the corridor beyond Zadok's bed-chamber, Enan heard his lord cry out. He stepped carefully over the sleeping figure of Zadok's manservant. Motionless and silent, Enan stood by Zadok's bed.

A few moments passed, then the sleeping Zadok called out again from his dream. "Yaffia! God's night will hide you. We shall meet again."

Though the hour was late, Enan went promptly to Ezamar's door. Akab bent his massive head at Enan's knock.

"Lead me to the queen," Enan said. "I have words of great interest."

Without a moment's hesitation, Akab led him to Ezamar's chamber where Enan bent low and recounted his tale.

"What more did my faithful steward hear?" Ezamar asked.

"Then my lord slept and his voice was silent," said Enan.

Ezamar glanced down at the steward who sat at her feet. "Were there no slaves in the courtyard the night when Yaffia fled?"

"The walls were dark," Enan replied, "and the house slept."

Ezamar measured Enan's words. All the world knew that Yaffia had fled with a lover. Now the question: Had Zadok deliberately concocted this tale to throw Pharaoh off the track? Perhaps the truth hides some-where, she thought, and not in Pharaoh's ears.

"Steward, observe my lord Zadok's steps closely," Ezamar ordered. "Press your ear to his door at every opportunity."

She placed two purses of gold in Enan's hand and called to Akab who led the smiling steward from the room.

Restless, Ezamar lay upon her couch after Enan had left. Consider this, she thought. If Zadok had purposely hidden his precious Yaffia from the eyes of Pharaoh, if she could prove this — how would the Great King react to such deceit and intrigue?

Wild thoughts churned in Ezamar's brain. Thunderous thoughts. Zadok would be disgraced before Egypt. Pharaoh would be merciless in his anger. Zadok's head would be forfeit. All Gaza would then bow before Ezamar, the Queen. She would be free to choose another to sit by her side.

She would have wreaked her full measure of vengeance.

Chapter Nine

Ezamar brooded. Weeks had passed and Enan had brought no further words of interest to report. She had hoped that Zadok would speak out again in his sleep. She considered adding a potion to his wine to loosen his tongue. Instead, she confronted Zadok near Jehovah's altar. She hoped to catch him off guard with a sudden question.

"In the dark of the night, I dreamed of Yaffia," she said with an innocent air. "In my dream, I saw Gaza's prince standing by her side. Where is she now, your desert flower?" She looked at Zadok as though her eyes could penetrate his deepest thoughts.

Zadok's heart skipped a beat. He was quick to realize the threat in Ezamar's sudden question. Only that morning he had learned that Akab, whip in hand, had queried every slave who might have served in the stables and courtyard on the night of Yaffia's disappearance. Zadok was certain that Ezamar had discovered nothing. He had taken the greatest care the night Yaffia fled. No slave was present, the house was asleep, the courtyard was black — not a shadow, not a lamp. Yet his blood ran cold. Without a word, he turned and left.

Ezamar followed him through the garden. She was determined to badger him. "The lover with whom Yaffia fled," she persisted, "who was he? Was he chief of a shepherd band, a wandering tribe who come and go like the wind?"

Again, Zadok refused to answer. He hurried to the gate and fled into the courtyard, but Ezamar had seen his frown. She knew her probing had disturbed him. She smiled. She felt certain that with time she would uncover the truth.

Soon, Zadok became aware that Ezamar's spies followed his every step. Through a maidservant he heard that Ezamar had questioned the ladies of the garden house not once, but twice. Then Zadok's chamberlain reported that the steward Enan had been listening outside the door to the royal bedchamber. A sudden terror rose in Zadok's heart. One slip of the tongue, even in sleep, could bring down Pharaoh's wrath upon his head.

Ezamar was the danger ever-present. He saw her as a serpent which lay in the dust of a path in the garden, an asp waiting to strike from ambush and bite him on the heel so that he suffer with her venom.

* * * * * * *

With the coming of the winter rains, it became clear that Ezamar was with child. Zadok was pained. He feared that she might bear a son who one day would rule in Gaza. He prayed that her seed be stillborn, the cord wrapped around its neck, its face blue and mottled, that it might not see nor breathe. He had expected her to be barren, like a whore who receives many and conceives nothing. He had thought of her as an empty barrel with no fertile soil in the darkness of her womb. But bloated and proud, she walked in the garden, her hands clasped about the swelling below her navel.

Ezamar enjoyed her state. Of course, it was a male child she nourished, so she declared before all. She was certain of it. The princeling already churned round and round and kicked her side. She would bring life and joy to the Great-House, she said.

"May your seed cause you no pain in childbed," offered the ladies of the garden who hid their envy.

As the weeks and months passed, Ezamar counted the days by the rising of the sun, and with the approaching hour of the birth of her child, thoughts of vengeance were swept from her mind. She thought only of the child she nurtured who one day might rule in Gaza's world. She took every precaution against the inroads of evil. Magic amulets hung about her bed to ward off demons.

Without fear, she lay herself down when her time was ripe. She tossed her head and jeered at the midwives who clucked concern that her bones were narrow. She scoffed at their hot bricks and towels. The infant knocked, and a red trickle issued from her thighs. "It is time," she called from her bed.

"Not yet! Not yet!" they replied. "There are no pangs. There must be pangs."

"Idiots!" she laughed.

To spite Zadok, she sent Enan to bring an Egyptian physician and the steward came back panting, the healer by his side. The Egyptian was full of praise for her composure. He threw up his hands in amazement at her swiftness. Such ease. In a twinkling the child, covered with caul and the silt of her womb, slipped out from her flesh and gasped.

Ezamar opened her eyes. "A son?"

"A maid," the midwives answered lowly.

Ezamar was stunned.

No comment from the garden house. Prudent silence was the byword of the ladies.

Not the fault of her womb, the physician insisted. Such strength and vigor as she possessed he had never seen. More likely it was the fault of the sire, the prince who had been defeated. Often a man defeated was weakened in his loins.

But Ezamar's pride had tumbled. It was not a princely heir. It was a maid who could only stand second to Yaffia's child, the Princess Tamuru. She thought she heard laughter ringing from the walls.

No sooner was her issue swaddled than she called out to Zadok with complaint. She accused him, her voice bitter. He was to blame. His feeble manhood had caused her to produce a princess, not a prince. She used obscenities to describe his testicles and phallus. She threatened to befoul his bed with others more potent to erase the failing in him. Even the steward, she jeered, would have been more successful. Even her black eunuch, gelded as he had been at an early age, would have been more equal to the task of begetting an heir.

"A foolishness," declared Zadok. "Have I the power of a god? Or a priest with a magic wand?"

"Ha!" she replied. No god. No priest. But who among his wives had borne him a male heir, she taunted.

Alarmed that he might be weakened in his loins, Zadok went in secret to a certain old hag who was known to have mystic powers in such matters. "And of what use?" cried out the hag, where she sat among her kettles and pots. "Of what use in these bitter times to beget a princely heir who could be reared only as vassal to the foul ones of the river land of Egypt. Dagon shut her womb to an heir. Such is the reward to those who whored with Egypt. May she be barren for all time with her shame!"

It had been with a lighter heart that Zadok returned and laid a deaf ear to Ezamar's daily complaints. At least it had not been a son, an heir who one day might have ruled on Gaza's throne. In his relief, he sent a fine gift to Astarte's temple.

*   *   *   *   *   *   *

Zadok's peace was short-lived. Ezamar was petulant in her bed. She was petulant while she sunned herself, as the Egyptian physician advised, to restore the freshness of her skin which she complained her confinement had marred. She looked back bitterly on the burden of the months now passed. "Like a sow have I bred," she cried, "and now my breasts are misshapen. With pain have I shed my blood, and my slender flesh has turned to fat."

She cast a malicious eye at the lady Copperakh, at her slender beauty and her hair like copper, who seemed to rejoice at Ezamar's pique and disappointment.

It was then that Ezamar demanded a healing brew from her Egyptian physician to restore her youth and beauty. The physician sent two flasks of greenish brew distilled from herbs and powders known only in the land of Egypt. One she retained for herself; the other she generously gave to Copperakh.

But the potion brewed to enhance beauty produced an opposite effect on Copperakh. In a matter of days, her bones and flesh began to ache. Her skin faded, and her copper-colored hair, which was her greatest pride, became edged with gray.

Copperakh hid her face, but she took her sickness in hand and rose up from her bed when Zadok sent for her in a twilight hour. Languid though she was, she answered his call and followed the steward as she had done many times before, but she fell behind a pace as the steward passed through the door into Zadok's chamber.

She leaned against the wall while Enan bowed to Zadok. A hooded cloak veiled her frown. Her breath was troubled. Not until she swept the hood from her copper hair could Zadok see the paleness of her skin. Even in the fading light, he saw that she was thin and drawn. He looked at her with concern. "Are you ill?" he asked.

Copperakh bent her head. "Merely a mild pain," she said. "Have no fear, Lord," she continued. She drew a small flask from her robe. "This potion will restore my health."

Zadok drew back, startled. "A potion?"

Copperakh nodded. "From the queen," she said. "From Egypt." She had brought it to share with Zadok. A magic potion to preserve his youth, perhaps forever.

"Ezamar?" repeated Zadok. "From Egypt?" Zadok sucked in his breath. He stared at the flask. It was as though Caleb, eyes squinting, stood behind him in the shadows with his warning to be wary of all potions. Zadok took Copperakh's hand and led her to the couch. "Rest," he said. "The slave Shatah shall provide your needs."

At the first light of dawn, Zadok sent word to Caleb, who took the flask carefully in hand and went again to the seashore, to the same secluded place near the dunes. Tipping the flask, he emptied the brew into the water. No fish floated dead in the waves but a dark cloud of death floated down to his feet. "Poison!" said Caleb when he had returned to Zadok.

"The lady Copperakh," Caleb whispered, "speak to her when she wakens. Should the queen ask," he advised, "let Copperakh explain that the flask was accidentally dropped, spilled out on the floor. Strangely, a cat which had licked some of the potion was later found dead. It will leave a smell of suspicion. Perhaps then the queen will desist and hold back her venom."

But Zadok knew that Ezamar was not one to give up so readily. Accordingly he made plans. Caleb, the merchant, would lead a small caravan south to seek out Yaffia's tents, where Copperakh would be safe. Four soldiers disguised as servants would protect the train.

Ezamar merely shrugged when she learned of Copperakh's departure. "It would seem," she said lewdly to the ladies of the garden who had turned to listen, "that two of my lord's consorts have been sorely disappointed by his phallic powers. First, the flower, Yaffia, fled with a lover, then Copperakh disappeared, perhaps she, too, with a suitor. Now my lord Zadok must choose another to scratch his back."

* * * * * * *

All Ezamar's probing for the truth about Yaffia's sudden leaving of the garden house had proved fruitless. Zadok still remained innocent in the eyes of Pharaoh. Ezamar was thwarted, for Zadok sat firmly ensconced on his throne.

Still she clung to the dream that one day she would rule alone as queen. She saw herself with an Egyptian honor guard leading her litter as she was carried through Gaza's streets. The highborn from Pharaoh's land would come to visit with praise for her beauty and wisdom. But as the days passed and her prospects dimmed, she grew irritable. Still determined to disgrace Zadok, she went back to her vindictive ways.

To gain her end, she chose to turn with her charms to the Egyptian captain Sakhiri. In this same way she had once turned to Pharaoh, but with Pharaoh the price she had paid was high. Egypt's king was sadistic. He had cost her bruises, and his breath was foul. With Sakhiri, it would be a different matter. She counted on pleasure. He was a handsome man. Her flesh tingled at the thought of the strength of his arms.

A feasting was arranged in the Great-House with Sakhiri as honored guest. Ezamar donned a revealing robe of the thinnest gauze. She welcomed Egypt's captain with a ready smile and sparkling eyes. At the banquet table, she deliberately crowded close to Sakhiri's thigh. She touched his flesh, then glanced at Zadok with taunting eyes.

Zadok grit his teeth at the sight of the Egyptian and Gaza's queen laughing side by side but, being a man of reason, he turned his eyes away and held his tongue.

The next morning, in the sunlit hours, Ezamar rode off with Sakhiri in his chariot. She had deliberately left a message for Zadok with the steward Enan. She knew that Zadok would be inclined to follow. "They ride to the south road and the sand dunes by the shore," said Enan.

Zadok nodded. He understood only too well. A private hour to be shared under the white clouds and the sun.

A brittle anger mounted in his eyes. Her purpose was to shame his bed, to cast his pride like dust before the wind. "Harlot!" he muttered to himself. He cursed them both, Ezamar and Egypt's captain. "May they rot as they lie with their heads and feet together!"

He followed where Enan had pointed. At a distance, from the shadow of a sycamore tree, he watched them. He saw Ezamar take Sakhiri's dagger from his girdle. She fingered the sharp edge for a few moments, then thrust it into the sand, and he saw Sakhiri shake his head as if he answered "No" to a question.

Zadok's breath caught in his throat. It was clear that she sought an ally. Who could know what was in her mind? Perhaps a plot to injure him in some way. Perhaps murder! A passing thought. He had no proof but with the thought he hurried back to the courtyard of the Great-House where he called out to Eliphas.

"Guard me well, Eliphas," he said. "Whether in the courtyard, the Great-House, in the streets or the market, guard my back. A plot may be afoot. We must be wary."

* * * * * * *

Zadok's life was barren in the garden house. He found no joy in the song and dance of the maids who painted themselves and put on transparent garments to please him. He yearned to be with Yaffia, to touch her, to hold her. He had found happiness with her and a passion he could not forget. There was a magic that drew him to her despite the danger. Many times, mingling with the pack animals and carts of a merchant caravan, Zadok led his camel towards the southlands and Yaffia's tent only to turn back. He feared a lengthy absence would rouse suspicion and Ezamar's spies or Egypt's would follow. Once he rode out in his chariot in a pretense to join a hunt, and turned back when a sudden wind swept up a whorl of sand and he took it for a sign of evil.

Until one night, when together with Ezamar, he joined with Sakhiri and others of Keme for a feasting at her father's house.Under a shady arbor, small tables were laden with cool fruit juice and wine, bowls of oranges, pomegranates and candied sweetmeats. Slaves stood side by side with torches to cast light.

Ezamar drank cup after cup of wine until she sat heated and bloated with drink. A colic gripped her ribs and liver. She gasped with the pain and was forced to retire. She sent for her Egyptian physician who administered a powder in a draught. It was an evil caught in the gall, he explained. Nor would it heal until the demon escaped. She was to rest for six days and nights. She was to eat nothing and drink only the purest water.

Zadok took advantage of the opportunity to excuse himself. He complained of a cough which was troublesome. The night vapors had seized his throat, he said.

While the eyes of the merrymakers were distracted and clouded with wine, Zadok rode out. Eliphas and two soldiers followed at a distance, watchful lest a leopard or lion leap out from behind. So Zadok rode through the night amid dark shadows, then in the early light of dawn he saw the fields and tents of the shepherds.

"Riders from the north!" sentinels called out from the high ground to the shepherds below.

"It is Gaza who rides to the shepherd's camp," Zadok said to the sentries who challenged him.

A guard with spear in hand led Zadok to the light of the campfires where the burly Asa, Yaffia's eldest brother, now head of the tribe, stood wrapped in a woolen cloak against the cold of dawn. There had always been few words between them, now even less than in the past. Frowning, Asa craned his neck and looked beyond Zadok into the shadows.

"No fear," said Zadok. "No one has followed. Only my captain and two soldiers who wait below the rise of the hill. Is she well?" asked Zadok.

"She is well."

At Asa's signal, a shepherd rose up and led Zadok to the higher ground.

Near the centre of her tent, Yaffia was waiting, her arms half-raised. A gentle smile broke from her lips. Then with a little cry, she flew to Zadok's arms and he cradled her head on his shoulder.

How long had he waited for this hour. How many times had she filled his dreams. Night by night he had whispered her name into the dark and repeated a song of love that swelled in his heart. He took her hand to guide her to the couch and spoke the sweet words he had prepared:

"When my love waits for me and I behold her

   I take her to my beating heart

   And in my arms enfold her.

   My heart is filled with joy divine

   For I am hers and she is mine

   And with her lips pressed close to mine

   I am made drunk and need not wine."

His hand passed over her body, her breasts, the mound of her belly, her thighs. Their passion was like a fire which burned deep in their souls. They lost count of the hours.

For passion is like a mask which blots out time.

*   *   *   *   *   *   *

Zadok led Yaffia from the tent into the light of a peaceful day. Downcast, Yaffia prepared the dried fruit and cheeses, provisions for his return journey. Her hands filled the waterskins Zadok's beasts would carry. Her every movement cried out, Do not leave! What joy there would be!

"Stay, my love," she whispered. "Stay with my people." She held his hands and kissed his fingers. "Stay," she pleaded, kissing his face and neck.

Zadok was silent for a moment before he answered. "My heart is saddened that we part again," he said, "but I must leave. There would be questions asked. Ezamar's eyes and Egypt's would search the world."

Yaffia's heart ached. A moist darkness filled her eyes. "One day we will be together again," she said, "in God's good time, with God's will." With arms outstretched, she bid him farewell and he rode to the north with Eliphas and the two soldiers who followed behind.

She turned from the field where she had waited until they were gone from sight. In the distance, under a tamarisk tree, there was an altar sacred to Jehovah. A sacrificial stone, oblong and rounded, with a ridge of blood caked on the rim. Devoutly, Yaffia laid her head against the sacred table and listened to the soft sweep of the wind in the leaves of the tamarisk, and she prayed to the God Jehovah.

"Blessed be Thy name, Creator of the Universe. Wake in Thy mountain and hear my prayer. Lead my lord Zadok as You have led me. Let the day come when we will walk together in Your light and bless Your name before all."

Chapter Ten

With Zadok's departure, a door had shut on Yaffia's life. A sadness filled her eyes, a regret for all which was gone and faded. Each day that passed was much like the day before, with little purpose or hope. It was two years since she had seen Tamuru. Only through the merchant Caleb did she learn of her child, how the little maid had grown, her smiles, her tears.

From the threshold of her tent, Yaffia watched as the brothers let the sheep pass under their staffs to make an accounting of the yearlings, then drove the flocks of goats and sheep before them as they made ready for the journey to market. With a maidservant at her side, Yaffia followed the herds in an oxcart. It was her habit to accompany the brothers, for the shepherd clan believed that she bore the blessing of Jehovah, which they thought requisite to prosperity and success. When she bartered for corn or oil, her voice was calm and the price she paid was usually lower than most, while demanding the highest profit for the animals and their wool.

Together with her brothers, she made her way to the towns and villages of the lowlands and fruitlands around the walled cities of the south. Everywhere in the farms and market squares, the oppressor Egypt had made its presence felt, and Yaffia saw want and hunger in a land of plenty. Egypt's tax collectors had descended like vultures and robbed each house of gold and silver as tribute to Egypt's god. The tax assessors were guarded by soldiers armed with long spears and wooden shields who seized the milch sheep and goats and beat the farmers with staves lest they dare to hide their goods and produce.

Near the gate of one village square, a mother carrying a wailing child caught Yaffia's attention. When Yaffia drew near, the woman bent her head slightly and reached out. "Great lady," she said softly, and pressed the weeping babe closer. "Help me," she begged. "My little one hungers for want of milk and bread."

Yaffia, moved with pity, took out cheeses and oat-cakes from the store in her oxcart and gave them to the mother. "Let the babe eat," she said.

Later, at the shepherds' camp, in the hour of sundown, Yaffia stood thoughtfully by Jehovah's altar. She listened to the bleating of a lamb in the field not far off, and it was as though she heard the child weeping at the woman's breast. The breath of the wind swept through the leaves and rosy blossoms of the tamarisk tree, and the cries of weeping children seemed to rise in a crescendo into the coming wall of night.

She looked to the sky and with her fingertips she touched the sacred stone of the altar. She raised her voice softly to the clouds. "Lord, you have opened my eyes to the new path of my life. My heart has heard Your call to aid the children who hunger, to stand up for the poor and the oppressed. Guide me, Lord. Let Your strength be as my strength against heathen Egypt."

The next morning a falcon alighted on the roof of her tent, then struck a robber-raven from its perch. The robber-raven fell to earth where it stumbled, then flew off. To Yaffia, this was a symbol of a blow to Pharaoh and his tax collectors, and she took it as a sign from God that heaven would lend her strength to stand against the oppressor, Egypt.

* * * * * * *

More than six months had passed after the sheep had been gathered for the shearing when tales of a warrior-queen began to spread throughout the land. A champion of the common people, those who suffered most from the heavy burden of taxes levied by Egypt. In the village squares, they spoke of a maid in warrior's garb, impenetrable to spear or arrow, who led a band of courageous warriors, giants of strength who rode forth on swift camels. A daring group who stood high in the stirrup and shouted "Hallelu-Yah! Hallelu-Yah!" as they rode. It was said the men of Egypt, the collectors of tax and tithe, threw down their spears and bows and fled, as if under a spell. Mysteriously, a few farm animals and some sacks of wheat grains had reappeared first in one house, then another.

Sakhiri, the commander in Gaza, counted Egypt's losses. Angered, he confronted Zadok not far from the outer gate of Astarte's temple. "Did Gaza's prince know that some of Egypt's tax collectors had been set upon and robbed?"

"I have heard it," Zadok replied. "Stories are rampant in the market." Though inwardly he rejoiced at Sakhiri's dilemma, he turned an apologetic face to Egypt's captain.

"I will search far and wide and seek out the transgressors," he offered. "I will put the question to the Lords of the Sands, the roving shepherd bands who appear and disappear like the wind. Even within the hour, my captain and I will depart. Those responsible will be apprehended."

Sakhiri appeared content with Zadok's answer. He bid Zadok safe journey, then turned back to Astarte's walled house.

With only Eliphas by his side, Zadok left the Great-House. They rode first to the east, then turned south. Though nothing was said, Eliphas sensed that Zadok had seized the opportunity to make his way to Yaffia's tent.

The sun shone their way into the twilight hours. By nightfall, they saw the flames of a campfire in the distance, but when they drew near, they were surprised to find only a few shepherds and one tent in the field.

In answer to Zadok's questions, the shepherds pointed to the east into the darkness. Gaza's prince was to be taken to another place. His friend was to wait in this camp. By torchlight, Zadok was led over rocky fields and through gullies, until voices broke from the distance. "She waits there," said the shepherd guide, nodding toward a path which turned downward into a hollow. Zadok counted ten more paces along the night-darkened path.

Then in the flaring light of a campfire, he saw Yaffia, but it was not the Yaffia he knew. Only her face was the same. She was dressed in a leathern jerkin, a warrior's garb, not unlike the armed band who sat round about.

Yaffia sprang up to greet him. "Come, sit by my side," she said. At her signal, a wineskin was brought, and breads and roasted meats and fruits. "Hear me now," she said to Zadok. "There is much to tell. I went among the people of the mountain villages and towns, and everywhere I saw the misery and suffering of the children. I walked on God's mountain," she continued, "and God's call came to my heart. I have answered His call to defend the young and the weak."

Zadok was silent. There were no words in his throat, but Yaffia saw the fear in his eyes. "The Lord Jehovah will protect me," she said.

She led him to a nearby tent, and in the dim light of a lamp, they embraced. He could feel the softness of her breasts beneath the heavy cloth of her cloak. And Astarte pierced them both with her fire.

When he awoke, he was alone in the tent.

Yaffia and the band had vanished.

* * * * * * *

Barely three days had passed when Zadok returned to Sakhiri's quarters in Astarte's sacred house. He had questioned both old and young in the plains and the foothills to the east, said Zadok, but he had discovered no one guilty of the crimes against Egypt.

"I myself met with some small success when I led my soldiers into the villages and farmlands," Sakhiri remarked, as he led Zadok to the outer gate of the temple.

Zadok watched with a heavy heart as a stream of oxcarts followed the street toward the road which led to the sea. An Egyptian lieutenant with his whip marched in front. A straggling column of soldiers formed a guard. Bound hand and foot, men, women, and children were huddled in the creaking carts which lurched as the wheels dug deeper in the sand. Captives from towns and villages to the east who had been found with Egyptian gold hidden in their cloaks, stolen taxes which the warrior-queen had turned back to the poor. Those who had not been slain and flung into the fields had been taken prisoner to be sent down to Egypt as slaves.

Downcast, Zadok turned back to the Great-House. Where was Yaffia? he thought. Is she safe? At Jehovah's altar he bent his head. "Shield her Lord, from the might of Egypt. Stand by her side," he begged. "Watch over her both day and night." But even as he prayed, what he feared had come to pass.

The merchant Caleb came running, alarm in his face. Yaffia had been taken, caught in Egypt's web.

Zadok stood up sharply. "How! Where!"

His hand shaking, Caleb pointed toward the north and east. "I found her tent in a valley higher up in the mountains. I had come to bring word of the Princess Tamuru's health and wellbeing to Yaffia but the tent was empty. I learned that Egypt's tax collectors had recently been beaten and robbed in a village nearby. Egypt's soldiers who patrolled the area recovered a few silver rings in the dust by the well and their captain had laid a trap. In the early dawn, soldiers waited for any who came to the well. Guilty and innocent alike were caught in the net."

Caleb went on to describe how he had bent his knees, his forehead in the dust before Egypt's soldiers, and begged that Yaffia not be taken captive. He had explained that she was his wife, the youngest of three and most disobedient. She had wandered from his tent, he said, though it was only water from the well that she sought. The Egyptians had pushed him aside and refused to hear his plea, nor would they be bribed with gold. When he turned toward her again, two soldiers had raised their spears in threat. Another had drawn a dagger from its scabbard before they drove him off with stones and shouts.

"We must hurry to save her!" cried Caleb.

"Softly," cautioned Zadok. He could not hide the terror in his soul, but he motioned with his hand. Egypt's eyes and ears were everywhere. All must be calm, above suspicion.

In the cool hour of dawn with a yellowed streak of light breaking from the east, a grim Zadok and ten chosen men disguised as merchants met with Caleb where he waited beyond Gaza's gate. He led a cart drawn by a sleepy-eyed white ass. They followed as Caleb took the bridle in hand and directed the beast from Gaza's road toward the foothills of the east. Two wineskins and good eatables hung from the cart. They kept up a leisurely pace which was the pattern among merchants set out to buy wool and corn.

That night they made camp in a grassy field and lay down to rest under the stars. In the wide breadth of darkness, Zadok imagined that he and his men had crept up on the Egyptian sentries and killed them. He imagined he searched the ground until he found Yaffia where she lay trembling, bound hand and foot. He touched her warmth, the softness of her flesh. Still bound, she returned his love, and in his fantasy, he took her where she lay under his strength.

The next morning they set out once more at dawn. They would reach the mountain village and Egypt's camp after nightfall, Caleb said. He was certain that Egypt's soldiers were still encamped in the field near the well and there would be no difficulty in overwhelming the small Egyptian force while they slept.

Long shadows had filled the black of stone and rock when Caleb turned into the hills toward the north. He tethered the ass under a cliff. Without a sound he motioned to the others. The camp was there, to the left and above, where the land was cleared.

They saw the flames of a campfire where it lit up the night. Zadok's heart pounded as they crept forward in the dark. Silently, with blades drawn, they approached the flames.

The campfire burned, but no sound, not a whisper broke the stillness of the night for the Egyptians' throats had been cut. All were dead. In the field, shreds of rope were strewn everywhere.

Like avenging angels, Yaffia's band of warriors had descended upon Egypt's soldiers and the captives had been freed.

Chapter Eleven

With Yaffia in the lead, the warrior band had mounted their riding camels and fled north into the hills to a hidden place, a cliff of caves. By the campfire they had built, they stood with spears upright and round about Yaffia like a cage, and with one voice they gave thanks to Jehovah. "Blessed be the Lord, Creator of the Universe," they intoned. Then, under the stars, they swore an oath to continue to aid the weak against the oppressor Egypt.

Later, in the hours while the others slept, Yaffia sat by the warmth of the fire away from the cool of the night. More than ten years had gone by since the fear of Pharaoh's lust had driven her from the Great-House. At first, the days had been unbearable, but she had endured and the weight on her heart had become less. In these latter years, she had been nourished by an inner strength and a feeling of content in her struggle to aid the oppressed. Time had dealt kindly with her. Her beauty had not passed. Her black hair was still the same, her fair skin without a blemish, but her dark eyes had saddened.

Alone, she listened to the beating of her heart. The thought of Tamuru was uppermost in her mind. Ten years, she thought. Ten years since she had last seen her. The child had been only four. The years drifted before her like a dream. All that she had learned since about her daughter's life had come from Caleb's mouth: How Tamuru smiled as she walked at her father's side, and how Shatah, the slave and second mother, told God-stories to the growing maid. And this night, as always, tears flowed on Yaffia's face.

So it was that Yaffia made plans to return to the Great-House to see Tamuru with her own eyes. In secret, she schemed with Caleb, who many times had brought word of Tamuru to her tent. They both knew the danger should she be recognized by one of the slaves who might inform Ezamar or Enan or Sakhiri of her presence.

She came disguised as a slave, an elder woman, stooped, a hood and a shawl to hide her face. She hobbled. With Caleb at her side, she passed by the scribe at the gate of the Great-House without suspicion. In the courtyard, she saw the steward Enan angrily berating a slave and she quickly turned away. A maidservant carrying a basket of pomegranates stopped and stared intently, looked back once or twice, then went on.

Caleb led Yaffia to the inner court and the garden. She approached gingerly, watching, still fearful lest she be discovered. She stood at a distance in the garden under the trees. The temptation to reveal herself tore at her heart when she saw Tamuru.

"My daughter!" Yaffia whispered.

The sun was already low in the west when reluctantly she turned and followed Caleb's steps from the garden of the Great-House, through the streets of Gaza to his house. "Here you will be safe," Caleb said as they entered. "My servant is without speech, and even could she speak, she would never betray us. I have spoken to the Lord Zadok, and he will arrive in the darkening hours when he can walk unseen among the shadows."

As he spoke, a flock of ravens gathered, clamoring over the rooftop as if they were demons out of Egypt intent on betraying her place. Yaffia hid in a darkened corner of the house. She drew the hood down over her face while Caleb opened the door. He took a goodly loaf and threw bread crumbs at their yellow clawed feet and the ravens squabbled amongst themselves, then flew away.

When Caleb returned, Zadok was following close behind. Yaffia looked up as he stepped through the open doorway. She drew back her hood so that she might see his face. The air was charged with emotion.

"I remember our days of happiness," he said softly, and he pressed a flower into her hand as he had on their first night.

"I remember," Yaffia said.

Their eyes spoke of their yearning, but they allowed themselves only the luxury of a single touch. Breath to breath, they lingered close to one another. They spoke of broken dreams, of lonely nights, and of time which had been wasted.

Yaffia sighed as he turned to leave."I am saddened that we must part once more," she said.

"You must take care," Zadok warned. "Egypt's eyes are everywhere."

"Lord," she begged, after he had left and the door was locked, "when shall we walk again hand in hand? When shall the waiting come to an end?"

* * * * * * *

As the days and weeks passed into months, tales of the warrior-queen spread again through the land. Storytellers beat on their drums and raised their voices to the crowds that gathered to listen near the village gates and in the markets. Applause greeted the storyteller's words, and copper coins filled their cups.

Zadok stood silent as he listened to the tales of Yaffia's exploits. He yearned to be with her. His life was empty without her by his side. Only one comfort still lived for him in the Great-House — the Princess Tamuru, the link to the past before Ezamar and Egypt.

Tamuru had grown from a boisterous child into a gentle maid of fifteen, an image of Yaffia. The same black mass of hair sweeping low to the shoulders, the same vibrant spirit in the shining eyes, the pert little nose, the curved hollow in the upper lip, the redness curling round like two rosebuds.

Zadok would press Tamuru's head to his shoulder, his fingers sweeping through the unruly blackness of her hair, and his throat would tighten, the tears starting from his eyes as he gazed backward to a memory. Often when he stood by the door to Yaffia's chamber which had been sealed with brick and mortar, his mind would reach back to the shadows of the past, until Tamuru would appear, touch his side, and he would rouse himself and his smile return.

* * * * * * *

From the first moment Ezamar had entered the garden, Tamuru had been a thorn in her side. She was a constant symbol of Zadok's love for Yaffia. But when Ezamar gave birth to the Princess Raanu, not a male child as she had hoped, it was clear to all who was first in Zadok's favor and who was second. Now that Tamuru, the favored, was grown, the thorn dug deep. Zadok had praise for Tamuru, yet none for Gaza's queen or her child, the Princess Raanu.

It was against Shatah, the second mother who had wiped Tamuru's childhood tears, that Ezamar dared to show her anger openly. "What right has Tamuru's nurse to live within the garden?" she asked the steward Enan. "She is a slave, a lowly mountain maid with roughened hands and graying hair. Her bed should be in the stable with the others!"

"She worships the God without a face as did Yaffia," replied the steward.

So! Ezamar sucked in her breath. The faceless God whose house was in desert and mountains. What was He in the light of Amun-Ra? Nothing! This she said aloud within earshot of Shatah who heard her and went round by another path.

At a distance, Ezamar watched as Shatah and Tamuru knelt at Jehovah's altar in the twilight hours. "A God-child is Tamuru," she sneered later to the bevy of the garden. "A child of moon-dreams. Perhaps her God has already sent a youth to visit her on a night of moonlight." Ezamar drew up her nose with her jibe. "Her breasts have grown enough," she laughed.

Alone in her chambers, Ezamar sickened with her spite. She retched with the bitterness of gall spilling over, her hate pouring out in the green and yellow water. And she swore vengeance on Tamuru.

She considered poison like the greenish brew she had offered Copperakh who miraculously survived. Too obvious, she thought. It must be a way without suspicion pointing to herself. The death of Copperakh was one thing, but the death of Tamuru could bring Zadok's wrath down full upon her head.

Akab provided the evil answer. "Witchcraft," he whispered. Sorcery from his birthplace of Cush, the land of steaming jungles. "No one would know," he whispered.

Ezamar set her lips firmly. "Then go, and do what must be done."

He chose the darkest of nights, for the moon often interfered, he said. Among the trees, the farthest from the house, where no light could reach him, he set his pot to boil. From a handful of clay, he began to form a figure. Deftly, quickly, the little mound became a head with eyes and ears and all the attributes of a maid. He had cut a few strands of horse's mane for the hair and a small feather for a cap. His nimble fingers formed two breasts, not the pendulant breasts of an old woman, but the young, firm, sprouting breasts of a virgin maid. Then the navel, the private parts, and the arms and legs and feet. So it was finished with only one thing left to do. He fashioned the sharpened barb of death from a sliver of bone which he set into the head slowly, not too deep at first, but firmly planted. Under a bush close by the wall, he left the figure to fester in its evil.

All the next day, Ezamar and her black-skinned slave watched and waited. Each time Tamuru raised her hand to touch her brow, they held their breath. At sunset, Akab drove the sharpened splinter deeper and deeper until it was completely through the figure's head. But no illness came of it, no pain throbbed in Tamuru's temple.

Akab was disappointed. At one point, in a flare of fury, he broke off one clay arm to add more pain to the threat of death. It was then that the witchery seemed to take effect. Tamuru accidentally scratched her arm. The wound was small but bled profusely.

Akab hurried to report the mishap to his mistress. "The evil has found the path," he whispered, his black eyes sparkling. "Soon! It will be soon!"

That night, Akab craned his neck and listened, waiting for Tamuru's screams, but he heard no moans. The Great-House was still. He opened Tamuru's curtain slightly with one black finger. "Come, evil," he coaxed, beckoning to the darkened air. "Come," he wheedled, sniffing the wind for a devil-stench.

He waited into the early hours, but it was all in vain. The demon would not work its way into Tamuru's head. Akab snuffed up his nose with his chagrin when Tamuru rose up smiling, unharmed except for the scratch she had bound with a cloth. The wound healed quickly, without pain. In six days, no sign remained where the sharp-edged stick had pierced her skin.

In the wan light of a horned moon, Akab made a second needle from the sharpened tooth of a strangled fox. With a vicious thrust, he drove it into the navel of the hardened clay. Dust flew from the wound. With spittle from his mouth he sealed the jagged edge. He was about to dig a deeper hollow when he heard a noise. His fingers froze. Behind him, he heard footsteps. A lamp! A swinging light! With his heart thumping in his throat, he crept away.

He left the figure where it lay. He had no thought but to escape. In Ezamar's chamber, he clung fearfully to her knees while he told his tale.

His bowel churned with fright that a soldier with a sharpened blade would find him and gash his thumbs and fingers for his part in the evil scheme. In terror he hid himself under her bed.

So the night passed, with Ezamar above and Akab below. The next day they learned that it had been the captain Eliphas and two soldiers thrashing through the brush in their search for an insubordinate slave who later was found hiding in the stables.

A week passed before Akab dared to show himself again, lest he be found with the doll of clay and be accused of witchery. And another week slipped by before he thought it safe to seek the figurine.

He crept near the wall once more and searched the ground. Gone! The doll of clay had disappeared! Then he found a heap of earth freshly turned like a grave. His trembling fingers scratched the soil. There it lay, the barbs removed, the broken arm set in place.

An owl hooted above his head. It was the sound of evil in the wind, he thought. The warning of some great god, perhaps Tamuru's God without a face. "I hear," he mumbled in his fear. "I obey." Leaving the figure undisturbed, Akab quickly covered it again. A second time he turned in fright. "I obey," he whispered.

But it was from a young maiden's hand that Akab fled, not the power of a god. Only two days before, Tamuru had found the doll of clay. With pity for the helpless thing, as if it were a child who had lived and died, she drew out the bony thorns, then buried the doll that it find peace in a proper mound.

Rolling his eyes in fright, Akab trembled before Ezamar in her lighted house. "A moon-spirit must watch over Tamuru's head," declared the eunuch. "We can do no more lest it mean our death."

* * * * * * *

Ezamar was silent in the face of fear. She, too, trembled at the hidden power of darkened spirits. She turned to the ways with which she was more familiar, the desires of flesh and the cunning of her mind.

It was a fortnight later, at the hour of sundown, when she appeared at the door to Sakhiri's private quarters in the temple, where they had met together many times over the past years. She had adorned herself in a skirt of white pleated linen, girdled at the waist with a woven band of red and blue wool, her breasts exposed behind the thin weave of her transparent shawl.

Sakhiri greeted Ezamar warmly. He offered his hand and ushered her inside.

She had brought a gift to please him. A sculpture of the winged goddess Isis, breasts and navel exposed, the traditional locks of hair falling freely about the shoulders. She knew Salhiri favored the goddess Isis above all others, and Sakhiri smiled with his pleasure as he set the sculpture on a carved wooden pedestal near his bed.

Ezamar pressed herself on Sakhiri's arm. "For me, these are bitter days," she said. "The thorn that plagues me is the Princess Tamuru. Daily Zadok brings gifts to the favored, but none to me." She sought the distraction of wine and Egyptian song, she said, and dancers and acrobats and musicians. She leaned forward. She let the folds of her robe open lower to expose the cleft between her breasts. She pressed her bosom to Egypt's flesh. The problem, she said, was how to rid herself of this thorn that pricked her side. "It must be a way without danger to myself," she added.

"I have a thought," Sakhiri said casually. He toyed with the ivory-handled dagger at his side. "Politics," he said. "The subtle poison of kings and princes." It seemed that in the northern cities, there was rebellion brewing against Amun-Ra. Should Thutmosis be given reason to believe that Zadok had been seen with the rebels, should the Egyptian commander point an accusing finger at Gaza, then there would be need of a child-hostage to Weset, Egypt's sacred city. Zadok and his maid would be forced to journey to Egypt, to lie with their cheeks and noses before the toes of Pharaoh who would sit in judgement.

Ezamar pressed closer to Sakhiri. Their eyes met for a moment. A knowing smile passed between them.

"So be it," Ezamar replied without hesitation. "Send the hostage deep down to Egypt."

BOOK FOUR

EXPECTATIONS

Chapter Twelve

Z adok knew of the insurrection which Sakhiri had indicated to Ezamar. A short time before, a group of northern princes disguised as shepherds had passed through the gates of Gaza to seek his support. "The time has come," they whispered, "to forget our petty quarrels and join as one in strength, which then will be greater than that of the foul Egyptian."

A congenial group, closely knit, each man ready and willing to take his part, to sit or stand, to live or die, whatever the circumstance demanded. Zadok counted twelve in the group, precisely twelve, twelve being an auspicious number in the horoscope of heaven. One prince for each year that Egypt had been their master. And provisions had been made for death. Should any one of them suddenly fall upon his back, another was to come up to take his place and so maintain the all-important twelve to ensure the success of the undertaking.

"The time is ripe," they whispered.

Yet beneath this mask of harmony there was an undercurrent of bickering which had always been the weakness of Canaan. In this case, it was a question of who should be leader of the group, who second, and third, all the way down to the end of twelve. The last six in the progression were far more disgruntled than the first six in line, a thing which Zadok did not fail to notice in spite of their friendly airs. Inwardly, he feared that the secret freedom-seekers would not be secret long.

As a result, no sooner had they made their appearance than Zadok abruptly decided he would have none of it. Out of courtesy he had listened to the secrets of their planning, then had urged the disguised plotters to leave Gaza as soon as possible. "It is not safe," he warned. "Too much of Egypt lives here."

A genuine concern, but more with a view to his own cares rather than their well-being. It was clear that Gaza would always be Egypt's gateway to Canaan. He was Pharaoh's slave, and he must bear it all his life. "Egypt has many eyes," he cautioned. "Even in my own house, I know not where one man looks and where he babbles."

The group of twelve had glanced at one another in alarm, then around at the windows and doors. Singly they rose up. It was their intention to meet again beyond the city. They would send word to Zadok of a secret place, they said. But no word had come. Three days passed. Four. Five. Zadok felt a strange brewing in the air. On the sixth day, his eyes were opened.

The Egyptian caravans which appeared at the gates of Gaza were not merchant caravans but disguised companies of Egyptian soldiers. As Zadok had feared, the secret plot had been uncovered. Almost before he knew it, the garrison in Gaza was quietly doubled. Then it was reported that most other cities had covertly received a similar double quota. Ships of Egypt appeared along the seacoast, each bulging with more soldiers, chariots, war equipment and provisions.

Clearly, Egypt's show of force had snuffed out the revolt before its beginning. Very efficient. No war, no bloodletting, no clashing of shield and spear. Whatever happened to the twelve freedom seekers, no thread of suspicion pointed to Gaza and Zadok counted himself fortunate that he had not been caught up in the net of treason against Amun-Ra and Egypt.

Nevertheless, he lived with apprehension. Days and weeks passed before he felt safe again, but just as he was congratulating himself on his foresight, a messenger from Pharaoh appeared in the courtyard of the Great-House. Direct from Thebes had the runner flown. He carried a scroll stamped with the official seal of the Kings of Egypt.

Zadok trembled even as he read, but the message was simple enough and innocuous. "Greetings! My Majesty is pleased to send an invitation to you. Your presence is requested at certain festivities which will take place at Weset, the sacred city of the sun. Come at once," it continued. "All things necessary for your comfort shall be provided. The presence of your daughter, the Princess Tamuru, is also requested."

Zadok let the scroll fall from his hand and sat down heavily in a chair. A finely worded invitation, very polite and pleasant. No mention of the word hostage, but that was the meaning, and quite clear without being written. Him, they would not force to remain in Thebes, but Tamuru they would hold in safekeeping to ensure Gaza's future loyalty to Egypt. He knew what Thutmosis would say: "The princess will be safe here at my Majesty's court. Trust us, Adoni. My Majesty will not allow her to wither away and die so long as Gaza remains loyal."

"But I am innocent!" wailed Zadok alone in his chamber.

That night he slept very little. On the morrow he stood before Sakhiri. "Why this call to journey down to Egypt?" he cried out bitterly.

Sakhiri put on a sympathetic face. He shrugged. Under the circumstance he could do nothing. There was insurrection against Amun-Ra in the land of the Kharu to the north. Did Gaza know of it? No? In any case, the stench had reached Pharaoh. A list of cities, princes and kings had been sent down to Egypt. It was Pharaoh who judged, not the commander of Gaza. Should Zadok's innocence be established, well then...

"But I am innocent!" broke in Zadok.

Later, behind the closed door of his chamber, Zadok hastened to set down the truth in a petition to Pharaoh, his judge in Weset. He denied any part in the rebellion. He denounced the group of twelve. He declared his loyalty to Amun-Ra till the end of his days and into eternity.

A squatting scribe, stylus in hand, set down Zadok's words on a scroll of papyrus and within the hour a messenger, already panting with the urgency of Zadok's petition, rushed through the gate to the roadway leading south to Egypt.

Later, when the sun lay deep and spread its gold upon the ground, Zadok went to Tamuru, his face a mask of cheer. "An invitation from Thebes has come," he said. He shrugged his shoulders casually. He said nothing of innocence or guilt, nor of rebels or rebellion. "A great honor," he added. "One of their festivals to worship the sacred waters of the river Nile." Though it was a long distance south and there were many discomforts, it was impossible to refuse.

He had planned to speak of the joys of travel, the wonders to be seen, the monuments, the temples, but he said no more. For some time they stood together beside the garden pool, then he urged Tamuru to make ready. He turned back and followed the path through the garden, and Tamuru watched his steps, her tears shining. She had kept them hidden until he left her.

* * * * * * *

Tamuru had not been deceived by Pharaoh's message and she wept alone in her hidden garden. It was her place for weeping, its pool edged thick with reeds and grassy banks. Beside the pool stood a stout-limbed tree, an ancient terebinth rough and gnarled, a few roots bared like fingers dipping into the water to quench its thirst. To Tamuru, the tree was sacred for she believed that the Lord Jehovah had opened the wood to a friendly spirit who made its home within the crusted trunk. Many times in a lonely hour Tamuru had looked upward and spoken to the goodness of the spirit's heart, and she had been certain that it had answered, that she had heard his voice in the wind sweeping through the highest boughs.

She scratched on the bark to waken the leafy spirit in its bed. Her fingers wet with her tears touched the bark, that the spirit might not be deceived but taste the salt. The wind stirred the leaves like a multitude of tongues. "Why?" the wind asked. Why did she weep the tears and salt?

"I weep because I fear Pharaoh and I must journey to his house in Egypt," she whispered. She thought of Egypt as the land of Satan, a land of blackness where stone idols lived in vast temples, where people were lustful, black of soul, and maids walked shameless with their navels bared. "How can I survive in that evil heathen place? Speak to my heart, kind spirit," Tamuru begged. "Tell me what I must do."

"Wrap your skirt tightly round your thighs," advised the wind, rocking the limbs of the tree and twisting its leafy fingers. "Bind up the cloth and lock the door to your womb against Egypt's hellhounds. In this way you will remain chaste for your betrothed."

Many times Tamuru had opened her breath softly to the wind and spoken of her yearning and of the youth whose name was Shuah, though it was still a courting at a distance, only with eyes, without words. "Not yet betrothed," she whispered.

"Not yet," echoed the wind, "but soon there will be a courting and a touch."

Only in her dreams had Tamuru thought of Shuah's touch. In her dreams, she would dance for him, her body wakening to the needs of life. She would dance with the cloth swirling, the opening in her thighs widening, inviting him into her flesh. She dreamed that like her mother, the desert flower, who had fled into the night, she fled with Shuah to the mountains or desert or wherever he chose, for his house was a tent not a dwelling with walls of stone.

He was a tall, broad-shouldered prince of the desert, high cheek-boned, lightly bearded. He was a distant kin to Yaffia and he, too, followed Jehovah. Because of this, Zadok had been generous with his hospitality and his house. Many times had Shuah come with his servants and herders and pitched his tents in the fallow field not far from the Great-House. He was a shepherd, a breeder of cattle and beasts of the field and he brought brood mares and stallions, sheep and camel, to trade for Zadok's grain and gold.

From the first moment Tamuru saw his handsome face, his full red lips, his dark sensitive eyes, her thoughts had turned to the moon. In her dreams she had called him Adam though he had not yet called her Eve.

Now she was to be swept away as hostage in the dark land where scorpion people lived, the evil ones of Satan's world. With her ear to the sacred tree, she wept to the wind. "What strength have I in the face of Pharaoh? What strength has a lamb in the jaws of a lion, or a hare in the talons of an eagle?"

"God's strength," replied the spirit whose breath rose and fell with the wind. "Have you forgotten the God-story of Sarah which you learned at your mother's knee?"

Tamuru remembered how her heart had fluttered with excitement as she had listened to the legend of Sarah captured into Pharaoh's house. In days long ago, in a time of famine, when a plague of locusts had consumed the green and left it barren, Abraham left the safety of the land of Canaan. Down into Egypt he went with his true wife Sarah, and her maids and servants and their children, and the herdsmen and their children, with all the flocks and tents. In a watered place they camped, where Abraham saw that Sarah's loveliness was like the morning star and grew afraid that Pharaoh would seek to take her from him. He hid her in a coffin that her beauty would be seen by no man's eyes, but the tax collectors perceived the casket and saw this one thing had not been opened and they required that its contents be made known. So was Sarah discovered and the men of Egypt gaped in wonder and ran to Pharaoh with word of her incomparable beauty.

So it came to pass that Sarah was taken to Pharaoh's palace where she was adorned in queenly robes and anointed with sweet savors. In her despair she prayed that the hand of Pharaoh not blemish her virtue, and God sent down an angel invisible to Pharaoh. In that night when Pharaoh came into her chamber and stretched out his hand to her, God's messenger struck him such a blow upon the shoulder that

Pharaoh reeled. Later Egypt's king came again to claim her beauty but instead received a clap of thunder which flung him to the floor. Whereupon he fled, for he knew that his life was cursed should he lay a hand on Sarah, the star-maid of Canaan. "Remember Sarah," whispered the wind." Remember Sarah."

The sunset spread its golden rays to the garden where Tamuru sat by the sacred tree. The wind had shut its breath, the leaves were still, and the night fell with its blueness on the pool.

Tamuru washed the salt from her face and in place of tears she turned to God. With her face to the eastern mountains she prayed that night to Jehovah, saying, "Leave Thy house and mountain and come down with us to Egypt's land. Do not forsake me in the house of Pharaoh. Deliver me as Thou didst once deliver Sarah."

* * * * * * *

The ship set sail. With the tide and the wind Zadok and Tamuru were swept out to sea. Behind lay Gaza perched high on her hill. To the south lay Egypt's river with its wide reedy mouth. For nine days, they journeyed up the waters of the Nile until they reached Weset, Amun's city, and the Valley of the Kings.

From the port docks they were carried in litters through the city but with the curtains drawn they saw little and had no wish for viewing. They heard the noises of the city, the hum of living, the hawkers and children, the poor milling up and down the narrow crooked alleys. The city stank in their nostrils — the porters with sweaty bodies, the smell of food in the markets, the oxen pulling carts rattling over cobbles, the sheep and cattle, and the mangy stench of camel. A vast city with scores of foodstalls to feed the many. Zadok sneered his contempt for its enormity; a greater city only made it a greater urinal and a higher dungheap.

They were carried toward the west, away from the poverty of the rabble and the rattling oxcarts, past the villas of the rich and favored, the trees rising above the walls guarding lush gardens. Then on to Medinet, Pharaoh's temple palace near the desert and the redfaced cliffs, where the litter stopped before the portico to Pharaoh's court and Zadok and Tamuru stepped down into the glare of sunlight.

An underchamberlain came out to greet them. A dwarf in a pleated apron, his arms folded across his chest. He sidled up to them like a dog with his tail between his legs. He nodded briskly, his bald head cocked to one side, an obsequious thin-lipped grin on his narrow face. He beckoned and Zadok and Tamuru followed past the guards, who admitted them with barely a glance. With short, quick steps, the dwarf led them into a hall of columns, past rows of stone rams and lions, through a garden, then to a pavilion, its floor covered with colored tiles laid in mosaic, where he pointed to the chambers provided for their comfort.

A second steward, eyes downcast, who never looked upon their faces, brought food and wine and fruits in a basin of beaten gold and a black slave was sent to serve them, her broad, flat feet pattering on the tiles. A white apron hid her thickened potbelly. When she knelt before them, her bared breasts, sagging and dried like wineskins, dragged upon the tiles leaving dust on her nipples when she arose.

For six days they were served in silence. No chamberlain came down to enquire about their comfort. The steward who brought the food was mute. He came and went without a sound, and the black maid only grunted. A black man had called out to her from a nearby garden, perhaps her husband, and they had spoken together with gestures and shrieks in their native tongue of Cush.

In the first six days this was the only voice they heard. No message came down from Pharaoh, no call from an underling or vizier who served in Pharaoh's court but it was no more than Zadok had expected. The servant must wait upon the master. Of what importance was Gaza? Of what great note here in this vast estate with its swarms of servants, slaves and soldiers who served the brilliance of their god? Gaza? Who was Gaza? And the hostage? Let her sit in fear. Of what importance was she or Gaza in the light of Pharaoh? The god was too high and they, too low.

And Zadok spat with the taste of bitterness in his mouth.

On the seventh day, they were suddenly discovered. "Ho!" came a shout from the garden. A familiar voice. Zadok turned. The sun glinted on the man's jewelled collar. It was Sakhiri, Zadok's plague in Gaza, the eyes of Pharaoh, with nose so keen that he had sniffed out the stink of rebellion even where there was none. Now Sakhiri had followed him down to Egypt to plague him in this underworld where a man was forgotten, neither welcomed nor chained. Sakhiri seemed surprised, though he must have known that they were somewhere here in Pharaoh's place since he had stood by when the ship had sailed.

"Gaza!" Sakhiri exclaimed. "We meet again in another world!" He clapped Zadok's shoulder. They were well met, he said, here in Medinet.

The greatest honor, this being at the court of god. Yes, he, too, had left his post in Gaza. A temporary arrangement. He had left the duties to an undercaptain who no doubt would be stern and efficient in his new importance.

Now and then in the past — and Zadok knew it — Sakhiri would take his leave from Gaza. He would come down through the desert, a swift route by chariot, then up the great river by boat. He enjoyed life in the sacred city near Pharaoh's brilliance. To him, Gaza was merely an out-post, a village, though its walls were stone not mud and its gate was bronzed and weighted, requiring five men to move it. Not that Gaza's towers were unimpressive. But what were they in comparison to Pharaoh's temples, the Avenue of Rams, some five thousand ells from beginning to end and the gates of Weset which numbered one hundred, a thing of wonder to all the world.

They were well met, repeated Sakhiri, here in Weset, the brilliant and hundred-gated, though he knew Zadok found little pleasure in the sacred city. He was about to turn, to excuse himself to Zadok when Tamuru appeared.

He stopped.

Was this the hostage, this flower? She was a grown maid of fifteen. She was no child of ten as he had thought. He had been deceived, or rather he had deceived himself. It had been only a matter of a thorn to be plucked from Ezamar's side. Ezamar had complained and he had found a way to answer her dilemma. Who could have known that the hostage would be such a beauty? Hair black as ebony, clear white skin. She still wore the foreign garments of her native Gaza. What a sight she would be in the pleated linen of cultured Egypt. He would send her Egyptian garments at his own cost, the best, the finest, with the thin-ness of woven air. It was sheer nonsense to hide the curve of thighs and hips and bosom under layer upon layer of heavy cloth. The beauty of a maid was a beauty to contemplate.

Ho! What a surprise for Pharaoh! Obviously Thutmosis knew nothing of this captive beauty in the small pavilion by the left side of his royal house. Much fairer by far than any of his imported Astarte-maidens, or the maids from the islands of Crete.

Sakhiri knew of the god-king's lust, his impatient phallus, and the pains Thutmosis took to revive his vigor. Warm within the hide of a newly slaughtered bull, Pharaoh would smear his thighs with the innards while he drank wine mixed with the blood of lions. Day by day he would stand before his mirror and view his nakedness with approval. If this lithe, demure maid could not revive his loins, then the god was truly dead.

Pharaoh would be pleased. Only one word of her beauty whispered into the godly ear and for Sakhiri, a moment of glory. A reward. A gilding with gold in showers from the god. And honor. To be publicly called Pharaoh's friend, that he might bask forever in the sunlight of divinity — this was what Sakhiri yearned for. To ride behind the god in the second chariot. Or if not the second, then at least the third. His importance recognized, brought up high in the eyes of the populace who would line the streets and shout "Sakhiri! Pharaoh's friend!"

With a grin and friendly clap on Zadok's shoulder, Sakhiri excused himself with no thought but to run off to Pharaoh and tell him of what he had found in the sun pavilion near the west garden.

So was Tamuru discovered, like Sarah revealed when the casket lid was opened and the princes of Egypt gaped at her radiance.

Chapter Thirteen

In his eagerness to see the beautiful hostage, Pharaoh sent for Zadok and Tamuru from his morning levee in the palace; from his lion-footed throne which had been widened to include his divinity-daughter, Hatshepsut. He sat above all his courtiers, the greater and lesser who were so favored to attend. Sakhiri was present, though he stood among the lesser, some distance from the god.

The chamberlain, flushed with excitement, came running to the small pavilion where Zadok and Tamuru rested. "Pharaoh summons you," he called out and urged them to make ready without delay for the god was waiting. He was fairly prancing up and down with his impatience, running off toward the garden, then back again, beckoning, rapping his knuckles against the pillars.

They followed him to a stairwell leading to an upper landing where a captain of the guard opened the carved cedar door for them to enter. The audience chamber was resplendent with flowers and sweet with incense and myrrh. Paintings of husbandry covered one wall — people ploughing and sowing the sacred land, wheat sheaves and ducks near a pond — and on the opposite wall, a painting of the goddess Isis standing toe to toe with her naked son Horus, his infant phallus exposed, his lips at the level of his mother's breast which she offered cupped in her hand.

Eyes downcast, Zadok and Tamuru entered, bowing toward the throne, having been previously instructed how to approach the god. In such and such a way must one salute Pharaoh, the chamberlain had said in the antechamber. Zadok had replied that he was well aware of these royal procedures; he had bowed to Pharaoh many times before. Good! the chamberlain had said, and turned to instruct Tamuru. He had bowed to her over and over and she to him, like puppets, which had angered Zadok, for he considered it an indignity and dishonor for his daughter to bow like a mere slave before the chamberlain.

But at the sight of Pharaoh, Zadok's anger was suddenly subdued. This was not the man of power who had left Gaza eleven years before. The years had sunk his eyes deep within the sockets. Age had stolen out his flesh. His thighs had withered. His face was wrinkled, hollow-cheeked; teeth black and yellowed. Zadok suspected that the excesses in Pharaoh's life had aged him beyond his years. It was well known that he drank to excess as was the habit of all Egyptians and that since the death of his royal spouse he visited his women's pavilion without restraint. From his cushioned throne Pharaoh studied Tamuru. "She pleases me," said Thutmosis to all his court. "Charming. A beautiful flower. It gives me pleasure to look upon her. She must be adorned," he said, "bejeweled. This exquisite flower must not remain hidden from Pharaoh."

Thutmosis rose up from the throne and raised his hands to Tamuru. He began to applaud, his fingers tapping lightly against his palm. He turned to all the guests, who joined in, for it was the king who applauded. Only Hatshepsut, the sun-daughter, did not lift her hands to clap for she deeply resented such praise not directed solely to her.

Pharaoh pointed to Sakhiri and all the levee formed a ring of acclaim around the captain for the well-deserved honor clearly indicated by Pharaoh. Now a whispered word went from Pharaoh to the grand-vizier. He in turn signaled to the keeper of the royal treasures who rushed to the door and returned with a chain of gold which Pharaoh flung to Sakhiri's feet.

Sakhiri kissed the hand of Pharaoh and bowed low with his head to the tiles. He pressed the chain to his throat — the first golden treasure of the gilding which hopefully awaited him.

* * * * * * *

Pharaoh had discovered Tamuru, even as she had feared. "Lord God," she pleaded. "Do not forsake me. Where is the angel who struck Pharaoh when his hand reached out to Sarah?"

Day after day, she waited hopefully, thinking that God's angel would come to stand by her side but invariably it was Pharaoh's steward who appeared, mincing and bowing. "Come this evening, he would say. "Gaza's lord, too, must come. A cheerful time is expected." And he would bow again, then run on ahead to announce their coming to mighty Pharaoh, who was exceedingly sensitive to delays and waiting.

Pharaoh would have gifts for Tamuru. Jewel-encrusted combs to sparkle in the sweep of her dark hair. Neckbands of lapis and gold and pearls for her milk-white throat. Two golden bracelets in the form of curled-up serpents and other bracelets of elephant ivory and mother of pearl.

Tamuru felt smothered by the many gifts from Pharaoh, who was pleased with the giving and her curtsy when she received them. A sweet child, he would say to Zadok. A modest maid. He found her shyness all the more enticing. He undertook the role of a second father. He called Tamuru 'daughter'. An unwholesome doting with an underlying incest-need within him. He nodded, reached out to touch her. "A charming daughter. A flower. Beautiful flower."

He squeezed her arm and it was like a flame had seared her.

Then, on a day when Tamuru sat with only her black servant nearby, it seemed that God had truly forsaken her in this heathen land. Pharaoh's steward came again to the small pavilion. "The great king demands your presence," he sang out. "You must come alone for your father is elsewhere."

Tanuru had no choice. She knew she must stand again before Pharaoh's appraising eyes. Despite her prayers, there was no angel of God, no shield. And now, no father.

She was tempted to run, but the steward stepped closer.

"Are you scented?" he asked, and sniffed her fingers. "Good," he said. "You must be scented. The god-Pharaoh is waiting. His majesty is resting in his chamber."

With wooden limbs, Tamuru followed him through the garden, then to Pharaoh's inner chambers where Thutmosis sat at a table laden with meats and wine. She waited behind the steward who made a pretense of arranging some silver goblets. Beyond the folds of a shimmering, tasseled curtain, she saw Pharaoh's couch.

Pharaoh beckoned. "Sit, Tamuru," he said and set a cup of wine before her. He told her how fortunate she was with her beauty. "A flower," he said, "so sweet and gentle." He was pleased that her noble father had brought her down from Gaza to the royal house at Thebes where she could feel the glow of Pharaoh's divine radiance.

Mechanically Tamuru raised the cup to her lips and drank. Stumbling with every word, she responded weakly to his many questions. He rose up from his place and graciously extended his bony fingers. He led her toward the centre of the room, closer to the tasseled curtain and the couch.

At a signal the steward disappeared, and she was alone with Pharaoh. His hand was upon her. She shuddered. Her skin grew cold. She was near to falling to her knees to beg for mercy, to plead with him not to take her by force, when the Princess Hatshepsut suddenly appeared in the doorway. She stepped inside and stern-eyed, she glanced at Tamuru, then stared at Pharaoh.

Pharaoh took his hand hurriedly from Tamuru's arm and turned to Hatshepsut. "You sent no word that you wished to join me in my private quarters." he said, hiding his annoyance. He leaned toward Tamuru. "Be patient. Soon you will come again to sit beside the son of Amun-Ra."

With relief, Tamuru bowed her head and left the chamber.

* * * * * * *

In her heart, Tamuru believed that God had sent His aid in the form of the Princess Hatshepsut, daughter of Thutmosis, who sat on the throne at Pharaoh's right hand. Tamuru could not have known that Pharaoh thought of his daughter as an asp who stung his aging hide with venom.

Since early life, Hatshepsut had plagued the palace with her intrigue. From her father she had inherited a will for power. She was determined to sit as Pharaoh. Fortunately, her two royal brothers of precedence had died — perhaps through misfortune — and she alone was left in the path of succession. By sacred law, the daughter of divinity had the right to share the lion-footed throne. The priests of Amun-Ra had agreed, certain nobles had agreed, but the king had agreed only as a last resort and at that, reluctantly.

Pharaoh's doting attention to Tamuru had set Hatshepsut's nerves on edge. The daughter of Thutmosis made it known that the women's house was already overfilled with foreign maidens seeking to be allied to the power of Egypt. There was no room for another foreign princess.

She resented this wide-eyed innocent who had wormed her way into Pharaoh's favor. Only she and her own divine progeny would sit on Egypt's throne. No foreign seedling with whatever royalty claims would rise up to that high place. And Hatshepsut resolved that Tamuru must leave.

A captain followed by seven spearmen came before Zadok in the small pavilion. The captain held a golden whip of office in his fist. He bowed briefly, his neck and back bending as one rigid bone. He had come with greetings from the Princess Hatshepsut. An audience had been arranged.

Zadok followed into the glare of sunlight to an open courtyard where Hatshepsut was seated in a chair of black wood placed well in the shade. She sat straight-backed, rigid with her dignity, her proud, strong-willed face thrust forward. In spite of her erect position, she could not hide that she was somewhat short and slightly fat. At a flick of her wrist, the maidens who had hovered near scattered out of sight.

The audience was brief and blunt. Hatsheput was impatient. "Zahi prince," she announced in a haughty voice, "only now have I read the petition which you sent down from Gaza in which you proclaimed your innocence in the attempted rebellion. In it, I have found truth and loyalty but the question of doubt has been raised and so the question will be judged by Pharaoh himself. "I will speak on your behalf," she declared. "You will be summoned." She stood up and turned her back to Zadok.

So the audience ended.

* * * * * * *

Zadok was confused, yet hopeful. He had little trust in the Princess of Egypt, crowned though she was. He knew nothing of the power Hatshepsut wielded or her motive but he sensed that his petition would be greeted favorably by Pharaoh. The truth, he said to himself, will win out in the end.

An hour later a chamberlain appeared before Zadok who was pacing impatiently. "Come up to us," was the message that he brought.

Zadok anticipated that he was to be taken to a higher level in the royal house but they went down, not up, and Zadok understood that the message 'Come up to us!' was merely the calling of divinity to earthly man. He followed through a sunlit pillared hall and into an inner court whose walls were covered with frescoes of courtiers and court life. The chamberlain pointed to a massive door and Zadok entered.

The hall of judgement was long and narrow. The walls of stone were etched with row on row of balance scales and the floor tiled with a design of balances, human hearts in one pan and feathers in the other. At the far end of the hall, Thutmosis and Hatshepsut waited beneath an array of white-plumed fans. The god-princess and her father sat together, their richly cushioned chair mounted on a dais.

Three times Zadok, the accused, bowed his head before the judges. Three times he scraped his nose on the tiled mosaic of hearts and feathers and scales of justice.

"Gaza." Thutmosis leaned forward. "I have been informed of your petition. It seems that all questions of doubt have turned themselves into misinformation. I am not surprised," he added. "You have always been a man of reason and a man of reason you have remained. Our judgement has been made. Zahi is reinstated in its loyalty and freedom."

"Amun-Ra is just," mumbled Zadok, his hands outstretched. In his relief, he would have gone on extolling Amun-Ra and his divine son and sun-daughter but Pharaoh interrupted.

"It is all for the best, this judging and judgement," went on Thutmosis. "All the better, for your flower pleases me. He had it in his mind to enlarge Tamuru's chambers, he said. He would have her closer to the son of heaven. He would provide her with more servants, an honor guard, all the comforts and the finest in foods and music.

"Are you willing?" he asked with a smile.

Zadok's face flushed. Great Lord of the Sea! The old man thought to make Tamuru a queen. Of course he was willing. Kin to Pharaoh! Tamuru, a Queen of the royal house! And he the father of a Queen!

* * * * * * *

That night Zadok slept in fits and starts. The next day he woke without the usual bitterness in his mouth, which he referred to as the bitter taste of Thebes. He walked again with long brisk strides. The sun shone with light and warmth. The color of growing things took on a brighter hue. He no longer yearned to leave this land of temples and tombs of stone. He was carried away with his expectations, carried high like an eagle in flight. As kin to Pharaoh, he would have power and stature once more. He would be free of Egypt's whims, free to come and go as he pleased, perhaps even free to bring Yaffia back to live by his side. One by one he would tear down the bricks from Yaffia's chamber which he had sealed. He would open her door.

Take care, he said to himself. Some twelve years before he had anticipated great things. He had seen himself as King of all Canaan and had received Ezamar instead. He would not make the same mistake twice. After all, Pharaoh spoke only of larger quarters for Tamuru, an honor guard, and such. But it was clear enough. Tamuru would be queen! Gaza's prince, father-in-law to god! Zadok slapped his thigh and laughed.

Then came a staggering stroke of misfortune.

Hatshepsut had understood too well what Pharaoh had in mind. She had anticipated it and she was prepared. The same lean-faced Egyptian captain came with a second message. "A ship waits in the harbor," he said curtly. "In ten hours it sails for Gaza. Both will board."

Then he turned, and left Zadok stunned.

"Wait!" cried Zadok.

But the man was gone.

Zadok ran out after him. But then he stopped. What could he say? To refuse was impossible. Hatshepsut sat high and arrogant, her rounded nostrils raised like a jackal's to the sifting wind. The schemer! She was determined from the beginning to be rid of Tamuru.

Two litters had been prepared, and from the gardens of the rich, Zadok and Tamuru were carried back into the crowds and noise of the narrow alleys.

At the quay Hatshepsut's steward was waiting. He followed as Zadok and Tamuru went aboard. "Farewell, Gaza," he said. "Divinity wishes you and yours a pleasant journey."

A vision of Hatshepsut's arrogant face swept through Zadok's mind. Wait, he thought, fuming. Pharaoh will rage when he finds that we are gone, plucked from his sight without consent. He will bellow and roar that his wig has been pulled over his royal eyes. He will call out again for Tamuru to return.

That night Zadok stood at the stern of the sailing ship. He raised both arms toward the south where Thebes lay far from sight.

"Egypt," he cried out. "It is not the end!"

Chapter Fourteen

“Egypt is a fine land,” Zadok said to Tamuru as the ship sailed under fair winds on their return to Gaza. “The land of Amun-Ra has no equal in all the world. The tombs and temples are a wonder to behold and their great river abounds with fish. The skill of their artisans with gold and silver is incomparable.” He regretted that their stay had been curtailed. “Pharaoh is a gracious man,” he said, “and generous.” Zadok was as full with praise as the sails were full with wind.

Tamuru listened with a faraway look in her eyes. She smiled because she was sailing home. Thoughts of Shuah filled her mind, but to her father she said only that she dreamed of a shepherd prince who one day would capture her heart on a moonlit night.

Zadok stroked his beard and cast down his eyes. “Childish fantasy,” he said. “Look into the burnished copper and see the truth. Look well at your form and beauty. There you will see power that will guide you to the highest match.”

Despite Hatshepsut’s opposition, he was convinced that Pharaoh would reach out to Tamuru again, but he said nothing of the golden prospects left behind lest he be mistaken and Tamuru be disappointed. As they drew closer and closer to Gaza, he could think only of success. So concerned was he with gaining honor in the eyes of Egypt and the world that he gave little thought to Tamuru’s inner feelings or her dreams. It did not occur to him that she would think Pharaoh repugnant. He imagined her in the palace at Medinet, crowned with gold, aglow with scent, attended by maids and servants with feathered fans and bowls of fruit. The world would ask, "Who is the father of this maid?" And the world would answer to every face, "Noble Gaza is the father of this queen."

With his excitement, Zadok pointed joyously to the walls when Gaza came in sight. On shore, he offered an eager hand and a smiling face to his captain, Eliphas, who had come down with slaves and oxcart. "We have returned!" he shouted. "All is well. Even better than expected." To himself he thought, "Yes, and things may turn out even better yet."

Slaves and servants gathered round and bowed down with their welcome. Litters were brought forward and Zadok and Tamuru were carried up the hill to Gaza's gate, then through the market square to the courtyard of the Great-House.

From the garden Ezamar watched with fists clenched as Zadok and Tamuru stepped down to the cobbles. Obviously, Tamuru had not been kept as hostage. The plan had failed. It was clear from Tamuru's good spirits that Pharaoh had not tasted her charms. Ezamar had hoped that Tamuru would feel the sting of his little golden whip on her naked thighs, until he grew weary of her tears and assigned some dandy of the inner court to teach her more of the cultured ways of Keme.

In a mask of cheer, Ezamar entered the courtyard and raised her hand in greeting. "The sweet child has returned," she said to Zadok. "She is safe." Would they return to Egypt? "Ezamar asked. "A great honor to stand in the royal palace of the sun."

"It is a fine land," Zadok answered. "Perhaps we will go down again at some later time. That will depend on..." Zadok was about to say Pharaoh but he thought better of it. "It will depend on circumstances," he continued. "Who can know what the future will hold?"

"Then you are impatient to return?" Ezamar asked.

Zadok fumbled with his beard and looked down to the ground.

Impatient? Well, yes and no. Yes, he was impatient, for it was a fine land, the land of the sun-god. And no, he was not impatient, for impatience only slowed the time of waiting. He would have liked to say: "I have in mind certain prospects," but in his caution he said no more. He must wait until Pharaoh called out — a month, a year perhaps, or however long it took.

But before a week had passed, Zadok was torn with the slowness of the passing time. When he met Tamuru in the garden his impatience would rise up like a swelling wave and thinking that she felt the same, he would say, "Wait. Soon Pharaoh will send you a precious gift." He did not notice that Tamuru turned away her face at the mention of Egypt's king.

It was in a moment of reminiscence as Zadok stood at the sealed door of Yaffia's chamber that his conscience came head to head with his golden prospects. In his heart Zadok knew that Yaffia would not approve of Tamuru living in Pharaoh's pavilion, but surely, he reasoned, Yaffia could not fail to understand the benefits to Gaza and Canaan. There would be food again for the children, a greater wealth among the people. The Zahi slaves could be freed to return to their families. Tamuru would have the safety and comfort of Weset, the warmth, the pride, the honor. She would be a Queen of the world.

Often, when Zadok sat alone at night, he dreamt of the royal court of Pharaoh. Wait, he would say to himself. Be patient. The day will come. Ah, if only Hatshepsut, the schemer-asp, had not interfered!

Slowly Zadok rapped his knuckles on the wooden table, and each rap echoed the same persistent thought: Wait. Wait. The time will come.

* * * * * * *

The time came sooner than Zadok had expected.

"The great Pharaoh is here!" bellowed Enan from the courtyard, where Egypt's runner lay breathless. "He stands on the shore below Gaza's hill."

Can surprise be described? Zadok's world suddenly turned around. Back became front, and down became up. He rushed from the Great-House into the court. Here it was then! Pharaoh, the chosen son of shining light, the heaven-blessed, had come to claim his flower, to adorn her with silver and jade, then float back to Thebes and proclaim her queen before all the world.

Elated, Zadok rode off in his chariot to Gaza's gate where he waited as a troop of runners opened the way before Pharaoh. Clashing cymbals and drummers led the procession. Gaza's people who had gathered in the market clapped their hands and shouted: "Glory to Pharaoh! May he live a thousand years!"

When Pharaoh drew close, Zadok dismounted and bowed down, a grateful servant at Pharaoh's feet. "Welcome, Great King. My house, my life are yours."

But Thutmosis refused the comforts of Zadok's house for the present at least. He would endure the hardships of a soldier's camp, he declared. Did he appear so sickly that he could not withstand the strain? Of course not. The echo was unanimous for who among his courtiers would have dared to say that the great Pharaoh was too old.

"But my precious lily is waiting with such eagerness and I have been looking forward to the great honor of your presence in my house." Zadok persisted.

Thutmosis raised his hand curtly and inclined his head. "Pleasure and wine must wait," he said. He was appreciative of Gaza's concern for Pharaoh's comfort. He would consider the invitation at a later time but for the present, No — and he would have none of Zadok's pleading. He made no mention of Tamuru.

Dark browed, firm lipped, arms akimbo, Thutmosis declared why he had come up to Gaza's world. "Reports have come to me that a tribe of Kharu in the mountains close by has refused to pay tribute. Is that true?" he asked sternly.

"True, O Lord."

"And furthermore that tax collectors have been robbed and soldiers slain"

Zadok's face paled. "True, O Lord."

"Then gather provisions," Thutmosis replied grimly. "We make war." He raised his hand. "Gaza, stand here, by me."

A noble at Pharaoh's right stepped aside to make a place for Zadok, who came forward, head bowed.

"Gaza shall ride in the second chariot, the place of honor," commanded Pharaoh. "Directly behind my Majesty. At high noon we meet at the east gate and join as one. To war!" Thutmosis cried out. "Amun-Ra leads us all!"

* * * * * * *

Zadok was disappointed that Pharaoh had made no mention of Tamuru but the thought of danger to Yaffia was now uppermost in his mind. He knew that Yaffia and her band of warriors roamed the countryside, even as far as the hills of the Kharu and he feared that she might be tempted to come to the aid of the mountain people. He directed Eliphas to gather an armed force to join with Pharaoh, then rushed off to Caleb's house but the merchant was nowhere to be found. Zadok was shaken. He had hoped to warn Yaffia through Caleb's mouth.

He was still troubled about Yaffia when he joined with Eliphas in the market square. At the east gate, they were greeted by Pharaoh who mounted his chariot and led the combined force out to the Jerusalem road, then on to the mountains of Kharu.

At sundown in a green place between two stony hills, the camp was made and the plan for war. Pharaoh was persuaded to spare himself the strain of battle. It was decided that the god would rest in the comfort of the camp while the others would see that the culprits, the Kharu tribe, paid with blood for their crimes against Egypt. It was for the soldiery of Gaza and Egypt, side by side, to win the battle on the morrow.

In the hours after sundown, Zadok was stricken with feelings of gloom. What would he do should Yaffia be taken captive! He prayed that she was in the lands of the south where Caleb had seen her last.

* * * * * * *

In a single day the men of Kharu were quashed, left strangled and maimed. Those who attempted to escape were struck down with arrows in their backs or taken captives in chains, their heads pressed down in the dust.

To Zadok's relief, there had been no sign of Yaffia or her warrior band. Agitated, he had watched with lips compressed while Sakhiri's officers questioned the Kharu captives about the warrior-queen. The captives had cried out in pain as they were beaten with whips but had denied any knowledge of her.

But the stroke of good fortune of one moment had been followed by disaster in the next. In the fury of battle, with arrows and spears flying from every direction, Eliphas, Zadok's friend, had been struck a fatal blow. He had raised his shield to deflect a spear from Zadok's back, when an arrow from the height pierced the captain's heart and he fell dead. Stunned with grief, Zadok had called to the sons of Eliphas and together they carried the dead to a grassy plot where they dug a grave and marked the place with a broken stone. Saddened, Zadok stood in silence with the memories of his friend and captain.

He was caught by surprise when a man of Kharu leapt forward, dagger poised. Zadok drew his sword to ward off the thrust but before the attacker fled, he dealt a blow to Zadok's arm and left a small wound in the flesh.

In the end, with the battle done, wounded though he was and grieving for his friend, Zadok gave thanks in his heart that Yaffia had been spared.

*   *   *   *   *   *   *

In his gilded chariot, Pharaoh led the triumphant legions from the east road back through Gaza's gate. Garlands were strewn along the way. The drums thundered in the temple court. At the temple, Egypt's nobles gathered round their great King with praise. Among them stood Zadok, a bandage wrapped round his forearm, the wound still fresh.

Pharaoh expressed regret for the pain, however slight, and regret that Zadok's friend and captain had been struck dead. He gave a gift to the sons of Eliphas, the heirs, though in his mind he would have preferred the role reversed: that Eliphas had lived and Zadok were dead. Then he could have given comfort to Tamuru. He would have held her head on his breast and, like a daughter, she would have clung to him and kissed his cheek. The thought stirred a feeling of intense pleasure in his thighs. It revived the lust within his aging hide.

If truth were known, it was for Tamuru that Pharaoh had joined the grinding wheels and journeyed to the battle, that she might see in him the strength and vigor of a youth. Elaborate arrangements had been made. In the temple, Pharaoh would receive plaudits for the victory against the Kharu. There would be a celebration with flute and horn, a great parade and a feast until the dawn. He would wear the traditional leopard skin, the leopard head draped on one shoulder and enlivened by large enameled eyes, the tail dangling in back, the paws hanging down over his thighs.

At the chosen hour, Thutmosis sent a message to Tamuru: "This is the day for which you have been waiting. The war is done. It is the time to sit in the brilliance of Pharaoh."

With the message he sent a gift of a jewel which was received by Zadok who promptly ran off to the garden with the joyful news. "Make ready without delay," he called out to Tamuru. "There is not one moment to waste." He could barely contain his excitement.

Within the hour, he returned to her chamber where her maids were arranging the folds of her robe. "Ah, yes," he said, approving. "But perhaps a little more revealing. You must know what I mean. Yes, just so." He would not have her beauty hidden.

He did not see the unhappiness in her eyes.

* * * * * * *

The dignitaries and other nobles of Pharaoh's inner court had gathered in the large hall of the temple. On a low platform at one end of the chamber, a small gilded figure of Amun-Ra was enshrined on an altar. The severed head of a defeated Kharu lay at the feet of the god. Nearby, Thutmosis sat in an armchair carved with lion's claws. Two more heads were perched atop pikepoles above the level of Pharaoh's chair.

From his place in the forefront of Egypt's lords, Zadok's attention was drawn to the severed heads and his heart filled with a sudden dread that Tamuru might sicken in the presence of Pharaoh and the guests. He could not shield her from the hideous sight.

Tamuru had been seated in a place of honor on a cushioned stool at the level of Pharaoh's knees. Pharaoh's eyes were set upon her. Proud and smiling, he rose up from his royal chair. He reached out a bony hand to bid her rise up and stand beside him.

When she stood up, she could not avoid the sight of the severed heads. Zadok saw her turn in horror. Her lips parted with each breath. Her eyes opened wide. She swayed. Zadok rushed to her side. She would have fallen had he not reached out to support her weight.

Two slaves quickly brought water to sprinkle on her forehead, then carried her from the temple as Thutmosis watched, frowning.

Shame was red, and red was Zadok. Tamuru was ill, he stammered in explanation.

"Is she ill like this often?" Thutmosis asked, his eyes cold and distant. It was obvious that he was angered.

Zadok's bowels quivered and seemed to drop. His hopes were crushed, his golden scheme was tarnished. "A minor complaint," he insisted. "Unimportant. Just two days past, she spoke of a pain in her forehead which was aggravated by the cool night wind." No player in a drama could have done better. He pointed where the pain was most severe. He leaned forward, his face a mask of sadness.

Pharaoh turned from Zadok and stared ahead. His eyes narrowed. He had always called Zadok a man of reason, a man of truth, a man whose reason had once saved his life. Tamuru was ill, Gaza had said — quite suddenly, but a trivial ailment. Thutmosis was disappointed. He had expected that Tamuru would smile close by his side throughout the feasting but what was a brief moment, he thought, compared to a life-time of pleasure.

"So be it," he said. He motioned to Zadok to approach, then spoke in a lowered tone that Zadok alone could hear. He had made a decision, he said. Tamuru would enter the royal household and a small house of stone would be set aside for her natural god. "Before three moons have passed, the royal barge will carry the maid in happiness to my side." He would announce it first in Weset; in Gaza, second. Pharaoh smiled as Zadok gasped. "Each thing in its own time," he continued. "My Majesty must sail for Egypt on the early tide for the great river's wave will soon rise and Pharaoh must be present."

The chamberlain of the royal court, who stood behind Pharaoh's chair, raised his gold emblazoned ebony staff, then thumped it down sharply on the floor. "Let the festivities begin," he called. He struck the platform twice more as Thutmosis raised his hand.

"Friends," Pharaoh cried out. "Welcome all to this sacred house on this day of celebration at war's end. My Majesty bids you sit." Thutmosis singled Zadok out and pointed to a chair and table in a place of honor at the forefront of all the rest. "It is with deep regret that my Majesty must leave Gaza before the dawn," he continued, "but on this night of feasting, there will be enjoyment of a drama brought especially from Egypt."

A curtain to one side was opened to reveal a stage. A drama by a famous troupe of players had been arranged. A jewel of Egypt's culture for the eyes of the world to see. "It is my Majesty's favorite," Thutmosis declared.

Trumpets blared. Then, to the sound of distant singing, a large round pot billowing smoke was carried to the stage.

...And in the beginning, there was waste and void, the still waters and a swirling cloud. So the drama began: Amun-Ra's Creation of the World.

A tall figure of a man appeared, covered wholly by a cloth that glittered like the purest gold. He glowed from head to toe like the bright of dawn.

This was the sun, the first eye of light, the first rising of the morning sun. So on the first day of life, Amun-Ra opened up his eye and dawn rose slowly above the waves. And the world was waste and void of gods.

A hawk-like cry burst from the hidden mouth of the figure enveloped in the cloth of gold and out of the swirl of clouds came the Earth and Sky in answer to the sacred call. The Earth was black, a flowing swathe from neck to calf. A woman followed who was the Sky. She was robed in blue with silver stars like the night. Her eyes were masked with stars, and between her breasts lay a silver moon. And the black of earth walked arm in arm with the star-filled night. The blackness kneeled, his black robe spread about his feet, and his consort, the night and moon, fell gracefully into his outstretched arms.

So the first day passed. Out of Chaos came Amun-Ra, the sun, who called forth Sibu, the fertile Earth like the mud of Keme and the sky Nuit with her stars and moon. And as yet, the Earth and Sky were as one.

The golden sun hovered, his arms sweeping up and down like the wings of a hawk. Once more the cry of a hawk burst from his throat. To the Wind he called, and the Wind, hair flowing wild, leapt and danced into the world. Thus the great god Shu, god of the Winds and Spitter of Rains, came out of Chaos in his turn. He slipped between the clinging Earth and Sky and he raised the blue to her place in the heavens.

And on this day the heavens were formed and the stars on high and the moon. Then according to his desire, Amun-Ra created mankind and all living things on earth and in water. Chanting hymns to the glory of his world, the golden disc floats in his sun-bark in its skyward course — great Amun-Ra, the creator of moon and stars and his shining son who is Pharaoh, god on earth.

The drama ended with loud applause. Gold and silver rings showered the floor near the feet of the players who bowed before the royal assembly.

Now platters laden with food and silver jars filled with wine were placed before the guests and the time of feasting began.

"Be merry," sang Pharaoh's chamberlain, a lettered man who knew the verses to be recited at a time of feasting, even as was done in Egypt's royal house in Weset. He dragged a small coffin and its mummy as he passed among the banquet tables.

"Wait not until the time of death. Revel in pleasure while your life endures," he chanted as he went.

"Deck your hair with myrrh.

Be richly clad in white and perfumed linen.

Like the gods anointed be; and never weary grow

Do as it prompts you. Celebrate this festal time

For no man takes his riches to the grave.

Yea, none return again when they go hence."

"Drink, therefore, and be merry!' cried the chamberlain over and over.

To Zadok, it was as though Pharaoh cried out, not the chamberlain. Be merry! The chant rang in his ears. He raised his brimming wine cup toward Thutmosis.

Before long, Zadok's thoughts whirled in his brain with the excess of wine he had consumed. Great was Pharaoh. Great was gold. Amun-Ra glittered. Amun-Ra glowed. Zadok clapped his hands. He thought in poems. Free was he, free and proud. Free and free, away the cloud. No more to bend, no more to fawn. The scene turned round. Ho! Up flew Pharaoh from his house and throne, the scheming Hatshepsut overcome. The old man who was Pharaoh ruled the world. Dance and sing, my lily queen. A crown to wear with sweet myrrh and precious gems at your feet. Dance and sing, my lily queen. A crown for thee and pride for me.

Once more Zadok raised his cup to Pharaoh: "May you live a thousand years, Great Lord, and may you prosper under Egypt's sun."

The priests of Amun-Ra had begun a solemn march round the altar while they chanted hymns to everlasting life and the glory of their Sun god, Amun-Ra, and Pharaoh, the divine son of the Sun. Behind them, Zadok followed step by step, and as he passed the god's altar, he bowed deeply, first to Amun-Ra, then to Pharaoh.

Then, in a final decisive gesture of undying loyalty, Zadok drew sword and scabbard from his girdle and laid them at the stony sculptured feet of Amun-Ra.

Chapter Fifteen

In the darkened hours before dawn, Zadok sat within his litter near the edge of the sea. He had followed Pharaoh and his entourage to the dunes and the rolling swell where Egypt's warship with banks of oars at each side waited at anchor not far from shore. A mound of provisions as well as Pharaoh's personal effects had been brought aboard the day before. Egypt's banner fluttered on a tall pikepole deep in the sand.

Zadok watched as Egypt's sailors manned the oars of a skiff and ferried Pharaoh and his nobles to the waiting ship. A gentle breeze drifted from the blue water. Zadok smiled and stroked his beard. His joy of the night before still swelled in his heart. He leaned forward, stretching his hand toward the sea where Egypt's red-striped sails dipped and swayed. "Hail and farewell, O mighty Thutmosis! In three months, Gaza and Egypt will be kin! Hail, O great god of Egypt!"

For a moment longer, Zadok gazed after the billowing sails, his lips parted in a triumphant smile. Then in the rising light, the litters bearers bent their backs and carried him to the Great-House.

Tamuru greeted him when he stepped down from his litter in the courtyard. She came toward him with a happy face as he dismissed the bearers. Smiling, Zadok took her hands in his, then pressed her to his breast. She smiled in return and when he asked about her discomfort of the day before, she dismissed his question with a light turn of her head.

Zadok pressed her hands again in his and nodded with his relief. "A father's concern," he said. "But you must rest. Let Shatah see to your needs. Avoid the night winds and seek peace in sleep. I feel it wise that you not attend the celebration at moonrise in honor of Astarte. Regrettably, Pharaoh, too, will be absent. It was necessary that he leave to greet the rising wave of his great river. The sails billowed with the wind as his ship headed southward."

He was about to tell Tamuru of the future, the joy and the sunny hours which lay ahead, but Ezamar had entered from the garden. She stepped forward with a thin-lipped smile. In the temple, she had been struck with envy when she saw that Tamuru sat close to Pharaoh, an honor which Pharaoh would have paid to his own royal daughter or a queen. She pointed to Tamuru, her voice sharp with contempt. "There she stood in a place of honor at Pharaoh's side and she swooned! Swooned!"

Zadok gave her no answer. He turned his back. Take care, he said to himself. Now is not the time to speak out. But his heart leaped in his chest as he imagined Ezamar's look of dismay when she learned the truth.

* * * * * * *

Zadok had grown wiser with the passage of the years. He knew that in the golden scheme of things, all is rarely as final as it may seem.

But what could happen in three short months? he thought. Day must follow dawn, and night follow every sunset. Day after day, night after night, full moon after full moon until three. What could happen in so short a time? Death? In one moment, a man could look up to the sun, the next moment fall upon his back, his heart stilled. Was Pharaoh so old and weak? Not quite. Away then, thought of death! And Tamuru? What could happen in the three months to come which would differ from the three just passed? Pestilence? Unlikely. Zadok shook his head. Her blood was strong. She was chaste and pure in her lungs. And she was safe in her garden. Three weeks, three months, it was all the same. Dance and sing. Away the fears. So thought Zadok, who was blinded by the golden sun. In his joy, he gave no thought to Tamuru's heart.

As for Tamuru, she hummed a merry tune by the waters of the pool while her father dreamed of gold and queens. She was deceived by the father who did not speak. She was deceived by Pharaoh's sailing away to Thebes. She sent up thanks to Jehovah, for she believed that it was God who had banished Pharaoh and blew the full wind that he might sail away. She thought no more of Egypt and his bony fingers. She thought only of Shuah who had come again from the southland two days before with his herders and flocks. From Shatah she had learned that the young prince had pitched his camp in the fallow field nearby.

In the morning sun, she felt alive and carefree. A soft wind drifted through the boughs of the trees in the garden. Tamuru pressed her fingers on the bark of the ancient terebinth. She bared her breast to the spirit in his wooden house that he might feel her touch and know the desire she felt.

The wind rose among the leaves. "Have you no shame?" the wind chided.

Tamuru loosed her robe to reveal both breasts, round and firm and full with life. She pressed herself against the bark. "I have no shame," she whispered to the wind.

She felt the yearning grow deep inside her thighs. Like a flame it burned. She pressed her naked flesh against the bark that the spirit might know the desire burning deep within her and grant the wish within her dreaming heart.

"No shame," sang the wind. "There is no shame in love."

Tamuru smiled and shook her head. "I am not ashamed," she said.

* * * * * * *

Zadok was looking forward to this festive night of the full, round moon of spring. The spectacle of the high priestess of Astarte dancing under the silvered light had always stirred his blood. Once again, the people of the land would join hands on the sacred mount and dance and sing in the fertility rite of the goddess Astarte. It was the time of blessing on seed and womb, the planting-time that the seed bear fruit. The seed would be covered by the earth and the cow by the bull; the ram would cover ewe, and man, the womb. So it would be in all the land of Canaan.

"Enan," called Zadok in a cheerful voice to the chief steward. "Only three litters with their bearers will be needed for the journey to the festivities on the mount. Only the Princess Raanu and Ezamar will accompany me."

"I hear," replied Enan and bowed his head. The fatness of his paunch quivered as he thumped his staff of office irritably on the cobbles. It had been a cheerful day for everyone — for those who dined in the great hall, for the slaves who carried the trays and nibbled the food and licked their fingers. Cheerful for everyone except him. Who had a thought for the steward? He could have had a demon dancing in his bowels and no one would have cared or paid him heed.

Enan put his hand to his head. A pain had begun to throb. From the moment of rising, his bones had felt chilled and began to ache. The ague, or some other plague, no doubt. Worst of all Zadok had ordered that Evihu, the understeward, guide the festive group. "Evihu shall lead us out," Zadok had said. "He shall carry the torch and lead the spear-men and guide the way." Enan was to remain behind and watch over Tamuru and guard the garden.

An usurper in the steward's place! Evihu, an understeward! A mere nothing in the Great-House. Enan grit his teeth. The steward's place was with the torch. Had it not always been so before?

Gripping his steward's staff which was still tight in his fist, Enan retreated from the court and gate into Gaza's bustling streets. From the market square he went down from Gaza's hill toward the sea to the grassy dunes and the shore where he could brood alone and curse the world at will.

The sun glowed like a ball of gold above the sea and as Enan walked he felt relieved though his fears remained. Close by the shore he climbed a sand-strewn hill to stand above the surf and scan the world below. There on the crest beneath a sycamore tree, he came upon a mound of stones laid three on three — a place of worship built by some poor fishermen where they prayed to Dagon, their patron god, for safe-ty at sea. They believed that should a man sleep with his head against these sacred stones a vision would come to him.

Enan was not one who dealt much in prayer but there comes a time to every man, godly or no, when prayer is the answer to fear and though he had brought no offering, Enan knelt to pray. Then, as was the custom, he lay himself down to await his sleep of dreams.

While he dozed in the shadow of the tree, his vision came. A dense white cloud descended slowly to his feet. A fiery ball of flame burst from the cloud. Though he could see no mouth, no ears, no face, the oracle of the fire spoke: "A king you could never be. A slave you will always be."

Darkness fell. There was no sound from the rolling sea.

The flame rekindled, and again the world grew bright. The cloud grew large and fell upon the sand. A second time the dream appeared and a second time it spoke: "To your heart of gold, revenge will be sweet!"

Then blackness swallowed the flame. Silence filled the sea. Twice it had appeared, then no more. It was spent like death.

Silence. No other sound. And Enan awoke.

The sun was low. The sand had cooled.

Enan scowled. He rubbed his nape. His neck was stiff where he had lain against the stones.

It had all been a waste, this sleeping and dreaming with his head upon the stones. Dreams! Ridiculous! Bah! What use were dreams when it was Evihu's hand which carried the torch instead of his?

He felt a sudden urge to escape, to leave the court and house never to return. To flee away from this festive night, anywhere, north or south, to the desert or the sea. But where could a slave escape? How to flee and not be caught? For a slave there was no escape.

Perhaps for the first time in his life, Enan wished no more to be a king. He would have gladly exchanged his steward's staff for a fisher's net, to live in a poor hut by the sea, if he could only roam carefree on this festive day with the drunken mob in the city streets.

*   *   *   *   *   *   *

All during this day of revelry the gutters of the streets of Gaza were clogged with drunken Egyptian soldiers who were pushed, prodded, and kicked by resentful, unknown feet. The milling mob, laughing, jostling, crowded the streets and market square. Tramping aimlessly, roaming in the darkening air, singing, dancing, the press of people waited for the night.

Shepherds from the nearby hills, the smell of dung clinging like a plague to their rough dirty cloaks, mingled with fishermen in tattered cloth fuming from last week's catch. There were tall black-skinned slaves. Mothers with babes on their backs or at their breasts. Hawkers bawling out their wares. Beggars with outstretched cups. Singing maids, jostling youths, all rejoicing. A jubilant, sweating throng.

By nightfall, Gaza's people were so filled with beer and wine that they went reeling along in the city streets. Here and there, a few soldiers raised their whips against the unruly crowd who thumped on tavern doors and rushed inside with cries of "Wine! More wine!"

The sound of bugles and thumping drums thundered from the temple walls as under the starry night, the high priestess rode out through the temple gates in her high swaying canopied carrying-chair, her face covered by a dazzling silver mask. On each side of her chair, temple maidens danced and swayed. At the head of the procession, maids with cymbals and castanets marched with a group of young boys chanting to the accompaniment of lute players and men with horns. Ranks of soldiers followed behind, with battle axes and swords strapped to their sides. Under a sea of torches held high in the hands of slaves, the multitude moved from the temple street toward the east gate.

Shouts burst from the mob:

"Remove your raiment, O holy maid!

"Queen of heaven, shine down with your light!

"Show us the way, O radiant one!

"Strip yourself, holy maid!

"Show us the way!"

Burly men, shrieking women, red-faced boys and younger children, fevered with drink and passion, sang and hopped and clapped in rhythm to the thumping drums and the clash of cymbals.

Zadok pointed to the stream of beacons rising to the sacred hill. "Take care," he warned Evihu who led the litters. "We have no wish to join the mob."

In an open place within the sacred grove near the crest of the hill, Zadok's guard was posted. A stout ring of six trusted men, each with glittering shield and spear of bronze. Eliphas' son, Jariah, who now was captain, drew his sword and pierced the earth, the blade at his heels.

This was the hour of moonrise, the hour when the light of the moon filled the sky and shone down on the dais, the altar of stones wide and round, bleached white by the moonlight.

The high priestess of Astarte stood on the altar, her face upturned to the shimmering light, her forearms extended, palms outstretched. She stood under the sacred gleam as her kind had stood many times before over the years and years since time began. Since the beginning it had been so, and the spirit-ghosts were waiting, the dead men and the dead gods in the shadows of the wood grove...waiting, waiting for her dance to begin.

The high priestess drew her beauty out of its cloth-husk, the robe that she wore round her shoulders, so that the dead could see her in the moon-glow. She let her beauty unfold. The cloth slipped to her feet. Her breasts and belly open to the moon, she danced on the stone.

With slow steps, the high priestess swept round and round, weaving to and fro, and the spirit of the moon ruled her, ruled her flesh, her thighs, and her steps on the stone.

All Gaza knew that a troop of dead gods, invisible to watching eyes, would come one by one from the shadows and the wooded slope to possess her soul. She whirled faster and faster to the tempo of the beating drums with both revulsion and passion in her eyes and face as the dead ghosts took her and used her flesh over and over. She opened her body wider with wild abandon, gaping to be entered, and her body obeyed. She invited the spirits and gnomes and all those of the night to her belly and thighs, to the flesh of her breasts she had slashed with her nails until her bosom was red with little streams of her blood.

Until she fell and lay panting on the stone.

And from the night came shrieks and shouts and laughter as the drunken throng scattered into the shadows.

* * * * * * *

White-lipped, the moon of spring, the full round gleam. It shone on all the earth, the sea, the soft green fields, the cooling desert, the mountain peaks, the wooded mount and it shone on Tamuru's garden. The house was still. Zadok and the others, carried in litters, had long since left the courtyard to join the festivities on the sacred hill.

Shuah had excused himself to Zadok, or rather begged to be excused. His explanation — and he was careful to give one — appeared plausible enough. A quarrel had broken out between two of his herdsmen. One had accused the other of robbing him while he slept. Both herdsmen were hotheaded and fierce and neither was of a mind to wait for the trial and judge to mete out justice in the matter. Shuah had held out one hand, palm upward in a helpless gesture and so had taken leave of Zadok and the festive group.

But there was no trial that night nor any quarrel. Shuah had excused himself with a lie only when he had learned that Tamuru was to remain behind.

From the first time Shuah had seen her, he was enthralled. Barely four months had passed since she had come through the gate from the garden into the courtyard and their eyes had met, then lingered. When their parting had drawn near, his heart had cried out to her: Stay! Do not leave! He had suddenly been afraid that she would be lost to him forever. One word had broken from his lips. "No!" In his mind, she had been like a bird on a bough ready to fly away with the wind, never to be seen again.

Now, in the night, he was drawn to the empty court where a lone soldier had been left on guard, and then to the garden beyond where Tamuru often sat. He wandered in the courtyard in the pale light of the moon and to the moon-white ledge of the garden wall.

But a shadow walked between the wall and Shuah. Enan's shadow. Enan watched as Shuah wandered through the darkness. At one point Shuah passed so close that Enan's outstretched hand could have touched him. A sudden breeze would have fluttered the steward's apron like a flag but Shuah passed through Enan's shadow as if he were blind.

It was a curious Enan who followed softly to the wooden gate, then through the trees to the garden. He was well aware that Zadok had ordered him to deny entry to the garden to anyone, but he was looking to praise and a rich reward from Ezamar when he reported the young prince's brazen searching in the forbidden grounds.

Tamuru sat beside the pool. The obedient maid had remained in the safety of her garden while the others had gone to join the ring of singing round the altar on the sacred hill. She sat alone. Her fingers dipped into the waters and ruffled the image of the moon. It was her place for dreaming, her garden within the garden, high-treed and sheltered.

A twig snapped somewhere in the distance. She turned her head toward the darkness. From the shadows steps came nearer, brushing through the fallen leaves.

Then she saw Shuah in the moonlight, as though God had heard her desires and had answered her prayers. Shuah came towards her in the garden and she waited beside the pool, calling "Adam!"

Hidden behind her was the serpent, the gnawing evil in the shadows, like the first serpent who beguiled woman with the fruit of good and the fruit of evil. And under the watching eyes of the serpent-steward, Tamuru found comfort in the arms of Adam, and he called her Eve.

Chapter Sixteen

The steward Enan, the spy-serpent of the garden, rapped sharply on the door of the house of women. "Open," he hissed into the darkness. "Let me in." He called again, knocking louder.

"Dog, cease your clatter," spat Ezamar's black slave Akab who appeared, lamp in hand.

Enan thumped his wooden staff on the ground with impatience. "I have news of the greatest importance for the mistress."

"My lady has just returned from the festivities on the sacred mount and is indisposed."

"Indisposed," the steward mimicked. "Fool, I am her eyes!" Since that humiliating day when Akab had lifted him like a sack of flour and flung him from Ezamar's threshold to the ground, Enan had seethed with anger at the black man. "Let me pass," he insisted, his face filled with hate.

Akab snorted his contempt. "Wait, then," he ordered, and turned with his lamp. In a moment he returned, sullen but subdued. "Come," he grumbled.

Enan brushed by him with a curse. "Idiot!" he hissed.

Ezamar was waiting near the open door. She beckoned, her nose tipped with interest.

Enan entered. The tale was bubbling on his tongue. "Tamuru and Shuah...in the garden," he began at once. The moon had been bright, and there had been much to be seen. Hidden in the darkness, he had followed Shuah to Tamuru's garden. He had watched them in the light of the moon. Enan turned to sordid gestures instead of words. Beneath his cloth he felt his manhood rise. He came quickly to the point and slapped his paunch. "The way of all flesh," he said. "The maid and the youth." They had gone the way of all flesh on this earth.

Ezamar clapped her hands, threw back her head. "A harlot!" she exclaimed.

This same word Zadok had flung into Ezamar's face and not once, but many times, always mocking at her relationship with the Egyptian Sakhiri. "Harlot!" he had shouted. "Take your wanton ways from my sight. Seek another love-nook for your lust. Take your Ishtar-inheritance from my house and squirm with Egypt in another place."

Ah, sweet revenge, she thought. A pleasant twist. Now her dear husband had two harlots before his righteous nose and her laughter would ring in his ears.

"Enan," she cried, "my lord, too, must hear. Now, this very night. Run," she said, and she placed a red jewel in his hand as a reward.

Enan paled. Zadok would know that he had stood passively by while Shuah had his way with Tamuru. A cold sweat broke over his brow. His heart turned cold. He saw the black hand of death before his face. A night's delay, he pleaded. At dawn. With the rising sun. But Ezamar adamantly waved her hand. "Go," she ordered.

Enan brushed by Akab without a word. How could he have been so witless not to have foreseen what would happen? It was his greed for treasure that had led him to this pit. He should never have told Ezamar what he had seen. The day had begun on a soured note and now had ended with this bitter plum.

He wished that he still slept on that lonely hill where he had dreamed, or even that he had drowned in the surf below. Better to have been blinded than to have witnessed what he had seen and now be forced to spit out the tale into Zadok's beard. As he walked into the Great-House, Enan cursed his eyes, his far-reaching sight in the glare of the moon. He cursed the feeling of his sex that had been roused in his thighs and he cursed his manhood which now hung limp with his fright.

He stopped at the door to Zadok's chamber. He hesitated, then tapped lightly, hoping that Zadok would not hear.

"Enter then, if you must," Zadok growled.

Meekly, Enan entered. His hand reached to his throat. He coughed.

He wavered. He pursed his lips. Until he was prompted by Zadok's impatient snort: "Well?" — at which Enan swallowed a lump of breath. He coughed again. "In the garden," he began. He was walking... And the words came out like stones.

No sooner out than Zadok in a fury sprang from his couch with one leap. He lunged at the steward and struck him a vicious blow on the fat of his cheek. "You were ordered to protect the garden! It was your duty to bar the gate! Yet you looked on with the eyes of a hawk while Tamuru was violated! Hawkeyes!" roared Zadok and seized a whip. "Watchdog of my household!" He snapped the whip down again and again on Enan's head and shoulders. "Hawkeyes!" With each lash, Zadok spat out "Hawkeyes!"

The steward crumpled to escape the scourge. "Lord, have mercy," he pleaded. "Gods, have pity! I bleed!"

He would have taken to his feet and fled but each way he turned, Zadok found him with his whip, until Enan, beaten senseless, lay still in a sprawling heap, blistered and welted, his blood in streams on the floor.

Zadok stood astride the welts and fat and threw down his whip. "Evihu!" he shouted toward the doorway.

"Here, Adoni," the understeward called out as he entered.

"Take up the staff," ordered Zadok. "Hold it up, and let it be known that all must follow its command. Henceforth, you are chief steward of my household. And this dog," he growled, prodding Enan with his foot, "thin out his hide, strip him of all his hidden treasure. Set him to labor in the fields like the lowest of slaves with no hope of freedom or reward. That, for his greedy heart will be the greatest punishment of all. Now take this Hawkeyes from my sight before I tear out his eyes with my own hands."

Two slaves carried Enan out, and Evihu followed, tapping his steward's staff lightly on the ground.

*   *   *   *   *   *   *

"I am ruined," Zadok announced the truth to himself. He turned his face toward the wall. He threw up his hands. Why had he let Tamuru out of his sight? Why? He should never have trusted the pot-bellied steward to guard her in the night.

Too late. His expectations were shattered. How could he offer the son of light a desecrated virgin? Impossible! Once the truth was uncovered, Pharaoh would would have him flayed alive and left to vultures. What could be done? What could he say to Egypt? What? He gave himself the answer: Nothing. Nothing could be done. "I am ruined," he groaned.

Shuah was the cause of his undoing. That thief of the desert. He had welcomed Shuah to his household and treated him like a son. The scorpion had kept his lewdness under cover until the house was emptied, then unleashed this outrage, his villainy committed in the very garden where Zadok had thought Tamuru safe.

With gritted teeth, Zadok bound himself round with sword and harness. He called to the captain Jariah, Eliphas' son. "Ring Shuah's camp," Zadok growled. "Surround the field with a hundred spears. Take the dog alive. No lamps, no noise. Let each man sit on his knees behind the hedge until the signal."

So the trap was set, and Zadok, bent on retribution, got some bitter pleasure with the setting of it. He thought of the flagrant tale of two fierce, unreasonable herdsmen that Shuah had concocted to explain his absence from the festivities on the mount and he looked forward to setting the lie before Shuah's face.

But the fallow field where Shuah had camped was empty.

"They are gone!" came the shouts of soldiers.

Zadok's brow grew mottled with anger. The swine had done his rooting work, then fled. Zadok slashed his sword against a stone. The blade splintered. The pieces fell ringing at his feet. He threw the hilt and scabbard into the field.

"Jariah!" he bellowed. "Gather provisions. We make war!"

"One thing more," he said, and his voice grew cold. "Take Tamuru to the highest chamber in the Great-House and bar the door. Guard her day and night, and place Dubinah, your younger brother, in command. And Jariah," he added with the bitterness in his craw, "take her not within my sight!"

* * * * * * *

Even before Jariah was able to carry out Zadok's order that Tamuru be taken to the tower, word had spread to every corner of the Great-House and garden. Zadok's shouts had echoed like the rising thunder of a summer storm. Everyone knew each detail — from the steward Enan's spying to his thrashing at Zadok's hands, and Tamuru's prison sentence. Shuah's love which Tamuru had kept hidden in her heart was open to the eyes of all.

Shame filled Tamuru's face with red, shame before all who passed, though discreetly they turned away. Shamefaced that they knew of her thighs exposed. Shamed by the light and Enan's eyes. And her tears spilled out.

Jariah, with a saddened face, met her in the garden. He was alone.

"Where is my father?" she asked.

Jariah coughed. He bent his head. Her father had turned his back, he said. A deep flame of anger had filled the lord Zadok's heart. So incensed was he at her choice of Shuah, the desert prince, that out of anger came the prison bar. Too low a match, perhaps.

Too low a match? Tamuru bent her neck with the weight of truth pressing on her soul. Suddenly she realized what had been in her father's mind. He had hoped to see her sitting as queen in Pharaoh's royal house. Through her, he would have gained glory and the power to sit a head-pride higher in the world.

She had been deceived by Pharaoh flying up and down his river. She had been deceived by her father's joyful mien which she had thought was like her own joy at Pharaoh's leaving Gaza's gate. She might have destroyed herself had she known what lay in readiness for her in Thebes. Disheartened, she was forced to admit that her father had little care for the needs she felt so deeply in her heart.

She pressed herself to Jariah's arm for she thought of him as a brother. "Why must joy turn to pain?" she asked. "Why must the world be so filled with tears?"

"In all things there is purpose," he replied. "Be it life or death or shame or serpent. In everything there is a purpose."

In a low voice he spoke of his own grief when his father died. How his anger had flared. How he had run amok at the sight of his father's blood. In the temple of the Kharu he had thrown down their god and burned the wood. There he had found a priest hiding in a niche, a man who had not fled with the rest for one limb was crippled and useless. The thin-boned priest had pleaded for his life and in return for mercy he had offered a sacred amulet which dangled from his throat. The amulet had a great hidden power, the priest had declared, the power to protect life from death. "My hands let the priest live," Jariah said, "and received the sacred charm. When your father, in his wrath, ordered me to imprison you, I prayed that your God Jehovah stand by you with His strength. In answer, I heard a thunder in the wind and God's purpose became clear."

As they stood together by the altar in the garden, he placed the charm on its beaded string about Tamuru's throat. An amulet, thin and flat; a curled-up babe etched in gold, knees drawn up and hands hung limp as in the womb; an unborn seed with the hope to breathe and suckle the sweetness of a mother's milk.

"This gift is from your God," he said. "It was ordained by Jehovah that you receive it through my hand to keep you safe."

Tamuru's fingers reached to the sacred amulet and with the image of a babe cradled in of her palm, she knelt at the altar and thanked the Lord Jehovah for His gift. Then she followed Jariah through a cheerless garden, to the Great-House, the stairs, the darkened tower and she was delivered into the prison.

The door was closed and the wooden bar thumped into place.

* * * * * * *

Fierce was Zadok's temper. He boiled with rage at his political health in ruin. He seethed with such fire behind his navel that his anger came rushing from his bowels. Tamuru at the side of Pharaoh had been the key to his golden scheme, the road to high favor in the eyes of Pharaoh and his god Amun-Ra. Only a few short months had remained until the highest match imaginable. Who could have guessed that Tamuru would play out her dreams of love with Shuah and that he, Zadok, would be left with an insoluble dilemma?

Zadok spat out foul epithets at Shuah — the rapine of a wolf, a he-goat astride a maid, a tomcat above a babe.

Ezamar's laughter rang through the halls. Her shrill voice echoed through the garden and the Great-House. "Of what use is a prison now? Too late. The deed is done. The birds have long since sung their song. Too late. The Shuah-bird enticed Tamuru to the nest, then fled."

Chapter Seventeen

It was evening. The last red-rimmed clouds hung low on the horizon. Night was falling. Only the sharp screech of a hawk broke the stillness of the heavens.

Tamuru watched as the lengthening shadows cloaked the ground. Dim, the earth from the prison window. Die, she thought. It is the time for death, the end to all things, the end to sorrow and broken dreams. Jariah's gift was nestled in her hand. A gift from her God, he had said. She looked down at the amulet. "Babe," she whispered, "speak to me, for I am wretched and in prison. Tell me when my tears shall end. How can this door be broken?"

She held the amulet up to the prison window that God might see. She twined its beaded rope between her fingers and it dangled downward. Then she loosed her robe. Before God's eyes she spread her arms like a gannet with its wings to the wind, and she lay back on the floor near the prison bed, her breasts and thighs exposed. It was for God to know all that had taken place. "Lord," she begged, "guide me. Open the path to Shuah's tent."

Fatigued, she closed her eyes and was swept into a river of sleep. She dreamed she was sitting in her garden. The walls of the tower had rolled and curled and changed into ivy-covered stone. The prison door had become the ancient terebinth. The image of the moon shimmered on the water of the pool. There was no sound. She plucked a leaf from the grass near her feet.

A twig snapped somewhere in the shadows. She turned her head.

"Shuah?" she called. "Is it you, my love. I am here."

Like an echo from the darkness, a voice came back. "I am here."

"Who speaks?" she called.

"I am your child. The fruit of your love. I am your love yet to be, nurtured in your womb. I am your promised seed."

"It cannot be," she said. "I have no child save this image of gold on its beaded string."

"I am here. Your seed and his. In life and in dream."

"Come then. Let me see you. Come out of my womb into the light."

Again the soft voice from the dark. "I am here, close by. Not yet to be seen. Between the naked toes of time my voice has been sent to you as a gift from heaven. An answer to your prayer. A sign to you that God will be your guiding hand and will light the path to Shuah's tent. Wherever you have need of me, There will I be. Tell no one of the gift within thee. Tell no one. No one. No one. . ."

The hollow echo faded in the dream and darkness. Then silence.

*   *   *   *   *   *   *

Hushed was the first light of morning. It glowed dim and red in the tower where Tamuru slept. She woke, the dream still clear in her mind, and swept out her hand to find the wall. The door was still a door, no longer the ancient terebinth. The prison room was still a prison and the door still barred, but when she stood up, she found a green leaf on the floor by her feet.

Was it the leaf she had plucked in the garden-vision? Tamuru had been touched by God, and she believed. "My child," she whispered. She stroked her flesh and she felt the warmth. She listened but she heard only the beating of her heart. She stood silent, lost in the depths of her musing, when the sound of steps and movement outside the door broke her train of thought.

Dubinah, Jariah's younger brother, opened the door wide for Shatah, the slave and second mother, who had brought food and drink. He watched as Shatah placed the platter of breads and fruit on a table, then closed the door and the bar thumped back into place.

Shatah looked about, shocked by the narrow window and the confining walls. "Why?" she cried. "Why the prison? Why this judgement? Has the lord Zadok lost his senses?" She was near to tears as she embraced Tamuru.

"Do not weep, dear Shatah," Tamuru said softly and pressed herself closer to Shatah's breast. "A wondrous thing has happened. I prayed that God would somehow break the prison bar and guide me to the safety of Shuah's house. The Lord Jehovah stands with me in my time of need. I felt His presence in the night." She said nothing of the hollow voice in the dark. She spoke only of the vision, of the pool, the moon.

A strange glow shone in Tamuru's eyes and face. She drew Shatah toward the bed where the twig and leaf lay nestled on the coverlet. "Shatah, see," she said. "A sign of God's miracle in the night. When Dubinah unbarred the door and I saw your face, I knew that God had brought you to me, that you would find the answer to unlock the prison and lead me out. We will go hand in hand to Shuah's tents, there to live in peace with my love."

Shatah frowned. What did a sheltered child like Tamuru know of the dangers in this cruel world? Even if they broke the bar and managed to slip out beyond the wall, they must still find their way and hide from beast and man.

Shatah shook her head. She turned her back, her eyes closed, and pursed her lips. She knew of evil men like Cain, and of Abel, her shepherd husband. Slain. Destroyed in war. Her village plundered, set aflame. Her own sweet babe dashed upon a rock before her eyes. Two men, bearded and full of stench, had dragged her from her burning hut. They had bared themselves, their manhood readied. First one had forced his weight upon her, then his brother. Ravished over and over while she lay frozen. For a purse they had sold her into the house of Zadok where she had been chosen as maidservant to Yaffia soon after Tamuru's birth. In the garden she had found peace for the first time since she had been taken from her home. She had no will to venture again into the world of pain and hate.

But Tamuru kissed her cheek. "Sweet second mother, do not fear. The Lord Jehovah shall guide us. He will keep us safe from the evils of this world. Hear me. Remember the days when I was but a child. Think of me now for I have need of a mother's heart."

Shatah had never been able to deny Tamuru any wish. Perhaps, she thought, the time had come for her to leave the Great-House. Perhaps it was meant that she return to her mountain village to begin life anew or to die and join hands again with her babe and shepherd-husband. She would seek a way to unbar the prison, she said.

And Tamuru wept her thanks.

* * * * * * *

Late that night the escape was launched, but first, a tragedy occurred at the prison threshold. Dubinah, Jariah's younger brother, who stood on guard outside the door, was caught in a web of mishap. Shatah meant him no harm. She meant only to lull him to sleep with a jar of wine steeped with a potion to make him snore.

Success hinged on an enticing hand. She chose the slave Araada, an artful maid with golden hair who knew the ways of song and dance. "Escape with us," Shatah said to her. "In Shuah's land you will be rewarded with gems and gold and you will be freed from a slave's life."

This was the crux of Shatah's plan — a jar of sleep, a pretty hand, while Shatah waited with Tamuru inside the prison until Dubinah slept.

Dubinah was easily bribed with flattery and wine from a willing maid. He was prone to taking liberties and this night with its joyful implications was no exception. To waste the night? Nay, not he. The memories of other nights which had not been wasted brought out a lusty grin. He forgot his post. He set his dagger down and his hand reached out to touch Araada.

"Drink again," Araada whispered. "Let me hold the cup."

With each touch of her golden hair, Dubinah's forfeit was another drink from the tainted jar. He drank more and more to please her. Soon his eyes grew heavy. He began to snore. But as Araada grasped the weight of the prison bar in her slender fingers, it slipped from her hand and fell back with a thud.

Dubinah woke. With arms outstretched he stepped forward to seek out pleasure, another touch. His arms spread wider to embrace Araada but instead of an embrace, he received his dagger; the blade thrust deep. He gasped. His breath gurgled in his mouth. He fell back and his blood spilled out.

Panting, Araada lifted the prison bar again. Shatah stepped back, heart frozen, when she saw Dubinah lying on the floor.

"He would have killed me," Araada sobbed.

"Hush, child!" Shatah warned. "Someone will hear!" She clutched

Araada's hand and beckoned to Tamuru. "Quickly! We must flee!"

A mist filled Dubinah's eyes. Three shadows hovered near him, then were gone. Running footsteps faded. Darkness fell.

* * * * * * *

Near-death and death are only a step apart. For some, Azrael, the Angel of Death, comes with swift feet, perhaps with wings spread. For others, the hand of darkness is not so kind; blood leaks out slowly, the last drop clinging to life as if its sole purpose is to prolong pain and suffering.

Eyelids half-opened, Dubinah peered in the light of the lamp at the cedar rafters above until dawn brought the guard to relieve the watch.

"Water," moaned Dubinah at the sound of footsteps. "Water," he begged as the soldier stared. "On the table."

The soldier filled the cup and bent down. A few drops reached Dubinah's tongue, then a thin river spilled from his lips. He coughed. "More water. I thirst," he gasped.

"Who has done this?" the soldier cried.

Dubinah turned his head. "She. . . the maid. . .with the golden hair. . ." Again he coughed. A trickle of blood ran from his mouth to his cheek.

"You bleed!" broke in the soldier with alarm. "Speak no more. Save your strength. I will bring your brother."

"Go. then." Dubinah sighed. "As for me, I shall never go anywhere again." And a drop of water, pushed from his eyes by the closing lids, dropped to the floor. No more nights wasted or not wasted would there be. No more comely wenches to caress. He could still see Araada's golden hair as if in a dream. He slept, then stirred and wakened at the sound of footsteps. "I see Jariah's face," he murmured as he opened his eyes. "Is it you, my brother?"

"I am here," replied Jariah in a trembling voice.

"They have escaped," Dubinah gasped. His breath was labored as he spoke. "The pretty maid, she struck the blow. There were three who fled the prison door."

"The desert prince, was he here?" Jariah asked.

"I saw no one else. No more question," Dubinah begged. "Pluck out the dagger and let me die."

"I cannot, my brother," Jariah said. The tears glistened like jewels on his face. "My lord Zadok must hear your words. Soldier," Jariah ordered. "Find the lord Zadok. Run."

"Run," Dubinah echoed faintly.

Jariah watched over his brother as he dozed and wakened and dozed again. Then, from the stairwell a glare of light and Zadok's voice.

"Great Lord of the Sea!" Zadok cried out with anguish deep in his throat.

Dubinah roused himself. "They are gone," he said slowly. "The fair-haired one. . ." He could say no more. "Jariah," he moaned. "The pain! There is a fire burning in my side. Pluck out the dagger. Let my life run out!"

"Draw it out," said Zadok. "Let him die."

Jariah seized the protruding hilt. A sudden pull, and Dubinah gasped as the blood gushed out. He turned his head with the surge of pain. Blood came from his nose and mouth and he moved no more.

Jariah bent his head and rent his cloak. "Strike me, lord!" He cried as he tore the cloth. "At the falling of dusk I sensed danger floating in the air. A winged shadow swept across my path, I heard a whispering in the wind, but I paid no heed to the warnings of evil. Strike me, lord! Cause my own blood to flow."

Zadok turned away. "I cannot. I am the guilty one, not you." He ordered that the fields be searched, the meadows, the woods but deep within him he felt that the three fugitives would not be found.

Zadok left the place of death. He walked slowly like a man whose spirit was weighted with the shadows of his life. From the tower he went on a familiar path to the garden which a father's love had built. There, beside the pool near the ancient terebinth, he stood alone in the still night air and he admitted his guilt to himself. His mind had been filled with his own hopes and needs. He had closed his heart to Tamuru's dreams. And silently, bitterly, he wept.

* * * * * * *

Caleb had left Gaza without delay to inform Yaffia of Tamuru's imprisonment and so knew nothing of the three fugitives and their escape. His heart sank with the sadness he had come to report when he met with Yaffia.

"Tamuru is imprisoned," he said in a low voice. He kneeled before her and hung his head with his words. "My lord was like a madman. His anger knew no bounds. Like the fury of a sudden storm. A madman," he said again.

White-faced, Yaffia turned her eyes to the north, toward Gaza's house. "But why such rage?"

Caleb bent lower and shrugged. "The Prince Shuah, blood-cousin to your shepherd tribe. Some have said it was a match too low in my lord Zadok's sight."

Yaffia sighed deeply, then frowned. Caleb was to wait, she said. She would climb the hills to seek out God's advice.

Staff in hand, Yaffia looked upward to the slope. She had always set her eyes to the vastness of the stone, to the grandeur of the mountain house of the Lord Jehovah. She had always believed that nothing happened on this earth without the wish of God, even to this present day of pain. God! she cried out within herself. Why must my child suffer in the first days of her love? Hear me. Lord. Hear my cry.

She had climbed to the height where the path between the stones narrowed. The slope was barren. A high cliff rose on one side, clusters of gray rock on the other, yet she climbed higher. Then, at a sudden turn of the path, she was confronted by a serpent lying on the stone, its head raised, tongue flicking in and out. She drew back, her hand and staff outstretched.

The serpent raised its head higher, and to Yaffia's surprise it appeared to speak. "Whom do you seek in this stony house?" the serpent hissed.

"I seek God," she answered. "I would ask why my child must suffer. What purpose?"

She listened, and for the second time, she thought the serpent spoke: "Foolish soul! God has more serious tasks than to heed such questions. What is there in the flesh and substance of man that he must forever badger and bark at the heels of God?"

"I would hear God's answer," persisted Yaffia. "I seek His advice."

"Advice! Advice!" the serpent hissed. "Then heed mine first! Go down the slope and make your way to Pharaoh's house. Unwrap your skirt from your thighs. Dance before Egypt and its king. Let him thrive on the beauty of your flesh which is even more lovely than the brilliance of the morning star. Submit to his touch, and the lord Zadok will be honored with new-won pride and precious gifts and Tamuru shall be spared more tears and shame."

Yaffia drew back from the serpent's head. She knew that it was Satan who spoke. He had taken the form of a serpent to cross her path. She had almost been beguiled by the Fallen One but he had revealed himself for the advice he gave was false.

With that, she questioned God no more. To question God's purpose was a blasphemy and a sin, an open door for Satan to lead a soul into a life of evil. It was for Jehovah to make His purpose known at the appropriate time and place.

She thrust her staff against the Satan-serpent as Eve should have done in the garden of the east. Satan scurried and slithered into a crevice. Again and again, Yaffia probed and struck the rock.. Satan's head and tail quivered, but he refused to come out.

"I have met with Satan face to face," she said to Caleb when she returned. "Your first duty, my friend, is to return to Gaza and speak to Tamuru in the high tower," for at this time neither she nor Caleb knew of the escape. "Tell her that it was Satan who spoke from her father's mouth. Satan's anger and Satan's words condemned her to the prison tower. She is to heed only Jehovah. She must put her trust in God."

So it was that Caleb returned to the Great-House where he encountered Zadok in the dining hall. He faced him with Yaffia's impatient questions.

Yaffia spoke these words, Caleb said: "Why is Tamuru imprisoned? What madness is this? Is her love for Shuah a crime?"

"He is a thief!" Zadok bellowed. "A robber of innocence. Tell Yaffia that!" He thumped the table with his fist. An earthenware jar scattered into shards on the floor. "Tamuru is gone. It was Shuah who plotted her escape. She is in his hands. Tell Yaffia that!"

"Evihu!" Zadok called loudly to his steward, who came running. "Prepare a riding beast for Caleb. The white ass or the gray. Choose the more swift and sure footed." As Evihu led Caleb to the door, Zadok thumped his fist on the table again. "Tell her we make war!" he thundered.

* * * * * * *

The chamberlain who served in the upper quarters where Zadok slept sidled in and out with cautious back-glances. He was an old man, long in service to Zadok, who prattled freely. In the corridor he beckoned to the steward Evihu who waited beyond the closed door. The elderly chamberlain wagged his head. "The lord Zadok's eyes are bitter and his heart is burdened. His sleep is restless. When the night was full and black, my lord called out Tamuru's name. The hidden truth lies ever on a sleeping tongue," he declared. "The master suffers deeply."

In the early hours of the morning, the old man said, the lord Zadok had met with the captain Jariah who reported that the searchers had found no sign of the three fugitives. No footprints, no sign where they had passed.

It is as I expected, the lord Zadok had replied. They have fled on speedy riding beasts to Shuah's tent. Zadok's eyes had saddened. "I regret my sentence of the prison tower," he had said in a low voice. "My heart has blundered. I drove my child into Shuah's arms."

Regret may well have been behind Zadok's saddened eyes but behind regret was his greater fear of Egypt's anger which hovered over his head. He thought of the moment when, trembling, he would bend before Pharaoh in the royal house at Thebes.

"And where is she now, Adoni?" Pharaoh would ask. "Your child, Adoni, is your responsibility. I am here but where is she? Insolence, Adoni! What has been done to rectify the matter? Has this desert prince, this Shuah, been trapped and cut and quartered? Has he been destroyed, Adoni?"

Zadok believed that to capture Shuah was his only hope of reprieve. "I have pursued him, great lord," he would say to Egypt as proof of his eagerness to make amends. "He lies in chains in the dust at Pharaoh's gate. The shepherd tribe has been conquered and made to pay heavily in sheep and cattle and grain as tribute to Amun-Ra's might."

Only with this, he thought, might Pharaoh be appeased and Gaza's honor be redeemed.

* * * * * * *

Two shepherds had brought word to Yaffia of the merchant Caleb's approach. They had raised the carpet at the entrance to her tent and called out: "The merchant has returned. He stands in the north field."

Yaffia came out into the light and looked to the north and the rise of land where the shepherds pointed. She waited impatiently while Caleb followed a familiar path into the shepherds' camp and to her tent. From her threshold she bid him welcome. "What report do you bring?" she asked.

Caleb bent his neck and spoke in a low voice. "On the second night, Tamuru managed to escape and fled into the dark. Shuah stands accused of the plot, and my lord Zadok is resolved to pursue him to his tent and make war."

"War?" Yaffia repeated, her voice shrill. She stood stunned and stared at Caleb. "What use is war? To what purpose?"

She was swept with despair at the thought of clashing shields and war between her shepherd kin and Gaza. A weight of sadness filled her breast. She thought of Zadok and the Great-House. She longed to reach out and touch him with her sadness, to kneel before him and beg him for the sake of their love to curb his anger. Eyes downcast, she stepped inside her tent and closed the flap. Alone, she knelt in the center of her house of hair and called out to Jehovah in his mountain house.

"Lord, hear me," she prayed. "Satan has done his evil work. Look down on Zadok in the Great-House. Melt his hate and drive all thoughts of war from his heart. Do this for me and I vow to turn him from Amun-Ra to a life devoted to the worship of God."

BOOK FIVE

TAMURU

Chapter Eighteen

Three days had passed since the fugitives had escaped from the tower of the Great-House. With the greatest care, they had stepped over Dubinah and away from the rivulets of his blood which had flowed into a swelling pool. They believed there was evil in blood, and out of fear they had turned this way and that to avoid staining their robes and feet.

They had fled through a hidden gate in the garden into the dark beyond the walls, into a world of violence and lust. They had crouched in fear beneath a hedgerow when a hound of the field lifted up his nose to sniff the wind and howl. At the sound of shepherds' flutes they had bent and skirted round and away by another path. From the lowland plain and the sea they had followed a path east to the craggy hills and climbed the slope to a stony ridge where they found a cave as shelter from the night and wind.

No pillar of fire had gone before them, no beam of light wavering toward the eastern mountains, but God had opened up the path and led them into freedom. So spoke Tamuru where they sat together in the shelter of the cave. Yet in spite of what she said, an uneasiness had grown in her heart — a gnawing fear that the evil of Dubinah's blood would follow.

Perhaps all would have ended well had Shatah wakened Tamuru at daybreak, which had been the plan. One more day would have seen them reach the safety of the village where Shatah was born, but in the first dull light before dawn, Shatah and the slave Araada rose up while

Tamuru slept and went off to search for food and water in a distant copse and Tamuru was left alone in the hollowed rock.

* * * * * * *

The yellow morn lifted its face above the mountains. In the first thin light it seemed a barren world of rocks and gorges, the depths still hidden in the shadows below. Against the dawn, the peaks stood stark. The earth was soundless, like the first earth before God created beast and man.

Then suddenly there was the clatter of falling rock. A startled blackbird flapped away from its hidden crevice. Black-winged, it floated across the lightening heavens, then veered sharply downward, its warning caw shrill in the early morn. The wind stood still and listened to the echo bounding from the distance as if mountain spirits carried back the warning call: Beware! Beware!

From behind the rocks a man appeared. An old man, small but stocky, with a back bent by age and labor. His head jogged and rolled with early palsy. He was unkempt, unshorn, his dry brown face half-covered in a mass of dirty gray hair. An ancient hunter of the hills, his cloak in tatters, feet bound in rags coiled round and round with strips of leather. He was armed with knife and cudgel. Age had made him a weakened hunter, a toothless lion, limbs rheumatic-stiffened, his vision dim. Still, hunger made him search every crevice.

The old man peered into the cave, then suddenly drew back with a gasp of fright. He sucked his lips into his toothless mouth with his alarm. He thought he had seen a demon in the cave. A whole troop might come flying out, clawing, screeching, the mother-demon in the lead!

He peered again into the narrow cleft. A maid! Sleeping, wrapped in her mantle.

He looked behind him and all about. She was not likely here alone, not in these barren mountains. Cupping his fingers around his mouth, he whistled to the higher slope. He waved his hand as a signal to his sons to come down. Swift and nimble, they clambered down the slope.

Yasuf, the elder, the taller and stronger of the two, was heavy, square-faced, thickset between the shoulders. "What have you found?" he rasped. "A fox?"

"Not a fox," wheezed the father. "A vixen. A black-haired vixen fast asleep." He pointed to the jagged cleft.

The two brothers stretched their necks and peered into the hollow.

"By the sacred stones!" Yasuf grinned. "What the old man said is true. A maid is there. Sleeping." He nodded to his brother.

"Yasuf," the old man whispered, motioning with his cudgel, "crawl into the cavern and bind this cloth around her mouth before she can scream and attract attention."

Crouching down like a mountain lion, the burly Yasuf crept forward, his coarse cloak dragging over the stones.

Tamuru woke with the crush of a hand on her face and lips. She clawed wildly at the foul-smelling rag round her mouth but Yasuf only pulled it tighter. Her fingers grasped and scratched the stone as she was dragged from the cave into the open. A sharp blade pricked her skin below the shoulder and a rasping voice warned: "Not one sound or this blade will pass you through."

They pushed Tamuru forward along a narrowed path that led up the mountain side. At each climbing step, she gasped for breath. Finally, the stony path led to a green meadow and a small running stream. Farther off, a miserable hut, wattled and thatched, stood in the shelter of a rocky cliff. An old brown cow bellowed at their approach.

The old man danced a jig on the meadow and ran toward the lowing beast. "See what I have brought," he screeched. "See the pretty maid." Squealing with glee, he clapped his bony hands together and pranced around the beast. He pulled at her tail and stroked the mottled hide. "The Egyptians say a cow has sacred powers of fertility," he shouted wildly, stamping his feet like a village idiot, prancing, jumping, unheeding the cow dung that smeared his feet. "Lend me some of your fruitful power," he begged.

"Look, my brother," Yasuf grinned. "The old fool has gone mad with one glance at this comely wench."

"Not so," the father shouted. "I am not mad. Wait. You will see."

Yasuf kicked up his heels in a hop and a dance to mimic his father. "You will see!" he mocked.

Tamuru winced as Yasuf pushed her through the doorway and the others followed. She drew back at the squalor: One room, dirty, foul smelling. One table, three blackened wooden benches. An earthen floor to soak up the water of men. Yasuf flung her down on a mound of straw

Children of God 161

in one corner and tore the gag from her mouth.

"Now scream if you will," he taunted. "No one can hear you in this place." With a loud coarse laugh, he reached out and pinched her breast.

Tamuru cringed back on the straw in horror. A plaintive cry broke from her lips.

"Do not touch the frightened wench," the old man cried out sternly.

Yasuf paused. His bushy eyebrows lowered, his black eyes blazed. He turned his head sideways and glared at his father. "I will do with her as I please!" he spat.

"No!" shouted the old man. "She is mine. I found her."

Yasuf spat on the earthen floor. Folding his arms across his chest he stood erect, towering over his father. "And what would you do with her?" he scoffed. "Play with her on the grass? Pet her long black hair? Old man, your loins are dry and wasted. This is a matter for strong men, not the old and feeble."

"But the cow. . ."

"Bah!" interrupted Yasuf. "The cow. Your stupid tales. The cow can give you nothing, only dung." He spat again. "But console yourself, old one. You will have a share."

"And I mine!" cried out his brother eagerly.

Yasuf thrust the youth away, knocking him to the ground. "Lie down, pup!" he growled and turned again to the father. "We shall all have our shares," he laughed.

The old man shook his bony fist in Yasuf's face. "There shall be no shares!" he shouted. "The maid is mine."

"There shall be, and I take my share first!" Yasuf took a step toward Tamuru who looked desperately at the half-open door and screamed in panic.

The old man drew his long sharp blade. "Yasuf," he warned. "Leave her!"

Yasuf threw back his head and laughed. "The old man threatens with a knife," he jeered. "Listen, old man. The strong take what the weak find. Out of my way."

The old man suddenly sprang at his surly son and Yasuf cursed as blood spurted from a wide wound to his shoulder. He had misjudged the father and his dagger. He drew his own knife from his girdle. With a sudden thrust, his blade struck deep and the old man crumpled.

Enraged, the younger son sprang forward. The point of his blade pierced Yasuf's chest. Yasuf drew back stunned, then lunged at his brother.

Tamuru screamed and hid her face in her hands as the younger brother fell, blood flowing from his nose and mouth.

Only Yasuf lived. But the two blades had stabbed him deep. His head was reeling. His breath came out with froth and bubbling from the wound in his chest. Blood dripped from his hand and ran in streams along his blade. Slowly his fingers opened and let the dagger slip away.

He took a step toward Tamuru but his body shuddered. He stumbled. Eyes opened wide, he pitched forward, his weight pinning her in the straw. His blood spread out in curling streams and stained her robe and limbs.

Frantically Tamuru twisted and squirmed against his weight until she freed herself. Moaning, she ran to the door and into the open where fear spilled from her eyes at every rush of wind, at the shadows behind every stone, as if the old man and his sons still lived, waiting to spring out and gag her mouth again.

* * * * * * *

The sun had barely risen above its bed in the mountain peaks when Shatah and Araada returned from their search for food to find an empty cave and Tamuru gone. A terror gripped their hearts when they saw the signs of struggle near the cave. They feared Tamuru dead, dragged off by a mountain demon or mangled by some wild beast.

Shatah ran toward a narrow path that led to a higher slope, then turned back and ran toward the cavern. Over and over they called Tamuru's name but each time only an echo answered. Finally, in despair, Shatah grasped Araada's arm and pulled her to the rise of a slope and up the narrow path that twisted and turned between the rocks and boulders. It was a long tiring climb before they reached the meadow where, to their great relief, they found Tamuru sitting on a grassy knoll.

"Safe!" Shatah wept. "You are safe!" Overjoyed, she ran to embrace her, but she stopped when she saw the stains of crusted blood on Tamuru's robe. "Ai-i-i!" she cried out. "What has happened?"

"The men are there," Tamuru sobbed wildly, pointing to the hut.

"They are dead. They fought with knives and daggers. The evil of their blood has touched my skin. Shatah, hurry! Take me away," she cried.

She rose up stiffly but her legs trembled even with her first step. Arm in arm, Shatah and Araada helped her where the path was steep and they went down to the copse below the cave. By a stream they stretched out her limbs. With great care, they carefully washed the blood from her skin, but there was a cold quivering in Tamuru's flesh. She feared the evil of Yasuf's blood had seeped to the bone of her limbs. Her legs grew weak. "Dear Shatah," she moaned, "my feet are stone."

"Flesh is flesh, and stone is stone," Shatah replied. "There is no more to fear. The mountain men are dead. The worst is done." In an effort to wipe out Tamuru's fear, she tore away the cloth where it was stained with red. "The evil in the blood has been cut away, washed into the stream. Come," she said. "We must go on." Her home, the village where she was born, was not far away.

* * * * * *

It was still early in the day when Shatah led Araada and Tamuru to the valley where she was born. She came as a stranger after twenty years. A slave returning home. Perhaps to a brother if he had escaped the sword. At least to a dead child, she thought. Her own dead child. Twenty years . . . home.

But the land was empty in the sun. Only a few sheep and cattle grazed untended in a silent world. No shepherd's flute, no children playing. No sign of life in the desolate ruin. Blackened hovels. Broken wood on the streets. Unclean litter and refuse. This char and pillage she had seen before. "War," she whispered. "Likely Pharaoh's recent war against the Kharu." She pointed to the well. "There. There is someone. At least one body has survived."

An old man stood pulling at a creaking windlass. He puffed through his white-tufted beard as he drew up the bucket. Though his head was shaded by a cone-shaped hat of straw, small beads of sweat lay on his blue-veined cheeks.

He was startled when Shatah came up behind him. He turned sharply, then recovering he clasped his hands, thumb on thumb and fingers together. He bowed four or five times like a grateful servant and offered water from a jar with a flaring spout in the shape of a bearded he-goat's mouth.

"This is a day of ill omen in our poor valley," he babbled. "Out of fear the villagers close their doors and hide. Our priest stood at the gate of the temple at the time of dawning. On the night before, he had seen the moon and it was horned, a clear sign it will be an unlucky day of undoing. A man must not stand on the left side of his ox lest it fall on him and crush his bones. Evil gnomes will come down in swarms to infest the fields and roam the streets in search of little children to steal away and eat.

"God will protect us," Shatah replied.

"God? Of which did she speak?" he asked. "The one above? Jehovah, the Faceless?"

Shatah nodded.

"In our village, we no longer worship the Faceless One. Baal, our god, has eyes to see. His face is cut in stone. I once knew a man who followed Jehovah. This man, a shepherd, fell and broke his hip. He died, and Jehovah was helpless. But what do you seek in this poor place?"

"We seek shelter," replied Shatah.

"Ha! Shelter!" the old man cried. "Where is shelter? Only poor huts charred with fire. The war has done this to us." And he spat a curse against Pharaoh and the Prince of Gaza. "Only ruins," he said. He shook his head when Shatah would have offered payment. "Even gold is worthless." He threw up his arms with the bitter comment. "But here comes my old woman to scold me. Perhaps she will know where shelter can be found."

His old woman had been watching, peering through a crack in the door. Slowly she had creaked the door open, prodding her cane into the air to drive away any gnomes that might be waiting. She was an ugly crone, white hair drawn back tight from her narrow forehead, hollow-cheeked, thin beaked nose, mouth puckered and toothless. She shook her cane in the old man's face. "Have you completely lost your senses, old man? Why do you speak with strangers who might be witches?" she cried. "Come away, husband, before it is too late!"

"Ha!" he grumbled with disgust. "Your words are stupid, old woman. Go back to your images of wax and the piece of pig's heart which keep you safe from witches' sorcery and such. No witches of the well are these. They seek only shelter from the night."

"Do not be afraid, old mother." Shatah smiled warmly. She would have touched her, but the crone drew back with fright.

"Away!" she shrieked. "You are Labartu, the evil witch who has cursed my life! You stole out the beauty of my flesh when my budding breasts refused to sprout. You caused the boiling pot to tilt when my thighs were burned. You create the pit of pain which grips my side in my impure times." The old crone raised the palm of her hand to Shatah. "Keep your breath from my face, Labartu!"

"We are slaves," Shatah protested, "escaped from a rich man's caravan which was attacked by roving brigands. All those in the caravan were slain, but we three escaped and hid among the rocks."

"Lies! All lies! I see a witch's evil eye in this. Old man, you stand near death. Come quickly, lest you be covered with blight and scabs!"

Her shouts had roused the villagers from their huts. Like a wind sweeping down a mountain, the whispers had spread from door to door, from ear to ear. Three strangers near the well! Three witches!

Soon one wary shepherd crept into the open. His brother followed, then his sister. Now other doors were pushed ajar. Some held back, peering at the women strangers. Others crouched in fear on this day of evil.

The old woman called out, her hands raised with fright. "Witches! Hide the children! Cover their eyes!" She pointed an accusing finger toward the well. "The witches must die lest a plague take us one by one. Stones!"

"Stones!" came the shouts round and round.

"We are not evil beings!" Shatah cried to the throng. "We are only slaves. In this same village I was born. Here my own babe lived and died." And she called out her name for all to hear: "Shatah! I am Shatah!"

The villagers shook their heads. Shatah? They knew no such name, no such face.

"All lies!" the old woman shrieked. She thumped her cane upon the ground. "We are not deceived. We have stones to cast against the evil eye!"

"Death to the three witches!" the people cried.

Down flew the first stone. It struck the earth.

"Wait!" cried Shatah, shrinking back.

A second stone struck the ledge about the well.

Shatah turned to shelter Tamuru and Araada. "Shield us, Lord," she prayed. "Hold out Thy hand."

And it seemed that her prayers were heard.

Cries of "Wait!" broke from the street. "The priest comes. Let the priest drive the evil from the well!"

In a circled crowd, they waited with one patient face for their priest was crippled in his hip and his steps were slowed. He was tall above the heads of men, bone thin, without flesh. A long face, thinning beard, eyes bulging beneath the bony ridge of his forehead. He wore his black woolen mantle wrapped round from shoulder to heels and tied with a sash. His right hip heaved and rolled as he toiled with each step.

The priest had a stone ready in his fist for the three witches who had been caught near the well. His hand was poised to cast the stone, but he stopped. His eyes had caught the glitter of gold. Out of weakness Tamuru had bent her neck and leaned forward and the amulet, dangling from her throat, fell free from her robe.

Surprise choked the priest's breath. He squinted and peered at Jariah's gift. His eyes grew wide. He knew this strength. It was his own. At least, it had been. His hand quivered with his excitement.

"Hold!" he shouted to the villagers. "Lay down your stones. No witches are these. No harm will come from these three. Away to your homes! Away from the evil spirits who roam the streets." And the villagers hurriedly turned their backs and fled, kicking at the dust to frighten any gnomes who might bar their path.

Shatah kneeled before the priest to thank him. His shadow, long and thin, fell across the open mouth of the well. There was no need for thanks, he said. He clucked concern over Tamuru's state of health. Her legs were trembling, her face was pale. "Come," he said. "In the temple there is comfort and shelter enough for all."

* * * * * * *

The priest was smiling as he limped away. Who could have dreamed that his golden charm would be returned after it had been lost into the world? Coughed up again by the earth after he believed it lost forever.

He could have clapped his hands when he saw the amulet. He could have taken the gold to his breath, kissed it, pressed it to his flesh.

How then did it come there, round the maiden's throat? Ah, it was not difficult to guess. No doubt from the soldier. A lover's gift. How else could she get such a precious power? Foolish soldier. To let such a gift slip away. Placing woman's flesh above this sacred gold. Well then, so much the better. Now again it would be his. He had but to open up his hand to get it back.

His crippled limb felt stronger with just the thought. For over twelve years he had borne its hurt. A sudden kick from an ox and his life was ruined. Each step he took dragged the aching twisted flesh in the dust, and the sound that the drag of his foot made was swish...swish... But in his mind, the sound he heard was weak...weak...

In weakness a man seeks a new strength, and the priest, Nabor, had found such a strength in the golden amulet. An old man near death had bestowed it as a gift when Nabor had given him bread. "Keep it," the old man had said with his dying breath. "It is from a time long ago, beyond the count of years. It has a greater power than words can tell."

With the old man's gift, Nabor had felt stronger, more complete, more a man. But when the soldier's hands had choked his breath, he had willingly given up the charm. Fool that he had been! The magic of the amulet would have saved his life.

Now, as though ordained, the amulet had returned. Suddenly, there it was around the neck of a maid. The need to get it back pressed deep in his heart. But how? To take it from unwilling hands would destroy its strength. Wait, he thought. A way will come. It was meant to be. It was ordained. Be patient.

Chapter Nineteen

At the temple steps the priest, Nabor, turned and waited for the three strangers. The wench would come to no harm, he thought. The amulet would protect her. He wondered why she took such care to hide the charm so deep beneath her robe. He could see only the beaded rope. She kept the amulet sheltered between her breasts as though she knew its precious strength. Perhaps she had learned of its far-reaching power. He coughed at the frightening thought.

He led them through the open court to an inner chamber. On a straw pallet in the center of the room, Tamuru lay down for her feet were numbed. Shatah rubbed her limbs, then wrapped her flesh in a cloth of woolen yarn. The priest brought water and a lamp and mixed a draught to bring her sleep.

Later, when Shatah came out to offer thanks, he made mention of a gift. If they could find it in their hearts, he said. Not for him, but for his god, Baal, who was in need of some repair. "As you can see," Nabor said, "his house has suffered at the hands of the warriors of Egypt."

He swept his arm about the court of prayer. Broken stone upon broken stone, pillars cracked. The carved wood charred and splintered. A mound of rubble in the center of the floor. Baal himself was sorely injured. The stump of one limb lay broken. The god leaned grotesquely on one foot supported by a pole of wood.

"We could not tolerate his humiliation as he lay on the floor," the priest explained sadly."We have lifted him as best we could."

He promised to pray that the maid regain her health, even though his god was not the one of her choosing.

He returned an hour later. "Is the maid asleep?" he asked. The potion he had mixed was full with sleep. She should be sleeping. "Is she your child?" he asked.

Shatah shook her head. No, she was not the mother. They were three slaves who had escaped together. They had made their way to this village, she said, for here she was born and she knew these mountains but after twenty years she had returned as a stranger. The young were too young to remember her face. The old, too old. Their memories had faded.

Nabor half-listened until she spoke her name. He gasped and caught his breath. The blood rushed to his face. Then in the hollow of his throat, he found his voice, stammering like a man who had lost the power of speech and now struggled to speak again. "Shatah...I...am...your...brother."

Nabor wept. In his young days, when there still had been compassion in his heart, his eyes would often fill at the sight of a broken wing or the cry of a child, at a sweet thought of happiness, of love, but his heart had hardened since the day his hip had been shattered. He believed that Jehovah had not been watchful just when he was needed most. Nabor had looked upward and raised his fist in anger at the silent heavens. Out of bitterness he had forsaken Jehovah to become a priest of Baal, for Baal was of stone and was strong and, unlike the Faceless One, Baal had eyes and ears with which he could see and hear. And since that time Nabor had wept no tears until this day.

Brother and sister embraced, then wept, then embraced again. Shatah's happy tears unending, but Nabor's were sparse with his embittered life.

"And how have you fared these many years?" Nabor asked.

"It was difficult at first," Shatah answered. "Until I found Tamuru." She faltered, then swallowed a word. "My own child was..." This one thing she had no wish to remember. She hesitated, then said quickly, "I must return to Tamuru. You and I shall have time to speak again."

* * * * * * *

Out of prayer had come the blessing of prayer. So thought Shatah. Not one blessing, but two together, like twins from a mother's womb. The first found them safe in the village of her birth. The second was sudden, unexpected. Nabor, her brother, restored to her after twenty years.

Despite the double blessing, Shatah's heart was not at peace. She saw an apprehension in Tamuru's eyes and face. Tamuru seemed distant, agitated. She constantly touched and rubbed her knees. From time to time she glanced furtively at the shadows as if Yasuf, the mountain man, might pounce out from some darkened niche. Even in the late hours after dawn she had not left the straw pallet where she had slept. Her hands quivered as she held the bowl of bread and fruit which Shatah had brought.

"Come," Shatah said. "Rise up." She bent down smiling and took Tamuru's hand but even with Shatah's help, Tamuru raised herself only with great difficulty. Her legs trembled. Alarmed, she looked down. For a moment she wavered. Then her knees collapsed. "Shatah! I cannot walk! My flesh is dead."

"Nonsense!" Shatah said sharply. "Likely a little numbness left from sleep." She kneeled and began to rub Tamuru's legs. They were safe in this house of god where her brother was priest, she reminded Tamuru. There was food and drink. "Calm yourself," she said.

"But my limbs are weak," Tamuru moaned. "There is a mark of red. The evil of Yasuf's blood has seeped into my bones. There. See the flesh? The ring edged with purple and black."

Shatah's face paled. "It is only a bruise," she said soothingly. "A thump. No more."

"The mountain men have touched me!" Tamuru cried. Her eyes grew wild. She clutched Shatah's arm. "They touched me while I slept in the cave!" she cried. "Shatah, my limbs are dead!"

"It is only a dream that you cannot walk," said Shatah, and she caressed Tamuru's head. "You are fevered. Your brow is heated. Sleep," she begged. "Sleep, then wake again. God will keep you safe."

* * * * * * *

Only a narrow band of light slipped through the drawn curtain in the room where Tamuru lay on her bed of straw. It streaked along the floor and struck the wall where it marked a red stain on the stone.

A dark sadness filled Tamuru's soul. She closed her eyes, but not in sleep. Sleep is for the peaceful, not for those in fear. She touched her flesh which was like stone. Never to walk again. No more to feel the grass or sand beneath her feet. Unable to go onward to Shuah's tents. To remain forever in the temple, a prisoner of her weakness for the rest of her days. Forever at the mercy of passing hands.

"Pity!" she cried out. But there was no sound from the darkness of the walls. She lay helpless on the straw and moaned.

She felt the golden amulet pressed against her breastbone. Suddenly she remembered her dream in the prison tower and the voice from her womb when God had touched her.

In her mind, she pictured her life with Shuah as she had once hoped it would be. The land was green. There were clustered tents and grazing sheep. She saw a bed of sheepskins and cushions in the center of a wide black-walled tent. Lighted lamps stood in all corners and bowls of pomegranates, dates and figs on small tables along the walls. Her infant had been swaddled and slept in a cradle hung low above the bed. The child had long lashes and smooth black hair, hands tiny and perfect. The babe grasped her finger when she reached out to touch it.

Like a wave, the need to walk rose up within her. She crawled from the pallet of straw to the nearby wall. Stone by stone, her fingers gripped every ridge. Slowly she pulled herself up and stood firmly on the floor, and she felt a surge of strength and warmth in the flesh of her limbs once more.

* * * * * * *

It was four days since Caleb had stood by Yaffia's tent. Now, sheltered like the yolk within the egg, Yaffia rode in the center of her warrior band, javelins stiffly at their sides. She had come down from the high ground to the clustered tents of Shuah's camp thinking she would find Tamuru.

Not far from the encampment in the low ground of the valley, a maidservant drew water from the well which was hedged by blocks of stone. An oasis of date palms was nestled by a running stream and beyond a narrow field of green there was a pasture for a flock of sheep.

Shuah greeted Yaffia warmly at the entrance to his tent. "Shalom, great queen." Clasping his hands before her, he bowed his head. "Come," he said, then led her into the dimness of the tent.

Yaffia's eyes searched every corner. Soft carpets were strewn here and there. An array of gold and silver trays and goblets glittered in the light of the flickering lamps, but there was no sign of Tamuru.

Shuah raised his hand, fingers pointing. "Gifts for my lord Zadok," he said with pride. "I will lay them at Zadok's feet and ask for Tamuru's hand in marriage when I return to the Great-House."

Yaffia frowned as she considered Shuah's words, then she spoke, her voice impatient. "But the merchant Caleb brought word to me that Zadok was greatly angered at the match which he deems too low, and in his anger he imprisoned Tamuru in the tower."

Unbelieving, Shuah stared at Yaffia.

"Even now, " Yaffia added, "Zadok prepares to make war against you and your people. He believes it was your plan which opened the prison door and that you stole her out."

"Not true!" Shuah protested. "It was not my plan nor did I steal her out."

"Am I then to believe that Zadok's words were false?" Yaffia asked. "Tamuru must be here. Show me where she rests her head," she begged.

"I cannot," Shuah said, "for she is not here. Tamuru is nowhere within my tents. Before God, I swear it." His eyes darkened. "She is hidden somewhere in Zadok's garden. His anger is merely the excuse to make war."

Yaffia's heart beat heavily with sudden fright. She thought of Tamuru wandering unguarded with lustful ruffians and scoundrels everywhere. Where would Tamuru find food and shelter from the night? What roads would she travel?

Yaffia hurried to mount her riding beast. She would ride to the north this very day. With her warrior band she would stop at every village gate to search. A reward of jewels and gold would be paid to those who uncovered the lost.

From the open flap of his tent, Shuah watched as Yaffia and her band rode off. At the last moment, he turned away. He had a vision of Tamuru imprisoned. Angered, he drew the sword from his girdle and thrust the point viciously into the earth.

Chapter Twenty

Enan, the ex-chief steward, had healed his wounds after his merciless beating at Zadok's hands. His well-oiled skin had repaired itself quickly, albeit the fresh red scars still pulled and stretched when he bent his back.

Enan was fortunate that he still lived. Zadok's anger boiled up again whenever he caught a glimpse of him. Even while he lay in pain, Enan was very nearly thrashed again and a second beating, however light, might have meant his death.

The steward Evihu, who was a gentle man, wisely kept him out of sight. He set Enan to work in the most northerly field which was somewhat hidden by a thick hedge of shrubs. It was not likely that Zadok's eyes would find him there.

So had Enan come down in the world, from chief steward to a common slave. Gone was all the fine white linen, the mantle elegantly draped across his breast from shoulder to shoulder. Gone was his staff of office with the cluster of silver rings round its middle.

At first, the slaves who worked beside him were afraid to speak. The high and mighty Hawkeyes set down and now no more than a lowly slave? They shook their heads. None dared to utter one word or look his way as they hoed the rows of corn.

Only Enan's cursing broke the silence. He cursed Ezamar, he cursed her black eunuch, Akab. That black devil he would never forget. From time to time, he flung down his hoe and pressed his hand to his head. The disgrace he bore, this standing beside these low ones — that was bad enough, but his gold had been dug up, all his jewels which he had buried in the farthest corner of the garden. Over and over he moaned of his treasure that was lost.

The slaves listened while they worked, their backs still turned, but inwardly they rejoiced at Enan's suffering. They had bitter memories of his whip on their backs and the sharp prodding of his staff.

A black slave called Hooknose was the first to openly show his hate. He had been given this name by his brother slaves because of the twist of his nose, three times broken by Enan's fist. It had been at his black skin that Enan had struck, as though it was Akab who had stood before him.

Hooknose stepped forward and spat a mouthful of foamy spittle at Enan's feet.

Enan looked up quickly. He spat in return and shook his fist. Had he still been chief steward he would have whipped this slave until he could see his bones.

Hooknose did not curb his jeers. He bowed his head to Enan in mock reverence. "Lo, my friends, a king I see, the oil of olives on his head."

At first, the jeers came from Hooknose alone. The others stood back. Fear started from their eyes. "Come, my friends," called Hooknose. "Be not afraid. He is like an asp that has lost its venom and can no longer rear its head. Like others, he must crawl upon his belly."

"Black devil!" Enan cursed.

"Fat devil," retorted Hooknose, and danced a jig.

With that, the others laughed and slapped their thighs. One joined with Hooknose in his dance. "See the painted staff in his hand!" he jibed, pointing at the hoe.

A pebble struck Enan's shoulder. Hooknose had thrown it to attract his attention. "Master," scoffed Hooknose. "Lend me one sliver of your stolen gold. One jewel. I promise to repay you double on some sunny night."

Enan stiffened. His face grew red, then white. He trembled with his rage. His hands began to quiver. Suddenly he uttered a loud hoarse shout and fell senseless to the ground. His teeth were clenched. Bloody froth blew from his lips with each breath. His body shook with violent spasms and a wet stain spread on his loincloth as he let his water out.

The sudden devil's fit stunned Hooknose and the others. They stood huddled in a small tight group. Then each man fled from the field. They rushed to the steward Evihu's side, and in a straggling, hesitant column they followed the steward back to the place where Enan lay stretched out upon the ground.

Evihu looked down at Enan who lay still, blood in the corners of his mouth. The sunlight glistened on the beads of sweat which had formed upon his brow.

"Are you in pain?" Evihu asked.

"My head," answered Enan weakly. "At the back. It pounds and aches."

"The sun was too strong," Evihu said.

"Yes. The sun too strong," mumbled Enan.

Evihu turned and called to Hooknose. "Carry him back to the slaves' quarters and lay him on his couch. Give him drink and treat him gently."

* * * * * * *

Evihu cursed this day which had begun like a plague settling on a field. Bad news had come that morning and Zadok's mood was foul. Two men had been led directly into his inner chamber. "Impossible!" was the only word that Evihu had heard. It was only later that he learned who these men were and what news they brought.

From the chamberlain who served Zadok's bed, Evihu heard that they were spies returned from the villages east and south, with the unexpected report that Shuah could muster ten thousand men at a moment's call.

"Impossible!" Zadok had exclaimed.

All his plans for war had been based on the assumption that Shuah could gather no more than half that number. But the desert tribes had formed an alliance amongst themselves since Egypt's recent battle against the Kharu to the north and Shuah was chief of the alliance.

Shuah would be no easy dog to catch. Ten thousand against Zadok's five was an accounting so lopsided as to border on disaster with the result that Zadok was forced to seek aid from Sakhiri, his only source of reinforcements. A necessary but galling task. Reluctantly, Zadok had ordered that his litter be made ready and had departed for Sakhiri's quarters in the temple.

Sakhiri's steward was waiting. He bowed stiffly, one hand on his staff, then led Zadok to the garden where Egypt's captain was reclining on an embroidered mat. There was a remnant of clothing, a woman's shift, transparent and pleated, wrapped in Sakhiri's fingers.

So began the meeting, with apologies from Zadok for the obvious interruption.

Sakhiri was accommodating. He waved his hand.

A look of uneasiness crept over Zadok's face at the thought of the request he was about to make. "I have need of five thousand of Egypt's soldiers," he said slowly.

"A fair round figure, five thousand. For what purpose?"

Zadok hesitated. "A family matter," he said, choosing his words with care.

Sakhiri smiled. "Ah yes, Ezamar has spoken of it. I understand you plan to deal severely with the knave. Of course, you must know that it is not Egypt's policy to become involved with local quarrels. Still, since it is a matter which concerns Gaza's household, the five thousand men at arms might be available . . . for a price."

"I am prepared to pay a measured chest of jewels and gold," replied Zadok.

"Agreed," Sakhiri nodded, "but I have an added treasure in mind. Ezamar's daughter, Princess Raanu."

It was not by chance that Sakhiri spoke of Raanu. He was convinced that the princess was Pharaoh's seed. He had reasoned it out. He had counted the time backward on his fingers, and he believed that through Ezamar's daughter he would become kin to god in this world and the next. Through her, he would slide into the sun-boat to sail eternally across the blue of sky. In Sakhiri's eyes, no greater honor could befall any man. "She will become first in my house," Sakhiri promised.

Zadok was startled. Raanu coupled with Sakhiri? Who could understand affairs of the heart? So be it. Let him take Raanu, if that was his wish. "Granted," he said without hesitating.

"I myself will lead Egypt's soldiers in your cause," Sakhiri declared. "I give you my hand and my word on it."

* * * * * * *

Like a shepherd concerned about a lost lamb of his flock, Yaffia had returned to the oasis of Shuah's camp. While her warrior band rested with their camels and drank of the spring waters under the date palms, she met with Shuah in the cool of his tent. "Has Tamuru reached this watered place?" she asked.

"I have not seen her face," Shuah replied. "It is in my mind that Zadok still keeps her hidden in the garden."

"My warriors have scoured the hills and the villages in the northeast without success," Yaffia said. "They found no sign of Tamuru and the two slaves who accompanied her but they brought back a strange tale of death. In a high meadow they came upon three men dead in their mountain hut. A cloak of fine linen stained with blood lay in the meadow. Near the cloak, a headband of woven cloth had been discarded on the grass. The warriors lit fires and called out loudly into the mountain rocks but heard only their echoes from the depths." She said nothing of her fears that the robe may have been worn by Tamuru. "We shall seek again to the north in the coming days. There are many villages in the rocky hills."

Side by side, she went out with Shuah to the place of Jehovah's altar where she poured a libation of wine and prepared a sacrifice of the finest meat for Jehovah's pleasure.

"Let the smoke of sweet savor curl up to the heavens," she said. "And may the Lord Jehovah hear my payers and keep Tamuru safe from all harm."

Chapter Twenty-One

"Rest awhile in this house of Baal," Nabor said to Shatah, who had approached him in the temple court. "Delay your journey. Remain at a brother's side until the full moon two weeks hence, for only the gods can know when we shall meet again."

"We will stay," Shatah agreed, and pressed his hand.

Nabor smiled. He was thinking of the amulet hidden beneath Tamuru's mantle and the time which might be required to get it back. "The maid will benefit from the days of rest," he said. "I see you still fear for her, my sister. Calm yourself. She will regain her strength."

And as Nabor predicted, Tamuru recovered. The paleness of her face was replaced by a glowing color. A quiet peace, a graceful calm unfolded about her eyes which seemed to become softer, deeper, a well of blue.

She had entered the court of prayer to receive their allotted portion for the evening meal when she saw a dark-haired youth, his skin browned by the sun, standing at Nabor's side. The boy was clad in a coarse gray knee-length tunic tied with a strip of leather at the waist. His face was narrow with a thin blade of a nose, his dark eyes melancholy and downcast. From time to time his fingers reached up and plucked nervously at the deep cleft of his chin.

He drew back as Tamuru appeared. Like a turtle in a shell, he tried to hide in the shadow cast by Nabor's figure.

Tamuru had seen a sudden fear in the boy's eyes. She smiled to disarm him, but as she drew nearer, the youth turned and fled.

"Raasban," Nabor shouted as the boy ran, "bring water from the well."

Nabor smiled as the youth glanced back and raised his hand in answer. "He is my servant and the apprentice in this house of Baal," he explained to Tamuru.

"But why does he appear so frightened?" Tamuru asked.

"He fears the evil ones the gods sent down to plague your blood and heart. He fears that demons still cling to your hair." Nabor saw the look of surprise on Tamuru's face. "I have taught him of the will and power of those who dwell among the clouds. A priest must learn to fear the gods."

Tamuru stepped back, but said nothing. She waited until Nabor returned with a basket of provisions. Glancing over her shoulder, she saw the boy hiding in a niche, terror stark and wide in his eyes.

Never could she have imagined that a day would soon come when this frightened youth, armed with a cudgel, would stand above her and threaten her with death.

*   *   *   *   *   *   *

In the court of prayer, the fledgling priest, Raasban, knelt before the sculptured idol of Baal. The carcass of a pigeon lay upon the altar, the smoke of the sacrifice rising in a cloud to the height of the open roof and into the blue of heaven. The boy's head was bent low, brow pressed fearfully to the stone of the floor. "Gods," he prayed, "look kindly upon your servant."

The youth was eighteen years old, and for ten of those years he had been living in this house of Baal. Nabor had found him drifting in the wreckage that follows in the wake of war and had taken the boy in and given him food and shelter. The frightened child could tell him nothing of his parents or the village from which he wandered. Nabor kept the boy and taught him how to serve Baal so that he could become a priest.

Raasban learned to fear all the gods, to make sacrifice daily without fail lest the heavenly ones feel neglected and give vent to rage. When thunder rumbled, Nabor told the boy that the gods were angered and threw curses at the people and all living things. When lightning flashed from the heavens and split a tree, Nabor would lean close to Raasban and point to the smoldering wood. "That tree would not bend its back.

Now it has been stung to death by a bolt from the gods."

A sense of power wakened in Nabor as he molded the boy's soul. Slowly, Raasban's heart became warped with fear. Nabor had gained a servant to do his bidding without question.

Often, by night, as they walked through the temple, Nabor would stop sharply and point into the dark. "See that evil spirit hovering near the wall? Watch him." And Raasban would cry aloud in fright: "O gods, protect me! Protect your slave!"

When Raasban had heard Tamuru's moans on the first night that she had come into the temple, he had covered his ears. He had pulled the hood of his mantle over his head to shield his breath. Mournfully he had prepared himself for her death and when she recovered, he could not understand. For two days he had watched her cautiously from afar, not daring to come too near. When he saw how she smiled openly, he was confused. How could she be so carefree when the wrath of heaven might strike her once again?

He had followed Tamuru from the open court to the wide stone stairs at the outer gate of the temple, then into a band of sunshine beyond the threshold. A grassy expanse spread out to the right and left. He came up behind her with quiet steps, stopping at intervals as if his feet were feeble.

Raasban waited until she turned. "Why do you not fear the gods?" he whispered.

"Higher than all the gods is the Lord Jehovah. He will protect me," Tamuru answered.

"I have heard the villagers speak of the Faceless One. But are not the host of gods stronger than the one?"

Tamuru's voice was firm with conviction. "The Lord Jehovah, creator of the world and all living things, is king over all."

The priest Nabor was not so far away that he did not hear the speech between them. He frowned. He was annoyed with Tamuru's words. She was poisoning the boy's mind. She was weakening his hold on the youth.

"Raasban!" Nabor called sharply. "Your duties are neglected. Prepare a libation for the altar. The god has been waiting."

* * * * * * *

Later, Nabor strolled idly on the grass. Tamuru had proved to be more of a burden than he had expected. Placing her notions about Jehovah in Raasban's head!

Still, she was beautiful, desirable enough to grace any man's bed. This he had thought of before. He had thought of it when he first saw the amulet dangling from her neck and he had thought of it many times since, but each time he had put the idea out of mind. He was afraid she would laugh at his age, his crippled hip. Nevertheless, Nabor decided that he would ask Shatah if she could persuade the wench. After all, pretty or not, what more was she than a slave and he was a priest.

But Shatah refused. "Nay, my brother," she said as she took his hand in hers. "I shall not try to persuade her. She bears a great love for another."

Nabor was silent, the corners of his lips turned down, fingers drumming nervously on the table. He sprang up and swung his crippled limb before his sister. "This is why she will not have me. My withered limb would not be to her delicate taste." He tossed his head in anger as he limped toward the door.

Bah! he thought. Why should he burden himself with such a one as Tamuru? In all likelihood she would chase after the younger men in the village which would bring nothing but shame to his bed. Besides, there were other ways to retrieve the amulet. He had a second plan in mind with so great a reward for Tamuru that she would certainly give up the amulet with its sacred power.

Without delay he went off to find her. But Tamuru was nowhere to be found, neither in the small room where she slept, in the food storerooms, nor in the temple courtyard.

Nor was Raasban anywhere in sight even though it was the time for him to see to the god's needs before the coming of night. Nabor called out several times to his underpriest, the last time loudly and tinged with anger. It was then that Shatah appeared and pointed toward the north pasture. Earlier, she had seen the young priest and Tamuru leave the temple together. They walked side by side, she said.

* * * * * * *

Nabor was waiting near the temple when Raasban and Tamuru approached along the path at sundown. The folds of Nabor's cloak were drawn up to shade his brow. His eyes were angered, his lips curled down. One bone-ridged hand reached to his beard. Then he smiled, for the plan he had in mind required smiles.

"And what new things have you been teaching my youthful priest today?" he called to Tamuru.

"I can tell him very little. His master has been an able teacher."

"True," Nabor said. "I have taught him well. He has learned to bend his will to the gods. Is that not so, my son?" He pressed himself on Raasban, one hand upon the boy's shoulder. "Leave us then, and bring wine to the altar table."

Discreetly Nabor touched Tamuru's arm to attract her attention. He chose his words with care. "Here you are," he said, "despite your beauty, a slave, lowly in the eyes of men, and what slave does not dream of rising to a higher place? What maiden in this world would not wish to become high priestess in a house of gods? In this temple, before Egypt's recent war against the Kharu, a priestess served the goddess Astarte, the consort of Baal, until she was taken captive to pleasure Egypt's nobles and captains. As priest, it is my place to choose another to lead the Astarte rites in the sacred grove. In return for that high honor, you are to present the amulet on its beaded rope, your gift to the welfare of Baal."

He expected that Tamuru would drop to her knees and kiss his feet. If it were the moon above them, not the sun, she might even dance before him and expose her breasts. Nabor smiled and counted on success.

But he gasped when he heard her words.

She refused!

Nabor tried desperately to restrain his anger. "Such an opportunity might not come a second time," he warned. "From a slave, you would become a queen. You would stand beside me. A priestess."

Again Tamuru refused his offer. She could not accept, she said. Her destiny was leading her to another path. Her voice was firm.

Nabor frowned. His frustration rose full in his throat. Take care, he said to himself. Show no anger. The maiden has a kind, gentle heart. Appeal to her compassion. Perhaps she can be touched with pity.

Nabor almost whimpered as he began his tale of woe. "Child," he begged, "there is something you possess that once was mine. the amulet that hangs from its beaded rope. Yes," he said, when she showed surprise. "Foolishly, I gave it up to a soldier in a moment of fright." He shook his head pathetically from side to side. His voice dwindled to a murmur. "I am a feeble man, tormented flesh, in dire need. Kind maid," he pleaded, "open your heart and return the amulet that I may live."

"I cannot give up God's gift," Tamuru answered.

"But I am an old man," moaned Nabor. "Return it to me lest I die. I am weak. My limb is crippled."

Nabor wept. He wrung his hands. The tears began to stream down his face. Yet nothing he could say would induce Tamuru to give up the amulet. He limped away, hating her for the despair she had brought upon him and the disappointment he had brought upon himself.

* * * * * * *

Nabor wore a sullen look. A week had passed and he had failed to regain the amulet. He grumbled about the world and life. He found fault with the sun, he found fault with the clouds. He was gruff with the villagers who came with thanks at having outlived another ill-omened day.

One by one the villagers trudged to the temple with their offerings. Some brought wheat, some brought honey. A shepherd brought an ewe to lamb; another a billy goat with beard and horn.

"Pray to Baal for continued fortune," they cried.

Nabor thanked each one for his generous offering. He was posed significantly near the god whose leg had been shattered in Egypt's battle against the Kharu, "Remember," he warned, "we do not yet have an unbroken image of Baal carved from good stone."

"The stone workers are searching the quarries. The very moment a fine stone of black and red colored granite is found we will bring it," the villagers answered all in a chorus. "Meanwhile take this lamb, this goat, that our god may not hunger in his home."

"He is thankful," replied Nabor. "No doubt his cracked limb aches severely as he stands but he is grateful for your gifts."

Nabor stood side by side with Raasban near the pen where the flock was kept and they counted the ewes and lambs. Later, when Raasban drove the flock to pasture in a nearby field, Tamuru walked behind, crook in hand. She took pleasure watching the lambs gamboling among the brush and rocks. In the pasture, while the flocks grazed, she sat beside Raasban on a grassy hillock where the wind was cool.

Suddenly a bee settled on a flower near Raasban's hand. The boy cringed and cried out with terror.

"Have no fear," Tamuru said. "The bee will not harm you. It is gathering the sweetness of the flower to make honey. It will not sting unless molested in its work. The sting is merely its cry of anger just as I might scold you for some mischief."

"But my master said it is an evil sent down by the gods. Its sting can bring death!"

"The bee is not an evil sent down by gods. It is Jehovah's creation, like the beasts of the field and the fish of the sea," Tamuru explained. "Like the rains that nourish the fruits and wheat."

The bee brushed near Tamuru and lit on her arm. Raasban gasped as he watched it cling for a moment, then dart away. "I must go," he said suddenly. "I must ask my master a question."

But when he sought out Nabor, Raasban hesitated to ask whether the bee had been created by Jehovah to fulfill a purpose and was evidence of Jehovah's good. He was afraid lest the gods be angered and thunder rumble from the clouds. He said only that Tamuru had spoken of the power of Jehovah, the Faceless One, and had denied the gods and the Baal of the temple.

* * * * * * *

That night Nabor lay thinking in his bed. Not only had Tamuru thwarted his every effort to retrieve the amulet, now she was twisting Raasban's mind and turning the boy from all that he had been taught about the gods. Nabor grit his teeth. He would teach Tamuru who was master and he would regain the amulet to boot.

A subtle plan had already formed in his mind, every detail plotted step by step. Without benefit of a lamp, he made his way to the court of prayer. In the black of gloom, he hid himself near the altar where the boy was praying. Then from the shadows, Nabor howled and bellowed. Screaking a stone along the floor, he crept stealthily to Raasban's side and reached out in the dark to the boy's trembling body.

"The gods," Nabor whispered. "Heed well each word they speak."

Raasban hid his face between his hands. "I heard them," he stammered. "I am afraid. What did they say?"

Nabor spelled it out so that there could be no question about the message from the gods. First, the amulet about Tamuru's throat. That charm was sacred. The gods had willed that the boy bring the amulet to the high priest in this house of Baal. "In the first hours of tomorrow's day, you must get the amulet, no matter how. Is that clear? Understood?" Nabor extended his hands, fingers half-bent, grasping.

"Yes, master. But will she give it to me?"

"Kill her if you must. Bring the amulet to me," Nabor growled, and clenched his fist. "It is the gods' will. Do you dare to question the will of heaven!"

Raasban cringed with fear. He put his head low between his knees and moaned.

"Obey the gods!" thundered Nabor in his ear. "Obey them, or a thousand knives will drive their points deep while you scream in pain for all your days."

"No!" pleaded Raasban. "I obey! I obey!"

"Good!" snapped Nabor. "Remember, kill her if you must. The gods have willed that you act the role of a wolf. Now go!"

When Raasban left him, Nabor gleefully rubbed his hands. The old man who had bestowed the golden power had said that death awaited anyone who dared to take the amulet by force. The gullible Raasban would kill Tamuru and then die. Clever, he thought to himself, extremely clever. Both Tamuru and Raasban destroyed with one blow, while he himself would remain with unstained hands, the amulet safely dangling from his throat. Shatah would grieve, that was true, but then again she would have no reason to cast blame upon him. He had already rehearsed the tale he would tell. Was it his fault that Raasban had suddenly gone mad? he would say. He would explain that for some time he had seen lust awakening in the boy's eyes whenever Tamuru stood by his side. When she had refused his advances, the boy must have raped and killed her. Who could blame the priest for that?

Soon the amulet would be his. Nabor reached down to touch his withered, twisted limb. Wait, you will be strong once again. Wait. One more day.

* * * * * * * *

As the first hours of light broke from the eastern heavens, Nabor watched Raasban and Tamuru disappear from sight over the rise of a slope as they drove the flock to pasture. He blew his breath in and out with his excitement. He would have liked nothing better than to follow after them and seize the amulet the moment Raasban tore the beaded rope from Tamuru's throat. But he thought it best to remain out of sight and so appear innocent of any wrongdoing.

As it turned out, Raasban was no wolf. He was full with fear. He slowed his steps and stalked Tamuru from behind. He bit his lips. He clenched and unclenched his fists.

Like an evil omen, a cloud suddenly blotted out the sun, and the sky darkened. Tamuru turned and saw him crouching on the ground, saw his bewildered eyes, his fright. Out of pity, she kneeled down beside him and touched his hand

Raasban began to weep. Like a child, he pleaded for the golden amulet. It was a message from above, he cried. The gods had sent a message to Nabor in the night. "It is the gods' will. Give it," he sobbed.

Tamuru's heart was torn, but she shook her head. "It is not the god's will," she said. "Nabor lies. He himself has begged me for the amulet which I cannot give."

"But I must obey the gods. Pain is mine if I do not obey. Give it in my hand, or I am dead," Raasban begged.

"Neither to you nor to him," Tamuru said. She repeated what she had said to Nabor, that the amulet was from God and she could not give up His gift.

"Then I must kill!" cried Raasban, springing up. He reached for a broken branch near his feet. He raised the stick above her head. "I am a wolf!" he cried.

Suddenly he threw down the wood. "No, I cannot kill a friend." He crouched on the earth and covered his face with his hands. He had defied the temple gods which could end only in pain and death. He thought to reverse himself, to reverse god-judgement but he knew it was too late. Already a great weakness seemed to fill his bones and flesh. Then a pain struck his side. It stabbed with fire. He lay curled up with pain and fear, his knees pressing on his chin.

"Help me!" he cried. He rolled on the ground and writhed. "Help me! I am dying!"

"Live," Tamuru pleaded. "Do not be afraid. I will be your shield. Let your gods strike me if they can. Your gods are stone and have broken limbs. Strike me!" she shouted in defiance to the heavens. "I have no fear! Where are the bolts from heaven?" she cried. "Where is the thunder?"

Slowly Raasban raised his head. Tamuru had not fallen to the ground! He saw no streaks of lightning; there was no sound of thunder from the clouds. "The gods are dead," he whispered.

"They have never lived," Tamuru answered. "They were cut from stone by the hands of men with hammers and chisels and sweat and spittle even while they chipped and chiseled to shape the beards of stone and noses as cold and dead as rock."

Raasban was silent. He lay still. Looking upward to the sun, he stretched out his arms to the clouds. "Send down your thunder!" he cried. "I am not afraid!" Wary, he scanned the heavens, but the skies above remained clear and calm.

He stood up, head erect, both feet firmly on the ground, new-found courage shining in his eyes. "I shall pray to the false gods no more," he said to Tamuru. "I am their slave no longer. I have no fear of their fire or pain. I shall leave the temple with its sculptured Baal. Henceforth, Jehovah shall be my guide."

* * * * * * *

At sundown, Nabor, hidden behind a tree, watched as Tamuru drove the flock before her toward the temple. She was alive! She must have given up the amulet willingly, he thought. But where was Raasban? He was not coming up behind the flock, neither to one side nor the other.

Nabor became alarmed. Something had gone wrong. It was useless to deny it. Perhaps the boy had been struck dead by the power of the charm when he attempted to pluck it from Tamuru's throat. In despair, Nabor decided that he must go and search for the boy. He felt certain that he would find Raasban lying dead in the field. His one hope was that he would find the amulet clenched tightly in Raasban's fist.

Nabor hobbled out along the path that led to the field but his underling was nowhere to be found. Nabor grew frantic as he peered through the darkness. He searched the meadow until he was unable to drag himself another step and he sank exhausted to the grass.

Only then did the truth begin to stir in his mind. Tamuru may have persuaded Raasban to kick up his heels and flee. All through the night he sat and raged and with the vehemence of a man gone mad, he cursed

Tamuru.

Nabor approached her in the first morning light. He had come back as soon as the sun had thawed his flesh. She was standing alone in the court of prayer where his limbless god stood leaning on its pole of wood. At the sight of her, Nabor's anger boiled over. "Where is Raasban?" he thundered. "You have turned him from me. First you refused to give up the amulet, now you have taken my young priest. You revel in my weakness but I will repay your malicious ways. You too will suffer!" He came toward her, his eyes wide with hate.

Tamuru drew back.

She turned sharply and ran behind the altar to escape him, but the hem of her robe caught on the rough edge of the god's stone.

For an instant the one-legged Baal teetered.

Then the god fell heavily to the floor and cracked his beard.

"Ai-y-y-ee!" shrieked Nabor. "Unbeliever! Desecrator!" He raised his fist as he limped close to Tamuru.

In his rage, he did not hear Shatah come running up behind him. "Nabor! No!" she cried out. "Do not strike her!"

Shatah's hands reached out and pushed him away from Tamuru. His weak crippled limb buckled. One sharp cry and he fell. His head thumped heavily against his fallen god and he lay still. Side by side they lay, the crippled Nabor and his broken god of stone. Blood trickled from his ears and nose. One hand quivered for a moment, then moved no more.

Shatah had pushed her brother to his death.

*   *   *   *   *   *   *

A veil of silence hung over the court of prayer. The air was still. An oak rubbed a creaking limb on the ledge of broken wall. A shower of dust and bits of rock came clattering down upon the floor. Then silence again in the tomb of ruin where Shatah grieved.

What words are there to describe the pain in Shatah's soul for her brother's death? Her heart wept. Even though Nabor had threatened to harm Tamuru, what had that to do with tragedy, with the breath of a life one moment and death the next? Shatah remembered Nabor's youth, the young years when life was good and he was not embittered. "My brother," she said, "has been dead for twenty years." And out of sympathy, Tamuru and Araada wept.

After the shock of grief came a haunt of fear. There was no need to put three heads together to discuss it. They knew what would happen should they try to explain Nabor's death to the villagers.

Hurriedly, they gathered cheeses and dried fruit from the storeroom. They searched for spare clothing but found only a few rough boyish cloaks. They left the dead lying where he had fallen in the open court. A coverlet of linen sheltered him from the rising sun. A day or two might pass before Nabor was discovered.

To avert suspicion, they drove the flock before them to pasture in a field not far from the temple. Skirting the village, they clung to the shadows. They ran from tree to tree. They took cover behind every boulder. Only when they had climbed well up into the hills did they stop to rest. Even then they were uneasy, looking down and backward for any sign of stirring in the village. Out of fear, they pressed on until the sun was at its peak and they were safely out of sight.

At a crossroads, a man clad in the coarse mantle of mountain folk approached leading a donkey and cart. He was a massive brute, his face covered with the black stubble of a beard.

Shatah sensed a threat as he drew near. She took the girls to her side and pressed them close. "We must limp and cough," she whispered. "Even in lust, a man will shun the sick." She stooped, like one ailing with the plague, and led them into the shade of an ancient oak on a slope nearby. The man glanced back once, then led the donkey and cart into a field and slowly disappeared.

But no sooner had one danger faded than a second appeared. More than a score of warriors mounted on camels, cane spears poised at their sides, approached swiftly on the road. A cloud of dust rose from their hooves as they drew closer.

"We must hide!" cried Shatah in alarm. "We have escaped one beast only to encounter a herd!"

They scrambled to a narrow thread of path which led higher between the faces of two cliffs. Here they crouched behind the rocks until the riders passed out of sight.

They could not have known that Yaffia had been searching from village to village and was the leader of the troop. Nor did Yaffia know that she had crossed Tamuru's path on this mountain slope.

Still shaken with alarm, Shatah looked to all sides and into the distance as she led Tamuru and Araada down from their place of hiding. "We must take care lest they return."

Tamuru grasped Shatah's arm. "Disguised as boys, we would be safe. We have the boy's clothing we brought from the temple."

Shatah was pleased with the plan. She bound their breasts and wrapped a cloth round their heads as was the custom in these hills. "Now only God can see that my boys are young maids," she said.

She mixed water with dust and made mud to stain their cloaks. "We shall be three beggars," she explained, "a mother and her two sons. Father and husband killed in the war. Who would molest us? What greater misery than the life of a beggar? Except perhaps a beggar who is blind," she added. She paused with the thought that had crossed her mind. Of course! She would play the role of a beggared woman who lived in a world of shadows. The world had compassion for the sightless.

In the next village, Shatah feigned blindness before all who passed. She walked with her neck outstretched and groped the wind. "Alms for the blind," she cried. She bemoaned her life, her fate, how she lost her sight, how her days were dark, forever night.

Copper coins soon jingled in her purse and new strong leathern sandals were purchased for the long journey south to Shuah's tents. They found shelter from the night in an abandoned hut and in the first hours of morning they broke their fast with crusts of bread, then followed a narrow path which led to a road bustling with people and crowded with goatherds and flocks and oxen-drawn carts laden with bundles of firewood and produce destined for market.

They made their way to a valley below and to a large, high walled town. They passed through the open gate into the hubbub of a market square lined with shops and stalls overflowing with grapes and figs and pomegranates and dates. Richly clad merchants hovered over their wares.

"Now here might be silver," said Shatah. "Perhaps enough for a cart and beast."

She chose a place near the temple of Jehovah — El Elyon, the Lord High God, as He was called in this town. There she sat, hand outstretched and bewailed her misery to all who passed, but she barely gleaned enough to buy their bread and no coin for shelter. Two days they slept in the open under the trees of an orchard grove.

Then, on the third day, fortune smiled.

"See there," Shatah whispered to Tamuru and Araada. "Yonder comes a well paunched soul with a happy face. Perhaps a piece of silver comes our way at last."

She raised her voice and began her tale of woe. She called piteously on the goddess of the morning star who had struck her blind in punishment for a misdeed for which she was not to blame.

The man stopped and listened. Then, reaching into his purse, he threw a coin into her bowl.

She groped the air, and found his robe. "Kind heart," she begged. "Help us reach our kin in the southlands. Take back your piece of silver with my thanks. Add some copper to your generosity and get us a donkey and small cart that our feet may not be worn away with the distant journey. Your robe has the rub of wealth. The small price of a cart and donkey has little meaning to a man of such stature as yourself. This good deed, this mitzavah, will be repaid with the blessings of God who watches from above. Any beast will do, old or small."

"I would gladly give such a beast to you," the man replied, "but only today I sold all those on my land to a trader from Gaza." He paused, then looked apologetically toward the heavens, as if he feared that a refusal to help the needy would be repaid with misfortune. "But there might be a way. It so happens that this trader is a friend I have known these many years. He has gleaned a purseful for himself this day. Even now, he prepares to lead a caravan southward at the break of dawn. I will speak with him and arrange your passage. He is good in heart and will certainly do me this small favor. Keep the piece of silver and hire a tent as covering from the chill night air. Wait here. I will send my servant with word."

He was gone almost before Shatah could cry out her thanks. "May the Highest bless you with two hundred years of life!" she exclaimed, hands upraised.

"A most worthy man," Shatah remarked after he had disappeared. "Surprisingly agile, too, considering his girth. Hopefully we shall have a donkey cart and the safety of a caravan besides."

Her hope was not wasted. For the portly man who was pious had gone directly to the trader, then sent his steward to find the three beggars to wish them God's speed and tell them all was arranged with the trader Damas.

"I will sing your master's praise into the ears of God," Shatah told the steward.

She thanked him as he went on his way, then following his instructions, the three beggars set out for the place where the caravan was camped.

Even at a distance they could see the rows of tents. Soldiers stood about with whips. Bustling slaves carried sacks and bales on their sweaty backs.

The trader received them graciously, led them through a maze of baggage, oxcarts both large and small, sacks of grain and fodder. Obviously, the mitzvah-duty had been extended to the trader that both might share in the reward which would come from the heartfelt giving. In any case, the trader's greeting was kindly, beggars though they were.

"We are not so by choice but through circumstance," Shatah explained with a twinge of shame.

"No matter," he replied gently. "In times like these, with wars brewing here and there, no one knows who will fall next. Even now the Prince of Gaza prepares for war against the shepherd chieftain Shuah. All this that you see, all these provisions have been gathered at Zadok's command and are destined for his soldiers' camp."

Under a coat of dust and grime, three faces paled. Stunned, Tamuru raised her hand to her lips. "Who?" Shatah asked in a shrill voice.

"Zadok, Lord of Gaza," the trader repeated, "and not a war concerning lands or tribute. I hear it is a family matter. Perhaps it will end peaceably."

"Perhaps," echoed Shatah. She bent her head down so that the trader might not see her eyes.

"In any event, we break camp at dawn. Take care," he warned. "Do not wander from your tent."

He left them there in a silent bewildered circle until they fully grasped what he had said. Then they hurried into the tent, and once again they formed a circle, squatting in the semi-darkness. To reach Shuah they would be forced to cross through a battleground. How could they survive the threat of death from every side! Their one hope was that the trader would show them how to circumvent Zadok's camp and find Shuah's tents.

Tamuru's sleep that night was fitful and broken. She was consumed by the thought of war and the threat to Shuah. She had a vision of her father, battleaxe in hand. If only she could place the amulet about Shuah's neck to secure his life.

Shatah, too, twisted and turned restlessly from side to side and mumbled in her sleep. Once she sat up and cried out sharply "It cannot be!", then woke to find Tamuru watching, still awake.

The time marched slowly, each hour clinging to the night. Then, at the first sign of light they heard the flurry of breaking camp. Before the sun had risen far up in the sky, the shout to move onward broke from the stewards and under stewards.

The caravan carrying Zadok's provisions began its journey south.

Chapter Twenty-Two

Though the heat and primitive facilities of a soldiers' camp had cost Zadok much discomfort, to say nothing of the price in gold, he had come down to the south and prepared for battle. Mounted in a chariot, Jariah by his side, he had led a double column of his archers and spearmen down Gaza's hill. A company of Egyptian soldiers had marched close behind. For three days Zadok had followed the coast road, then two trusted men sent to spy out the land had directed him eastward to a wide expanse of desert and a trail rutted by the wheels of oxcarts rolling over the hardened earth. After two hour's journey, the column had halted and the two guides had pointed south. From the vantage point, Shuah's tents were barely visible.

Looking in every direction, Zadok had surveyed the position. Shuah had entrenched himself firmly, with an escarpment on one side and a hill on the other. A wide band of soft sand strewn with a myriad of rocks stretched out in front to hinder the assault of chariots. So formidable an obstacle to chariot wheels was the deep desert sand that Egypt, even with her dread battle chariots in the thousands, had not been able to subdue the roving shepherds known as the Lords of the Sands.

Zadok had decided to build a wall facing Shuah's tents and at a distance the flight of an arrow from a good strong bow. For two days soldiers had gathered large stones and raised the wall to the height of a man's waist. A hundred paces behind the wall, rows of tents were pitched to shelter Zadok's troops. His own tent, as command post, stood in the forefront.

The company of Egyptians had been directed further to the rear where the land was filled with dunes and hollows. Under the lead of Egypt's captains, they had made their camp and set up their sentry posts at regular intervals. It was obvious that Sakhiri had assigned the scum of the Egyptian garrison to Zadok. Such a rabble Zadok had never before encountered. No sooner had their tents been raised than half the soldiers wandered about the countryside in small groups, raping, burning and pillaging, while the others loitered about the camp, indolent and lazy. Only two things kept them from returning to the garrison in Gaza — the thought of plunder and the pleasures of desert women.

Despite Sakhiri's word, it had soon become clear that he was not particularly anxious to endure the desert sun nor to assume command of these undisciplined ruffians. Sakhiri's aide had come a second time from Gaza with a message from Sakhiri that was little more than an excuse. It seemed that he had developed an aching in his head, a throbbing in his right temple and neck. More likely it was his liver which was not soaking up all the wine properly, Zadok mumbled.

Uppermost in Zadok's mind was his future relationship with Pharaoh. Barely two months remained before Pharaoh would set sail for Gaza from the royal palace in Thebes. Zadok had morbid visions of his head rolled in the dust or perched on a pikepole when Pharaoh discovered what had taken place. Each time that Zadok thought of Shuah who was the cause of his misfortune, his anger flared. "There sits the scorpion!" he spat, pointing across the stretch of sand.

Still convinced that Tamuru was held prisoner, he sent an ultimatum, demanding that Shuah surrender himself and release Tamuru.

Shuah sent a herald in return, a young shepherd who carried a scroll to the barricade of stone which Zadok had built. Shuah requested a face-to-face meeting when the sun had reached its highest point.

Zadok clenched his fist as he read the words. "Tell your master," he growled, "that I agree, though it will solve nothing. Tell him also that were it not for my daughter's safety, I would forget the propriety of war and have your head lopped off to show my contempt."

With that, Zadok abruptly turned his back as a sign that the audience had ended and the messenger, young as he was and not inclined to death, hurried away before Zadok changed his mind and carried out his threat.

Midway between the warring camps, a line was drawn on the sand, a spear dug deep to mark the place of neutral ground where Shuah waited. He was clothed in a burnoose with diagonal black and white stripes, a felt circlet bound round his headcloth. A sword in its scabbard hung from his left shoulder. Brazen arm bands circled the strength of his upper arms. Beside him stood a young shepherd with a studded bronze shield, an iron tipped spear in one hand, a bow and a quiver of arrows at his back.

At high noon Zadok made his appearance with drums and bugles blaring. Four slaves carried a large white canopy to shield him from the blinding sun and Jariah followed with spear and blade.

"Foul youth!" Zadok shouted, his voice twisted with anger, "I demand that you release Tamuru and surrender yourself. You will pay tribute to me of ten thousand head of sheep and a thousand camel with their foals, or the blood of your shepherd kin will run as freely as the sacrificial blood on an altar."

"Is Gaza so poverty stricken that he must seek excuse to make war and plunder the shepherd tribes? You know that Tamuru is not within my tents."

"You lie!" cried Zadok. "You who wrenched the innocence from Tamuru's soul, then stole her away."

Shuah's voice was low. "I stole nothing," he said. "Only my love did I give. I confess it was the wrong hour, the wrong day, and without a father's consent, but my love for Tamuru led me to my misdeed." Shuah knelt before Zadok. "Father, I regret that we pledged our love without your consent. Forgive me," he begged. And he bent his head.

Zadok was silent. At Shuah's words, it was as though he heard his own voice on that day long ago when he had stood on the height of Gaza's walls and called down to Yaffia's father: "Kadesh! Forgive the deed! Forgive!"

Zadok shut his mind to memories of the past, and turned back to Shuah. "Do not speak to me of childish love," he roared. Release Tamuru at once."

Shuah stood erect. A sudden burst of anger flashed in his eyes. "You know she is not hidden in these tents."

"I will not argue the matter further!" shouted Zadok. "You have heard my terms." And he stalked away.

Not entirely by chance did Zadok turn abruptly on his heels. A faint suspicion of the truth had already begun its stirring. A second listening to Shuah's denial might have shaken his belief that Tamuru was confined in some darkened tent, with the result that he would have been forced to ask another question: "If she is not with you, then where is she?" From Shuah's tongue would have come a bitter answer: "You know full well that she is not here. You have chosen this lie as an excuse to wage war. A deliberate lie so that there can be no turning back from a siege of bloodletting." It might have turned into such a well-rounded argument, but Zadok did not stay to round it out.

With the blazing heat, the raucous antics of the Egyptian soldiers and his morbid thoughts of Egypt and Thutmosis, Zadok was more inclined to anger than vague suspicions but for the present, he could do no more than wait. The caravan, with the much needed horses and equipment which had been arranged with the trader Damas, was still two days off.

*   *   *   *   *   *   *

The trader Damas, the leader of the caravan, was riding well out in front of the leading oxcart. He rode bestride a sleepy, gray-haired ass and every now and then turned head and shoulders half-way round to view the procession of vehicles and laden beasts moving methodically down the slope. More than a day's travel still remained before they would reach Zadok's camp.

He fixed his eyes on the donkey cart which had been provided for the three beggars. Not that he was overly concerned about his charges but his curiosity was aroused and Damas was a curious man as well as kind. Accordingly, when the caravan came to a halt and the tents were pitched, the fires lit, and here and there songs were breaking out through the night, he came to visit the three beggars and brought a little food — a few onions, a string of garlic, and a roasted leg of mutton. When Shatah rose up to answer his greeting, he saw that she was limping.

"Your foot?" he asked solicitously.

"Only a scratch from a jagged splinter on the floor of the cart," Shatah replied with no concern.

"A wound in the foot may be a serious thing," Damas warned, and proceeded to give advice on herbs and various medicaments, which ended only after a long-winded treatise on disease, the varieties of demons and how to coax them out of hiding.

Subsequently, Shatah's foot was not forgotten, even after Damas left the tent, and when Tamuru saw her limping once again with obvious discomfort, she became concerned.

"Must you believe all the horrors that kindhearted windbag tells you? I say it is nothing," Shatah reassured her. "Only a scratch. I will bathe the evil from it, apply the proper herbs and tomorrow the pain will be gone."

But the throbbing in her foot grew worse through the night. Despite repeated applications of the best and greenest leaves, the demon clung and refused to release its grip. A stubborn, willful demon who allowed her little sleep, and when morning came there was a fever in her eyes which alarmed Tamuru.

"It is nothing," Shatah insisted, though her body was already heated and restless. "Another day and the pain will disappear."

"Nevertheless," replied Tamuru, "it would please me more if we had the benefit of a good physician."

"Ha!" retorted Shatah. "Physicians are useless but if it will please you, my child, I will consent to seek the advice of a healer when there is one close by. However, the pain will be gone by then." But as the day wore on, her indulgence turned to a self-concern. So swollen had her foot become that she was forced to remove her sandal and consented to have a cloth wrapped round the wound. By nightfall the evil had extended higher to her calf and a turbid, brownish fluid of offensive odor was draining from the edge of the bandage. "See!" she cried. "The demons leave my poor foot. Now it will be healed."

But the early hours of the night brought no relief. Shatah lay back and moaned. In alarm, Tamuru ran off to bring the leader of the caravan.

"It is nothing," Shatah persisted as Damas knelt down beside the infested limb. Though in pain, she still attempted to make light of it. "The evil drains away," she explained. However, she was grateful for his kind attention and permitted him to remove the bandage.

Tamuru stifled a cry of horror when she saw what the cloth had hidden all that day. The skin was blue and black and green, and the devil's wind blew from the cut. A bubbling evil seethed and fumed within the ugly swelling.

"It is not serious," said Damas, without looking up. His voice remained calm. "Not serious," he repeated. He smiled to hide his fear of death while he quickly rebound the wound. "Tomorrow, when we reach the soldier's camp, I will arrange for a physician to come and cure it." It was unfortunate, he added as he stood up, that there was no physician traveling with the caravan. Many was the time that he had been forced to be his own healer while he camped beside some lonely path. "Perhaps she will be improved by morning," he told Tamuru. "Meanwhile, I will prepare a potion which may be of help to ease the fever. My servant will bring it to your tent within the hour."

Tamuru nodded heavily. She followed Damas a step or two. "Will we reach the soldiers' camp and the physician by midday on the morrow?" she asked.

Damas shook his head. "Not until sundown," he said. "Do not fear, my son. Healing is often aided by the night. You will see," he added in a cheering tone as he walked away.

But at dawn Shatah could not rise up without assistance. She took her place with the aid of a staff. Damas ordered that a canopy be raised to give her shade from the midday heat and she lay in its shadow, her eyes dull and glazed. She was growing weaker. At times she suffered agony. The pain had extended higher to her thigh and was almost unbearable with the jogging and bumping of the cart.

All the while Tamuru looked on, helpless. Had they been back in Gaza there would have been no jarring wheels, no stifling heat. Shatah would lie in the ease of a soft bed. Slaves would sweep feathered fans back and forth above her brow. And Tamuru looked sadly toward the west and the setting sun, to her garden where the wind was cool, where she might have given Shatah aid and comfort.

* * * * * * *

In Gaza, the paths were shaded in the garden of the Great-House but there was little comfort. Ezamar ruled in Zadok's absence and she ruled with a whip. With Sakhiri by her side, she often walked among the tall trees where the air was fresh with the breeze from the sea, and pointed to the garden walls and Tamuru's rippling pool. "The thorn is gone," she would say and she would nod and smile at her success.

From time to time she stopped and tapped at Yaffia's door, the empty chambers which Zadok had sealed with brick and mortar. "Where is your Tamuru now? Is she fled to her love to be caressed and fondled?" She would tap again and cock her head with a smug air. "Now it is I who rule in this house."

One day, carried in her litter, she went out of her way to jeer at Enan sweating in the fields. That was a sight to see. His fat was sagging above his rags. His feet were bare. She laughed aloud. She could not resist the opportunity to ridicule her fallen rabbit. "Enan," she called eagerly. "Enan. Are the field mice obedient to your every whim? I can see that the corn stalks bow and bend at your command."

Enan did not have to look up to see who called. He would never forget that taunting voice. He grit his teeth and set his nose down to the ground.

As she passed in her litter, Ezamar threw a ring at his feet. "Add this to your store of gold and jewels," she mocked and laughed aloud, then motioned to her litter bearers to move on.

Enan's face flared crimson with rage. His fury mounted to a pitch that seemed to crack his skull. Every scar on his back smarted again with the remembered sting of Zadok's lash. The weeks of jibing, the laughter of the other slaves, the mocking Hooknose and his cronies, seared his brain and pounded in his head. A thousand black faces seemed to leap beside him, puffed lips opening wide to show their colossal teeth.

And Ezamar! Her ring, half-buried in the earth, glittered in the sunlight. In a mad vision, he could see her standing disrobed before him, swaying, tantalizing, begging for his touch, then slipping from his reach and lashing out with a whip as she screamed into his ears: Akab! Akab! Then Akab laughing as he flung him to the ground from Ezamar's threshold and contemptuously threw her gift, the chain of gold, at his feet.

Enan clutched his throbbing head. The sweat stood out in giant beads. He could endure no more! No more! The wild flame of madness burned in his eyes. He flung the ring away from him into the field. He had no need of her gold and rings. He would find his own.

But vengeance first. He must have vengeance. Ezamar to give up all her jewels, grovel at his feet and cringe in pain. And Akab — Akab dead and torn to bits. Yes, revenge! Revenge! He glanced upward to the sun. There was still time.

He left the field before the others. He slipped stealthily through the courtyard. It was a simple matter to enter the garden. As chief steward he knew all the hidden paths.

He reached down for a heavy piece of wood. Silently, he crept toward the house of women, the cudgel grasped firmly in his hand. His eyes narrowed as he peered out from his place of hiding and saw Akab coming toward him through the trees. Black devil!

Slowly Enan crept forward. As Akab turned, Enan swung the club down on the black man's head. Akab moaned once. Then he toppled like a falling wall. Again and again Enan struck at Akab's face until the black man's lips and teeth and nose were crushed.

Enan spat on the bloodied flesh. No more puffy lips! No more Akab! Akab was dead!

Ezamar's door was open. Boldly Enan drew the curtain to one side. He drew back in surprise. Raanu, Ezamar's daughter was sleeping in her mother's bed.

Enan smiled. The man-lust in him was roused. Holding his breath, he crept to Raanu's side. For a moment he leaned over her, then he pressed upon her with all his weight.

Raanu woke with a start. Quickly Enan put his hand on her mouth before she could cry out to rouse the household. How she squirmed! He could feel her breasts upon his flesh. He laughed with his delight.

Raanu's eyes were wide with fright. A cry broke from her throat. Then she swooned. Her arms fell limp. Her head lolled to one side.

Enan scowled like a disappointed child "Open your eyes, my pretty," he begged.

A piercing cry behind him froze his tongue. "Enan, she is your own daughter! Your flesh! Your blood!"

Enan leapt to his feet. He whirled. Ezamar was standing in the doorway. His flesh? No! It was a trap. Ezamar meant to snare him twice.

With a wild cry, he sprang forward and seized her by the throat. "You lie!" he howled. "She is not my flesh! Not mine!"

Ezamar struggled to free herself but Enan's hands squeezed tight. Her face reddened, then mottled blue and black. Frantically she clawed his arms and neck. Her mouth gaped as she fought for breath. Then she shuddered once and grew limp.

Enan let her lifeless body crumple to the floor. For a moment he stood silent. Then a raving laugh broke from his lips. "She is dead!" he shrieked. His eyes were wild. He laughed and laughed with the piercing laughter of the mad. He tore the curtain from the doorway and dragged the cloth across the threshold into the garden where he flung it to the wind.

The steward Evihu saw him, called out his name, but Enan could not hear. "Gold! I must have gold!" Enan cried. "My treasure was stolen, all my wealth. But the sun is gold. I can get riches from the sun."

Once beyond the walls of the Great-House, he began to run, stumbling, then walking, then running again. Through the city gate. Down Gaza's slope toward the sea and the setting sun. "Wait! Golden sun, wait!" he called. "I am coming to you."

Striving to reach the sinking flame, he ran to the edge of the rolling surf. He stumbled into the surf, his apron floating.

The waters swirled above his head.

And Enan disappeared.

BOOK SIX

GOD IS MY SHEPHERD

Chapter Twenty-Three

Down came the caravan from the mountain, down into a gully. In the lead, the trader Damas rode upon his gray-haired ass whose ears were drooping for the beast's nose was dusty and he was wearied.

Far off in the distance, Zadok's camp came into sight, and Damas blew on a ram's horn as a signal to alert his servants that they were approaching the journey's end. With the urging of the drivers and the thumping of their sticks upon the beasts, the carts creaked forward at a faster pace. The sun was low and red before the caravan came to rest and the tents were pitched by the side of the road.

Beyond the resting beasts and the row upon row of carts, war opened up its face before Tamuru. She was stunned by the vastness of Zadok's camp. Concern gripped her heart lest one among Zadok's soldiers approach the caravan and recognize her face. From the overseers of the caravan, she learned that Shuah and the shepherds were gathered further down the road where they planned to take a stand against Zadok's force. If only Shatah had been able to walk, Tamuru thought, they might have been able to find their way to the safety of Shuah's tents.

This last day of travel had been an agony for Shatah. It was only with great difficulty that she rose up and left the cart. With assistance, she hopped on her sound foot and dragged the other with its stench of rotting flesh. She was grateful to lie down within the tent, though the ground was hard and strewn with rocks.

Night fell into the shadows. Fires were lit between the tents. In the growing darkness Tamuru watched anxiously for Damas who had promised to bring the physician from the soldiers' camp.

Instead of Damas, his servant came. Near the tent he stopped, raised his nose as a fox might sniff the wind, then backed away. "Young boys," he called from a distance. "My master is gone to bring the healer. He will return in due time." With that, he turned and fled.

Damas, the generous hearted, had gone off to find Jariah to announce that the caravan had arrived intact which was his first duty. They had arrived with all the provisions and beasts of burden as commanded, Damas reported. "We are safe," he said, "and the provisions intact." Such and such had happened, an axle broken, this and that, but nothing out of the ordinary in such travel.

It was only as an afterthought that Damas mentioned a blind beggar woman whose foot was so badly infested that she could not walk. "Ah, dear captain," he said sadly, "here I stand gabbling while a soul lies dying. My heart is torn for her two young boys." With that, he excused himself and went off to find the physician.

For the physician's benefit, Damas retold the tale — the blindness, the sickness, the sadness, and finally ended with a treatise on the blessings inherent in goodness-giving. Then both were silent as they followed a sandy path toward a small clump of trees. Like Damas' servant, both stopped short and raised their noses to the stench of rotting flesh.

The physician shook his head, then touched the trader's shoulder as they went on together toward the tent. "It is an infested wound," he said quietly. I promise nothing. Her death cannot be on my hands."

"No one will cast blame your way," replied Damas, who had sensed that death was near unless a miracle of healing could be produced from the physician's box of herbs and powders. "I give you my assurance," he said again, his nose pinched between his fingers, then hurried off.

The physician hesitated before he entered Shatah's tent. He knew what he would find even before he cut away the cloth. He clucked his tongue with deep concern when he saw the seething mass of brown evil dripping from the blackened wound. The flesh was dead, the limb eaten halfway to the knee. A demon blew its vile wind through the open sores in the discolored skin.

The physician cupped his chin in one hand and slowly rocked his head. He knew that the demon who had made his home inside that rotting flesh could not be driven from its den. "I have seen many such wounds following battle," he said sadly. "If the wound were fresh, searing would help to kill the evil. As it is, only one hope remains."

Shatah raised herself weakly. God had always been the healer of her choice, not sour-eyed, bony-fingered physicians. "What must be done?" she asked.

"The limb must be cut off and cast away before the demon can climb higher and reach your heart."

"Cut off my limb!" cried Shatah, shrinking back. "To be lame forever! To say nothing of the pain of cutting. No! It is better to be dead." She fell back gasping with her effort. "Let me die," she moaned.

"It is your one hope," the physician said quietly. Despite his soured looks, his heavy vein-ridged hands and inured as he was to pain and suffering, he was a kindly, gentle man who preferred to deal with men who cursed in pain rather than women weeping. He was a mender of cuts and bruises of the battlefield. In his time he had seen grief enough and so spoke no more of cutting away the infested limb. "I have seen miracles of cure before and hope to see them many times again," he added.

He gave Shatah a small flask with a tapering neck. "This potion will bring you comfort. One half will ease the pain. To drink it all will bring you eternal sleep. May your God heal you and grant you life and health." With that, he turned abruptly and left the tent.

*　*　*　*　*　*　*

It was the time in time, the appointed hour. The time for the descent into the abyss which was a darkness forever, unless a miracle intervened.

Tamuru, kneeling in the silence, bent her head in prayer. "Great God of life, Ye who made both dark and light, Ye who created heaven and earth and all the creatures of this world, be merciful and grant Shatah life and limb. Be merciful and grant her health. Grant her to see the dawn, grant her peace..."

Her prayer was interrupted by Shatah who called out weakly where she lay. "Tamuru," she called, stretching out her hand. "Tamuru, my own sweet child. Hear me and heed my words. Darkness calls and my time grows short. Promise me that you will not weep. I know that it is a difficult thing to ask," she said as Tamuru hid her face. "If you love me only half that I love you, there would not be water enough in the great sea to measure all your tears. But child, this earth is not for me. I have lived long enough. You have been the sweetness in my life but now your own love is near. Promise that you will not weep. There must be no mourning, no renting of cloth. Promise me this. It is my dying wish."

"I promise, Shatah," Tamuru said, then bit her lip.

"Let your disguise lead you safely to Shuah. Weep your tears when your gate is shut behind you and you sit near another pool and an ancient terebinth. I shall be watching from my place. Now leave me. Take the lamp. Do not return until the night is deep. I love you, my child. Go now. Leave me."

Tamuru's throat swelled with a band of grief as she pressed her lips to Shatah's cheek.

Shatah lay still. Her eyes were closed. Her last thoughts lingered in a time long ago. A faint, almost breathless whisper: "Twenty years. Twenty years. My brother and my child."

And Tamuru took up the lamp and closed the tent.

Inside the light was gone. Eyes that cannot see have no need for fluttering flames. Now comes a final peace in darkness, a silent peace that no living heart can feel. In place of dreams comes a breathless sleep, a simple sleep that knows no sound nor fear. There is no need for light. God with hands outstretched and fingers soft with an unearthly glow will lead a slipping soul from darkness into the eternal shining fields.

* * * * * * *

Tamuru had stepped out into the darkened walls of night and turned her back to the burning fires. She saw nothing for her head was bent. She heard nothing for her ears were deaf to sound. Beyond the roadside where the caravan had pitched its camp, she wandered to a clump of trees which drooped and seemed to sleep. Past a narrow waste lay Gaza's encampment with its rows of flames and black-peaked tents. Further south were Shuah's tents and the end to her tragic journey.

But no tears, a promise made, Shatah's dying wish."Perhaps a few tears to ease my heart that breaks," Tamuru whispered. "Just a few. There is no one to see or hear but the trees and the desert sand."

A grief that stores the water must break and leak, if only a little, and Tamuru wept. Quiet sobs as she leaned against a tree and the grief seeped out to ease her broken heart. "The promise to Shatah," she whispered to herself and she stemmed her tears. She wiped the water from her face and where the little rivers of grief had washed away the dirt, she hid the streaks with earth that lay about her feet. Then she turned back toward the caravan.

Araada had remained waiting in the shadows nearby their tent. "She is dead," Tamuru said to the question in Araada's eyes. "We must lay her down to rest in a lonely mound. We must let her sleep in peace."

Tamuru had already chosen the place to dig Shatah's grave, the hollow to lay her head. To Tamuru, there was no more fitting place than beneath the trees near the strip of sand where she had wept.

But when it came to seek out a helping hand among the slaves and servants of the caravan, there were none who would brave the stench of death. All shuddered and ran rather than stand near the demon who had caused such a malodorous death. They were afraid that some winged creature would fly out from Shatah's foot and light upon their flesh to cling with its claws and teeth and suck their blood. Had Shatah died of age or sadness, or had a rock or a spear thrust out her life, they would not have been afraid.

Even Damas, who had taken the orphaned charges to his heart, was reluctant to face the stench. Suddenly he remembered something urgent he had left undone. His hands he could not lend them, he said, but he did consent to lend a cart and donkey and gave them implements with which to dig the grave.

Tamuru bent her head in thanks. Trembling, Araada helped her lead the beast to the tent of the dead.

"Be not afraid," Tamuru said softly. "No evil dwells in Shatah. She was kind and gentle and full of love. Be not afraid, Araada."

Together they raised up Shatah's body into the cart. Then, past darkened tents which stood like mourning shrouds, they made their lonely way to the waiting trees clustered near the strip of desert. There they broke the crust of sand and dug a hollow.

"No tears," Tamuru whispered as she swept away the sand. "No tears."

The grave was dug and Shatah was laid down in her bed. The shallow grave was covered quickly and her tired body was hidden beneath the sand. Then Tamuru kneeled and with arms outstretched she begged that the waiting heavens grant Shatah peace and quiet rest.

There was still a need to hold the shifting sand with stones and boulders as a barrier against the fierce desert wind. With that in mind,

Tamuru took up the lamp to search for stones but there were few near-by. Together with Araada, she wandered further into the dunes and hollows to search for more, unaware that they strayed close to the edge of the Egyptian camp.

A sentry at his post saw Tamuru's swinging light in the distance and relayed a signal to his captain who came with other soldiers, six or seven, all Egyptian.

"Spies," whispered the sentry, pointing.

From the ridge of a dune they watched until the light came near. Then in a group they crept forward and suddenly, like evil spirits of the desert, they sprang from the darkness and seized Tamuru and Araada.

"Only two boys!" cried one soldier. "Two youths with dirty faces can mean no harm."

"Why do you wander so near the camp?" demanded the captain.

Trembling, Tamuru pointed to the trees. "We search for stones to cover our mother's grave," she said hoarsely.

The soldiers freed their arms. "True," they said. "A grave must be covered to hold the sand."

"Comrades," said their leader, "let us help them, for stones are heavy in such young hands. It is a blessing to aid the dead on their journey."

One by one, the soldiers scattered along the strip of sand to search for boulders. With an air of sorrow they gathered many stones and placed them near the grave for the benefit of the two orphans. They were sad to note that Shatah's tomb was but a beggar's grave without monument or the slightest finery. She had been carried to her place of rest without flutes, without a funeral procession of thumping drums. They felt the least they could do was play the role of kin to the departed, and form an exulting mourning circle. "She is deserving!" they cried. "No harm has she done to anyone. Judge her justly and with mercy."

Some even raised a lament in regret that the dead mother must go hungry since they had no food to leave beside her mound. She must go hungered, for she was poor, the Egyptians said. Without water she must thirst. They spoke of her as though she still lived for, in Pharaoh's land, to die was not the end to life. It was a passing down and through judgement by the god of the underworld and so to live again in a sun-strewn fertile land where there was no want or sorrow.

Meanwhile, their leader, a literate man, stood near the grave and recited a solemn verse from the Book of the Dead to assist the deceased woman on her journey.

Then came a blunder, almost at the moment when the soldiers would have left off mourning and departed to their post, almost at the moment when Shatah's grave was safely sealed from wind and beast. As Araada bent to pick up the last of the stones, her mountain cloak, already loosened by exertion, fell open and a soldier who stood nearby saw her bosom. Startled, he bent forward to peer closer. "Comrades!" he called with excitement. "This youth is now a maiden. I can see her breasts."

Another promptly seized Tamuru. "This youth, too, is a maiden."

The soldiers crowded round, grinning at such an unexpected prize.

"What say you to this valuable discovery, my captain?" cried one.

The captain laughed. "A choice find indeed. Four breasts hidden by men's mountain clothing is not to be sneered at on a night of need."

Tamuru fell to her knees. She clung to the captain's robe and begged that he let them go unharmed. "Have pity on us," she cried in despair. "Have pity on our dead mother's heart and spirit."

The captain frowned and looked up to the starry heavens. Veneration for the dead was deeply set in his soul. He considered a moment longer and his heart began to weaken. He called out a warning to the soldiers. "The dead mother's spirit must hover near to prevent demons from entering her body. Some great evil may strike us if we molest her children."

The ruffian pack grumbled their complaint and disappointment. To find two choice maidens alone on a strip of sand and then let them go untouched! Not to taste the charms of two so young and ripe!

"Let us take them to our camp," cried one. "The dead mother's soul must remain here on guard. She cannot strike us at the camp."

They were all agreed and before their captain could interfere, they had reached out for their prize.

Araada screamed as they dragged her across the sand but Tamuru did not resist. She had no heart left to struggle. As she bent her head, the golden amulet fell out swinging. Its glitter quickly caught one soldier's eye. His hand shot out like an adder's tongue. He clutched the gold with a shout of triumph. A sudden pull and the beaded rope snapped. Grinning, he broke from the others and ran off with his booty. His brother-soldiers laughed and jested at his choice of treasure.

In a hollow of the land not far from Shatah's grave, they stopped, crowded round, every man in his lust impatient, growling, pounding his feet, demanding his share.

One soldier, angered by Araada's incessant screaming, flung her roughly to the ground where her head struck a stone. Her screaming stopped.

Only the shouts and the laughter of the men remained.

Chapter Twenty-Four

Mounted in his chariot, Jariah rode through the Egyptian camp and saluted the groups of bowmen where they stood on guard. Halfway between one sentry post and the next, he heard the rough shouts of soldiers and he heard a woman scream. Probably some desert wench the Egyptians had captured, he thought, to be raped and beaten, then cast away at dawn. Meanwhile a sentry post was being left unguarded. "What trouble from those foul dogs now." he muttered under his breath, and lashed his steed to a gallop.

As he drew near, he saw the shadowy figure of a soldier kneeling by a lamp. "What mischief at this post?" he called, swinging down from his chariot.

"No mischief, captain," returned the soldier. He pointed to a hollow barely visible in the rim of light. "We have snared two maids who were disguised as boys." The soldier grinned and held up the prize he had gleaned from one of the maidens as his share of pleasure.

Jariah recognized the swinging nugget of gold in the light of the flame. He drew in his breath. His eyes filled with fright. Tamuru! She must be there in that darkened hollow! Down came his blade with a piercing stroke and the Egyptian died. The power of the amulet could not shield him, for it had been taken from an unwilling throat.

Bellowing like a bull with neck outthrust, Jariah roared into the wind. "Egypt! The maid is Zadok's! Should she be harmed, each man is dead!"

The soldiers scattered like twigs in a sudden gust. They feared that the voice from the distant dark was the voice of death. They fled without their lamps lest evil follow the twinkling flares which would serve as guiding eyes in the night. Behind a rising dune they cowered from the vengeful spirit of the dead and locked their fingers above their heads to shield against a rain of fire or claws or demon-power.

Even Egypt's captain followed where the others scattered, though he was least to blame. "No intent," he called over his shoulder. "No intent."

* * * * * * * *

Tamuru had not heard the voice when Egypt fled. She lay numbed in the bed of sand, her eyes closed. She sobbed, a soft lament. An agony of suffering was waiting, she thought. Perhaps even death. When she felt the amulet pressed into her hand, she turned her head in disbelief. "It is a dream," she whispered and opened her eyes. "It cannot be. How is it possible? Jariah? Is it truly you?"

"I am here, and God's gift is in your hand."

Tamuru breathed a deep sigh of relief and clasped the amulet to her breast. "My heart called out to God, and you came to my side."

"I heard a woman scream," he said.

"Araada!" Tamuru cried. She raised herself and looked about. Araada was lying close by in the sand, her golden hair stained red with blood where her brow had struck the stone.

Jariah's eyes turned down and away from the sight and he bowed his head. In his silence, Tamuru knew the truth. Araada was dead. Another blow. Another weight to carry.

With Jariah's aid she mounted the chariot. He snapped the reins and the horses leaped to a gallop. As she was carried through the dark, the rushing wind was like a stream of sand whipping at her skin. Her father would be waiting, his anger like a sword above her head. Her heart was weary in a world of gray despair. In her deep pit of depression, the feelings of a daughter's love toward her father were drained like the water from a broken pot. She had no will to feel his touch or his arms about her.

Like a black hill in the night Zadok's tent loomed before them. A groom with torch in hand stepped forward and took the reins. Jariah dismounted and extended his hand to help her down. "Tamuru is found!" he called out loudly and drew aside the carpeted entrance.

Startled, Zadok watched Tamuru step across the threshold into the light. He stared at her earth-smeared face, the rags of her cloak, the cold, dull weariness in her eyes. He waited for her to rush to his arms with her love as she had always done in the past but she stood like an empty shell, indifferent, as if she had no desire for his embrace. He desperately wanted to comfort her, to hold her, to caress her, but fear of her rejection lay like a stone in his heart. He turned away abruptly, his face to the wall.

"Take her to the womens' tent." His voice was low. "Place a guard, then return to me."

Step by step, Tamuru followed a pace behind Jariah. The sand slipped beneath her sandaled feet and once again the black of night closed round her. Her father had turned his back to her. A wall. Unyielding. There was no care in his thoughts for her needs, her dreams. Shuah's tent was forever beyond her reach.

It had all been a waste, she thought. Her escape from the prison tower in the Great-House to this bitter end. Once again she could hear Araada's screams. Once again, she could hear Shatah moaning where she lay sickened in the darkened tent. Two lives sacrificed. A waste.

* * * * * * *

Unbent, head erect, Zadok had remained facing the wall. In his mind he saw a vision of Tamuru, without love, mute, a shadow of her former self. And he wept, the tears in streams glistening into his beard. He drew a deep breath when he heard Jariah's footsteps behind him. A warrior, especially a prince, must have a lion's strength and make his heart like stone so that none will see the sadness he feels. Zadok squared his shoulders and stood erect, then turned to face his captain.

It was a strange tale that Jariah told: Of two maids disguised as boys, of Damas the trader and Shatah's death, of the tragedy of Araada, and of how he had freed Tamuru from the Egyptian soldiers. Neither Shuah nor his shepherd kin had played a part in the escape from the Great-House and the journey south, Tamuru had said. "There is no more that I know, my lord," Jariah added quietly.

"It is enough." Zadok's voice was strained. "Damas must be given gold. See to it that Shatah is buried in a proper mound. Now leave me."

* * * * * * *

With eight trusted men, Jariah rode toward the sentry post. He feared that the Egyptians might seek retaliation for their slain comrade and create a disturbance in the camp.

Egypt's soldiers had been driven off by the roaring voice from the dark, but they had returned to the hollow. Jariah saw them in the light of their lamps and he drew his blade but the Egyptians were somber, silent. Subdued, they squatted on their ankle bones. They had dragged their dead comrade to Araada's side, then looked up toward the dome of heaven. They had counted justice to the dark, one for one, one soldier and a maid. It was enough.

Stepping closer to Araada where she lay in the sand, Jariah saw the bronze hilt of a dagger which an Egyptian, in frustration and anger, had plunged deep into her side.

Jariah knelt in the glow of a lamp. His fingers closed round the hilt of Egypt's blade. A gentle pull, and he cast the knife away. It was as though he heard his brother's words again: "It was she, Araada. . Pluck it out, Jariah, and let me die."

Strange, he thought, how retribution is the need for a bitter moment, then fades when death fulfills the familiar scheme. He touched his lips to Araada's cheek. "Sleep in peace," he said.

* * * * * * *

Zadok had left his tent and stood alone in the night. "Run," he had said to himself. "Seek the dark." But there was no escape. Tamuru's shadow followed, her eyes defeated, cold.

"O gods, what have I done? Have mercy. Let me see her eyes shine again with love for me."

The ridging sand drifted from a nearby dune and it was as though Yaffia's voice had suddenly called out to him in the wind.

Zadok turned toward the south, her name already formed in his throat. "Pity me," he whispered to the wind. "I have lost Tamuru's love." His soul cried out from the depths of his being."The guilt is mine," he said. "I have failed." He had looked into his heart and found himself wanting.

If Yaffia were standing before him face to face, he knew what her reply would be: "To have failed is only to have known failure," she would say, "but you can begin again. God has stretched out His hand. He has returned Tamuru unharmed, but you must touch her heart and waken her love for you once more."

Zadok knelt in the cooling sand and his heart broke under a wave of tears. He had been blind. He had walked as though he were greatest in this world. He would have bartered their child for the sake of his vanity, his need to sit in high places. In the end he had proved as unyielding as Yaffia's father, the old shepherd Kadesh with his curses.

"Not too late," he mumbled.

Urgently he stumbled across the sand toward the womens' tent. He walked, he ran, with no care to the stones which bruised his feet or to the hollows where a man might fall.

His hand reached out and drew the tent flap to one side and he saw Tamuru. She was standing alone, her head bent. Maidservants had washed her clean of sand and crusted earth and scented her with nard. She turned toward him and stared, her eyes still distant, cold.

"Forgive me," he begged. "I have wronged your heart, your dreams, your love. I am consumed with anguish." He fought back his tears. "Give me your hand and embrace me. There is still time to undo all that has been done." With a sob, Tamuru rushed into his arms and he caressed her.

"Come," he said, "follow in my steps," and he led Tamuru into the dark of night. He called to the servants to bring torches. "Guide us," he ordered. "Light the way to the shepherds' camp."

They followed the flame of the torches across the strip of sand to Shuah's tents. "Comrades," Zadok cried to the challenge of Shuah's sentries from the darkness. "It is I, Gaza's prince. Send word to your master. I bring peace. There will be no war."

The sentries stared in surprise. They threw their lances to the ground, then with shouts to rouse the shepherd band, they led the way to Shuah's tent.

*　*　*　*　*　*　*

From the inner walls of his tent, Shuah had heard the tumult and came out into the night. Then, from the blackness, he heard Zadok's voice: "No war! I bring peace."

Where is peace? thought Shuah. What treachery is this? What trick? But in the blaze of light from the torch in a sentry's hand, Shuah saw Tamuru at her father's side, saw her face, her black hair, her cheeks, the full red of her lips. And his eyes moistened with joy at her nearness and the sight of her.

"Tamuru is found!" Zadok cried, his voice shaking with emotion. He reached out and grasped Shuah's arm. "I was wrong. She was not in your tents. For a time she was lost and hidden from my sight but she is safe. In this place and from this hour there shall be no quarrel between your house and mine. Between us, there will be a joining with my full blessing."

His eyes full with smiles, Zadok turned to Tamuru. She pressed closer with her caress and leaned her head softly on her father's shoulder. To Shuah, she stretched out her hand. "At last," she sighed. "I have reached your tent at last."

When she turned, he took her head between his hands and kissed her cheeks and beneath her eyes. His voice was choked. "All this time, I despaired that I would never see you again. All hope had left my heart. I had thought that a joining with your father's blessing would never come to pass. But we are here side by side and you shall be mine." The depth of his feeling glistened in his eyes.

Shuah faced Zadok and bent his head low. "Welcome, Adoni. Welcome," he said. "I give you my hand, and to Tamuru I give my love. My deepest wish has been to have Tamuru at my side. Her bloom and beauty speak to my man-desire. I will cherish her forever. I will rejoice to give her children."

He reached out to touch Tamuru's hand in an intimate gesture. "My love," he whispered, then turned back toward the tent and called out loudly to his herald. "Spread word to one and all. There is to be no battle, no war. Wake the priests from their slumber, even before the dawn. Let them make sacrifice and give thanks to Jehovah. Then let their clashing cymbals ring out the tidings. Send word to Yaffia in the caves to the north. A wedding. A joining between the shepherd tribes and Gaza. On that happy day, we will lay ten bullocks upon their backs that the feasting guests may share in the joy."

Shouts of "Peace! No war!" rang out from all sides among the shepherds in Shuah's camp. By the fires' edge they gathered with flute and drum and they blew the ram's horn in thanks to God. They danced and sang and drank wine from flasks, and they heaped wood high upon the flames which shone like beacons until the dawn made the fires pale.

* * * * * * *

On the stretch of sand before the entrance to his tent, Zadok waited for Yaffia to arrive. He peered impatiently into the first shadows of sundown. He was thinking of Yaffia's face, her shining eyes, her smile. He remembered her sweet scent as she stood close. He turned at the sound of a riding troop of camels and, in the soft flame of a torch, he saw her as she dismounted. With arms outstretched he came toward her.

How many times had he looked up to the sky and prayed to Jehovah for this moment? How many times had he heard Yaffia speak of the day when they would be joined together hand in hand once again? As he stood by her side and touched her with his caresses, tears of joy ran on his face. She took his hand in hers. She could say no word. She held him close and clung to him, her own eyes brimming.

Later, in the dimness of the house of hair, Yaffia sat at Zadok's feet. She rested on cushions for her comfort in the centre of the tent. The light from a nearby lamp shone full on Zadok's face. In an intimate gesture, she fingered the hem of his robe.

She sat erect and raised her eyes to Zadok. "Hear me, my beloved. Let me speak. The war is no more, you have said it. Peace has come to all the land. Though Tamuru is found and rests again in your arms, though the sheep has been returned to the fold and by the grace of God, unharmed — yet my eyes see a weightiness of concern in your countenance and the dark of a cloud in your face. I have brought to you the flame of my life and my breasts cupped in my hands but I was met with a sadness which bled from your soul and your eyes. Tell me, love, what pain lies buried deep."

Zadok pressed his bearded lips together as if hesitant to speak. "There is a fear like a thorn deep inside me. I fear that my days and nights are numbered. I have dared to thwart the great king's will. Pharaoh's lust reached out to Tamuru. She was so young, so beautiful and ripe in the old king's eyes. It was Pharaoh's decision to have Tamuru as queen in the palace at Thebes but I have given her up to her dreams, to Shuah, her love. The choice is made and lies behind me but the payment is yet to come. Soon Pharaoh's anger will rise against me like a whirlwind. Before two full moons, Pharaoh's ships will sail from his great river to claim Tamuru. Then will Egypt's king reach down from Gaza's walls to seek me out, the royal axe poised and ready above my head. There is no escape. My days will be no more."

Zadok drank in the cool darkened air of the tent. A sorrow went from him to Yaffia.

"You must pray," Yaffia said. "Place your trust in God."

"I have prayed through the years" Zadok whispered, "but God has not heard my voice. Where can I find God so that He can hear what lies in my heart?"

"If a man is to find God," Yaffia answered, "he must learn that there is more to life than what he can see or feel with his fingertips, more than the high places where he might choose to sit, more than his gold, and more than a god hewn out of rock, or a gilded statue encrusted with jewels. In what you have done for our child Tamuru, you have ceased to seek after glory and power and you have become one of God's children. Tomorrow when we sacrifice and stand by His altar, God will hear your voice and the needs of your heart."

*   *   *   *   *   *   *

With the first sign of the yellow rays of the rising sun, Yaffia and Zadok greeted Tamuru at the entrance of the womens' tent. Her face was vibrant and there was a soft glow in her eyes. She was robed in a blue-fringed mantle gathered at the waist with a red and blue woven belt. She took her father's hand in hers, pressed it gently for a moment, then kissed his fingertips.

Between them, Zadok and Yaffia led her to the wide high-peaked tent where Shuah was waiting. She took her place close by his side. Their hands reached out and touched.

The shepherds and elders of the tribe pressed close to watch as Shuah and Tamuru bowed down before Zadok who then asked Shuah the questions according to custom: "Shall this woman be your wedded wife and you, her husband?" — to which Shuah answered "Yes." Asked whether he was well-born, whether he would make the woman rich, Shuah answered that he was son of a shepherd chief, rich in flocks and would fill her lap with silver and gold, that he would treasure her more than rubies and make her fruitful like the fruit of the garden. Before all those who watched, Zadok touched the foreheads of the bride and groom, then stepped between them and laid hands upon them. Then he bid them stand up and embrace each other and declared that they were wed.

Having blessed the bride and groom and wished them long life, Zadok and Yaffia left the tent and crossed a narrow meadow to Jehovah's altar which was sheltered by a mound of craggy boulders. With the aid of a priest of the shepherds, they poured out wine and sacrificed a quail upon the altar stone.

As the smoke of sacrifice rose from the sacred table, Zadok stood humbled, his face upturned to the heavens. He renounced Egypt and Amun-Ra and he pledged himself to Jehovah: "Blessed be the one and only Jehovah, king over all gods, creator of the world and all living things. Look upon me with favor in this my hour of need."

* * * * * * *

Clustered round shaded tables in front and behind the tents, the wedding guests, dressed in festal garments, toasted the bride and groom and praised the boundless mounds of food and jars of drink. In the midst of the rejoicing, a cry from Shuah's sentries rose up: "A chariot from Gaza! A herald with a scroll from Sakhiri's hand to the prince Zadok."

Zadok's hands trembled as he held the papyrus. His face paled. Death! he thought. Pharaoh's ship must already be waiting near Gaza's shore. He wavered, then broke the waxen seal and the scroll opened.

"I regret to inform my friend Zadok," he read, "that Pharaoh is dead. The Great King Thutmosis has passed into the world of his ancestors and has joined the divinity clan who sail in the sun boat. Queen Hatshepsut, who now sits as Pharaoh, has expressed no interest in maintaining the foreign dominions at the point of a sword. The troops have been recalled. I shall return to Egypt where Raanu will be mine in Thebes as planned."

"Pharaoh is dead!" Zadok cried out to Yaffia.

"It is God's doing," she replied.

"The Lord Jehovah has heard my voice," Zadok said softly.

* * * * * * *

In the first hours of the next morning, Zadok and Yaffia watched from the brow of a hill as column after column of Egyptian spearmen and archers followed by pack animals and laden oxcarts plodded southward toward Zalu and the coastline where the ships of Egypt would carry them up the Nile to the city of Thebes.

Later, Zadok and Yaffia, lighthearted and with smiling faces, prepared for the return to Gaza.

At Zadok's command, the camp was dismantled. "Let each man gather provisions for two days march," he ordered. Then, in his chariot, with Yaffia at his side, he led his troops on the road back to Gaza.

On the third day of their journey, they reached Gaza's hill and Evihu, the chief steward of the Great-House, came galloping astride a donkey. He dismounted and with staff in hand came towards Zadok.

"Welcome home, Adoni," he cried and raised his staff in greeting. "In your absence, much has happened in the Great-House." And he told him of the death of Ezamar and how the Egyptian captain Sakhiri, before he departed for Egypt, had arranged that the queen be laid to rest with an elaborate funeral procession led by chanting priests of Amun-Ra.

Zadok was silent, musing at all that had happened. "My thanks for your tidings," he said finally. "Leave now. Return to the Great-House and see that all is prepared for the homecoming."

At the foot of Gaza's hill, a heavy two-wheeled oxcart carrying two huge drums and their drummers led Zadok and Yaffia in their chariot toward the high walls and the gate. Slowly the cart rolled higher, the drums throbbing louder like the first call of thunder in a summer storm. Not far below the double gate, an honor-guard of one thousand spearmen stood at attention on each side of the roadway leading up. As the chariot passed between the glittering spearheads, the cry of Zadok! Zadok! went up from two thousand throats. Behind, in a show of strength, Shuah and Tamuru rode in their chariot at the head of the shepherd clansmen. Ten abreast, the shepherds filled the width of the road as they marched upward. Above, the city gates swung open and the people burst forth by tens, by scores, and hundreds, dancing, singing, each man and woman with hands raised and the cry of Zadok! in their throats.

The press of people made way for the oxcart and the rumbling drums at the head of the procession, which passed through Gaza's gate, then into the crowded market square.

Hand in hand in their chariot, Zadok and Yaffia smiled and turned their eyes to the welcoming throng. The cries of Zadok! Zadok! rose everywhere. Young girls dancing back and forth flung flowers from wicker baskets to the horses' hooves and the chariot wheels. Zadok responded by raising his arm above his head as a salute to the cheering mob. He pressed Yaffia's hand and smiled.

He had regained the honor which was his before the days of Egypt.